# I KNEW HE WAS TROUBLE

# BY AMANDA SCHIMMOELLER

**Royal Hearts Series**
*A Royal Obligation*
*A Royal Competition*
*A Royal Arrangement*
*A Royal Promise*
*A Royal Possibility*

**Sweeter Than Fiction Series**
*I Knew He Was Trouble*

# I KNEW HE WAS TROUBLE

## AMANDA SCHIMMOELLER

1
SWEETER THAN
FICTION

ISBN: 979-8-9926045-0-4 (paperback)

Cover Design by Melody Jeffries
Edited by Caitlin Miller

Visit www.authoramandaschimmoeller.com for more information.

*For all the Swifties. This series is for you. Enjoy it, capture it, remember it for evermore.*

# CONTENT WARNING

While the overall tone of this story is light-hearted, this book contains a few heavy themes, including: divorce (past), cheating (past), parental abandonment, and a narcissistic mother.

But, rest assured, a happily-ever-after is guaranteed.

# CHAPTER ONE

## KELSEY

THERE ARE VERY FEW reasons I would be okay with being woken up at four in the morning.

One: Jesse McCartney is at my door telling me I'm the beautiful soul he wants.

Two: I'm leaving for a week-long, all-expenses-paid trip to Hawaii.

Three: My besties wake me up to tell me that Taylor Swift dropped a surprise album overnight.

All of those are perfectly acceptable reasons—great, even. But nowhere on my list would it *ever* include waking up to my neighbor blaring hip-hop music for his workout session at this unreasonable hour.

"For the love of biscuits," I groan, slapping my hands on my bed. I reluctantly push myself up from the warmth of the heavenly comforter and immediately wrap a blanket around my shoulders to stave off the chill of early fall air.

I slip on my fuzzy mocha slippers and shuffle over to my window, brush my curtains aside, and glare at my despicable, uncivil jerk of a neighbor.

I've despised Tyler Reed since the first day I met him. Or should I say, *heard* him.

Of course, he couldn't be a normal person who goes to the gym. Nope. Instead, he works out every morning at four-thirty in his home with hip-hop music blaring before going to work. Who does that? Psychopaths, that's who. There has to be something pathologically wrong with him that makes him choose to wake up before the roosters crow.

Did I mention Tyler's had this routine every single morning for the past two years? Every. Single. Morning. *Lucky me.*

After the first month of it consistently happening, I tried using earplugs, but I actually got *less* sleep because of the weird feeling they gave me having something shoved into my ear canals.

I've debated pounding on Tyler's door a million times, wanting to berate him for his inconsiderate nature, but something has held me back every time. I guess I'm just a kinder human than him. Or maybe it's the fact that letting the dogs I walk use his yard as their restroom feels like a better form of revenge.

It makes me smile just imagining the confusion and disbelief written on his face when he sees all the dead spots in his front yard courtesy of dog urine. I'm not a terrible person, though…I always pick up their poop, even if the thought of him stepping in it makes me excessively happy.

The next song on Tyler's playlist comes on, and I groan. A girl can only take so much Busta Rhymes before sunrise.

Bless his early morning, hip-hop-loving heart.

In case you didn't know, in the South, that's the equivalent of the middle finger, but I try not to curse…so Tyler is the lucky recipient of all my internal *bless your hearts.*

Tyler and I have hardly interacted in the last two years I've lived here. The only reason I even know his name is because my roomies and I got a piece of his mail right after we moved in that I *graciously* returned to him along with a loaf of banana bread—my attempt at being a kind, new neighbor.

Instead of accepting it like a normal person, Tyler told me he doesn't eat a lot of carbs. I'm not sure I could ever trust anyone who doesn't eat carbs.

The chorus hits, the beat pounding against my eardrums. If I'm going to survive the morning, I need a cup of coffee.

I grimace. It sounds like Tyler turned up the volume a few notches, instantly making my head throb.

Scratch that, I need an entire pot.

My barista job has made me a bit of a coffee snob, but today, I don't care what form my caffeine comes in as long as there's *a lot* of it. I trudge my way to the kitchen to get a pot of coffee brewing, my eyes only open wide enough so I don't fall down the stairs.

I revel in the sweet silence while I wait for the coffee to brew. I can only hear Tyler's obnoxious music in my bedroom—probably because my window is right across from his workout space—but I'm happy it doesn't disturb my roommates' sleep schedules.

The scent of freshly brewed coffee overwhelms my senses, and it smells like pure heaven. I grab the largest mug in our antique cabinet and fill it with the steaming java goodness before adding a splash of cinnamon dolce creamer.

I take a giant sip, ignoring the scalding sensation burning my mouth and throat. I'm too tired to care. I need caffeine more than I need my taste buds at the moment.

My steps are light and careful as I avoid the creaky spots of the wood flooring up the stairwell and down the hallway back to my bedroom. I may be awakened at this unusual hour every day, but I don't want my three besties to suffer the same fate.

I would do anything for the girls who have stuck with me faithfully, like an old pair of jeans, for the past decade. We all met when we were sixth graders at a Taylor Swift concert. Each of us was in the front row, our moms as chaperones. We bonded throughout the concert, screaming our tween hearts out. By the end of the night, we had dubbed ourselves the *Long Live Girlies*, and a forever kind of friendship was born.

I run my finger along the wood frame, showcasing a picture of the four of us from that night, our arms around each other's shoulders and giant grins pasted on our young faces. Even though she's blurry, Taylor is mid-motion performing on the stage behind us. I'm grateful for that day—the one that forever changed my life.

We discovered that we lived within a thirty-minute radius of each other, even though we went to different middle schools, and thus began the tradition of Friday night sleepovers. And we never turned back. We even maintained our ritual during college, thanks to video calls and the group watch feature on our favorite streaming platforms. We were so set on keeping this tradition that, whenever any of us started dating, the boy quickly learned that Friday nights were off-limits. No ifs, ands, or buts about it.

I'm already dreading the day my friends fall in love, get engaged, move out, and live their married lives. I'm the independent one—the girl who would rather be forever single than tied down to a person or place. Especially after watching the demise of my parents' relationship as a child. Just the thought of marriage makes my skin itch.

But, for now, I'm enjoying the fact that we four girls made a pact during our senior year of high school that we would move back home and live together after we graduated college. And here we are, two years into being roommates in a quaint, historic house in Louisville, Kentucky.

I successfully steer clear of the squeaky floorboards and reach my bedroom. After settling onto my bed and taking another long drag of coffee, I grab my computer off my nightstand. Most days, I clock in a few hours for my virtual assistant job in the early morning hours—thanks to Tyler's music. While it's not an ideal way to start my morning, at least I can knock some hours off my workday.

I spend the next two hours getting the weekly newsletter for the author I work for scheduled to send out tomorrow morning. I also create some marketing videos for her latest books. After emailing them to her, I head to the bathroom I share with Alyssa to get ready.

There's a faint floral perfume scent lingering in the air, letting me know she's already gotten ready for the day. I take a quick shower and blow dry my hair before applying minimal makeup. Looking at myself in the mirror, I see the exposed red brick wall behind me and smile. It's always been my favorite original feature in the house.

Once I look presentable enough for work, I walk to my closet to select my go-to fall outfit: a sweater, black leggings, and white sneakers.

Today, I throw on the first top I can find—a soft, cropped tan sweater with balloon sleeves—that looks great paired with my high-rise leggings.

I head downstairs and smile at Alyssa, who automatically pours a cup of coffee into a to-go mug and adds the perfect amount of creamer. She passes it across the counter to me.

"Lyss, you're the best." I inhale the glorious smell before taking a sip.

She waves a hand in front of her like it's nothing. "Where are you working today?"

Alyssa is the definition of a blonde bombshell. Not a single strand of her long locks of blonde hair is ever out of place. It's usually half up in a high pony or space buns, always wrapped in silk scarves. Today, half of her hair is up in space buns with ditsy floral print scarves tied around them, the remainder falling past her shoulders in gentle curls.

She always looks like she's ready for a photo shoot or walked straight out of an Anthropologie catalog, but really, she's a hairstylist. If she wasn't one of my best friends, I would still choose to go to her in hopes that she could get my hair to resemble anything close to hers.

"I'll be at Rise & Grind Café from eight to two, then I'll walk Winston, Brutus, and Lilo before heading to Sunrise Springs from four to eight." I slide my phone into my purse and put the strap on my shoulder. "I already clocked in a few hours this morning for my author assistant gig, so I should be free after my time at the assisted living facility."

"Thanks to Tyler?"

I nod, rolling my eyes as I take a sip of coffee.

Alyssa shakes her head, her long blonde waves swishing around her with the movement. "I don't know how you do it all. One job is exhausting enough for me. I can't even begin to imagine juggling four of them." She wraps her fingers around her coffee mug. "Will you finally be able to quit one soon? You have to be close to paying off your student loans by now."

My lips pull up into what I hope looks like a genuine smile. "Hopefully."

I hate hiding things from my friends, but I haven't found the courage to tell them the real reason behind why I have four jobs. They think I'm simply trying to make ends meet and pay off my student loans, but I paid those off a long time ago. I have four jobs for an entirely different reason, one that I'm not willing to share with them—or anyone else—yet. Not while it still feels like an unattainable dream.

A quick glance at the oven clock has me grabbing my coffee cup and adjusting the strap of my purse. "I've gotta go. Will you tell Mal and Shay good morning for me?"

She nods. "Have a good day, Kels."

I walk out the front door and down the porch steps to my car parked along the curb. Out of my periphery, I spot Tyler walking to his car. He's wearing his stupid scrubs and a smug grin that I'd love to wipe off his face. Then there's that rogue curl that always seems to fall onto his forehead...I'd love to cut it off while he's sleeping.

I pick up speed, hoping he didn't see me. But I've never been that lucky.

I'm fumbling with my car keys, trying to unlock my door, when his masculine voice calls out, "Stop letting your dogs in my yard."

I press my lips together to bite back a laugh. Just yesterday, I gave all the dogs I walk an extra treat for peeing in his yard and all over his bushes. I can't help it if all the dogs hate him, too. That sounds like a Tyler problem.

"Stop blasting your music before the sun is up," I yell back as I finally get my car door unlocked.

Tyler's expression falters and his brow furrows.

I roll my eyes at the audacity of that man to not even care about waking me up every morning. I don't wait for a response and instead climb into my trusty white Honda Accord. After placing my travel mug in the cupholder, I shrug my bag off my shoulder, set it on the passenger seat, and carefully maneuver my way onto the road.

As I pass Tyler's car, I glare at him.

"Bless your heart, Tyler *freaking* Reed."

# CHAPTER TWO

## TYLER

"Feel better soon, buddy," I say to the four-year-old boy I just diagnosed with influenza. His mother mouths the word *sorry* to me, glancing at the new addition to my scrubs.

I offer her a curt nod. It's not her fault her son threw up on me.

Once I get back to my office, I head to the attached bathroom. I do my best to wash my top in the sink and dry it off with the hand dryer, but it doesn't do much—the brownish stain is still visible on the light blue fabric.

I slip it back on, cringing at the dampness of the material against my skin. I always keep an extra pair of scrubs at the office for this very reason, but this *was* my extra pair.

That's right, I had *two* kids get sick on me today. I already stripped off my dark blue scrubs this morning after the first incident, so I'll have to make do with these for the rest of the workday.

Flu season is an unwanted welcome to cooler weather. I love the reprieve from the warmer months but could do without seeing so many children suffering from illnesses.

I throw on my white doctor's coat for the remainder of my appointments, attempting to hide the stain, but the smell sticks with me all day. Luckily, five o'clock hits without making it a trifecta.

As I pass the welcome desk, my receptionist, Nadine, gives me a pitying smile, further accentuating the wrinkles around her mouth.

"Rough day, Doc?"

I lift up the plastic bag holding my other pair of soiled scrubs like a prized trophy. "Just the yearly rite of passage as a pediatrician."

"I guess you need to start keeping *two* extra outfits in your office during flu season." She laughs, running a hand through her graying curls.

"You might be right."

"Go get cleaned up and have some *fun* tonight." She wiggles her eyebrows, lacking all subtlety. "You know, my granddaughter is still single."

I shake my head, laughing under my breath. "Goodnight, Nadine."

Since my receptionist is also my great-aunt's best friend, I'm surprised Nadine doesn't know that I typically stop by a flower shop and deliver a fresh bouquet to my great-aunt on Thursdays. I'm not sure that's the kind of *fun* Thursday night she was referencing. However, I think I'm going to have to skip that part of my routine today. I don't think Aunt D would appreciate the vomit stain on my scrubs and the smell accompanying it.

"I'll get you to go on a date one day," she declares.

"Good luck with that," I call back over my shoulder at the relentless woman. If she wasn't such a good receptionist, I'd fire her for her continuous attempts at matchmaking. But she's become like another grandmother to me. Plus, Aunt D would tan my hide, so I'd never actually follow through.

I step out onto the curb. Before the door closes behind me, I hear Nadine tutting. "Such a waste of a perfectly handsome face."

If enjoying peaceful evenings at home means I'm wasting my *perfectly handsome face*—her words, not mine—then so be it.

I do want to get married one day. Honestly, I thought I would be married by the time I was thirty. I even came close in my last serious relationship. Yet, now I'm thirty and have been single for a few years, but I don't plan on resorting to set-ups anytime soon.

When I reach my SUV, my phone buzzes in my pocket with an incoming call. I pull it out and see my sister Tess on the screen with a picture of her mid-sneeze that I refuse to delete. Everyone needs blackmail photos of their older sister to embarrass her. It's pretty much guaranteed that she has worse pictures of me, anyway.

I usually prefer to sit in silence on my car rides home, decompressing from the workday, but I know I should answer. I haven't had a chance to call her back after she reached out yesterday, and if she's calling again, it's probably important.

The incoming call continues to ring over Bluetooth as I start the engine. I press the answer button on my steering wheel. "Hello?"

"He lives," Tess practically screams.

I grimace and turn down the volume as I turn onto the road. "Is it impossible for you to start a conversation at a normal human decibel?"

"How else would I make sure you're actually listening?"

"You could give me a pop quiz after…or just trust that if I answer the phone, I'm giving you my undivided attention."

"Undivided attention, huh?" I can practically hear the gears in her head turning. "So, you're focused solely on me and not on the road then?"

I make a right turn, heading toward my house. *Busted.* "I could drive home with my eyes closed."

"Ugh, please don't do that. I need you alive for the teeny-tiny favor I'm about to ask you, oh favorite brother of mine."

I'm her *only* brother.

"Why do I have a feeling it's not going to be a small favor?" I groan as I pull up to a stop sign, scanning both directions before rolling forward.

I can nearly see the eye roll she perfected as a pre-teen. "I need you to watch Evie for a little bit."

Maybe it wasn't that big of a favor after all. "You know I'm happy to hang out with her."

I've always looked out for my sister, but I've tried to help as much as possible over the past four years after her scumbag of an ex-husband cheated on her and gave up all parental rights to move to Berlin with his assistant.

Evie needs a male figure in her life to look up to, and I'm happy to fill that role.

"Just remember those happy thoughts when I tell you the rest."

The rest? The rest of what? My fingers grip the steering wheel. What did I just get myself into?

I try to remain calm while I wait for her to explain her *teeny-tiny* favor and what the rest of it entails.

"I have a great opportunity at work that I can't pass up. They picked me to travel with our team to Africa to open a medical center. Isn't that crazy? Who would've thought we'd have two people in our family working in the medical field?"

I press my lips together, keeping myself from saying something stupid about how I went through four years of undergrad, four years of medical school, and three years of a pediatric residency to get to where I am in my career. She works for a nonprofit organization. It's noble work, and I'm proud of her. But saying we both work in the medical field is like saying apples and oranges are the same thing.

I feel like I'm walking into a trap, but I trudge forward anyway. "You know I don't mind helping out when it comes to Evie."

"That's a relief because I already registered you as the person who will pick her up from school for the next three months." Tess's words come out so quickly that it takes me a minute to piece together everything she just said.

"Three *months*?" I bellow, rubbing my temple. "I can't pick her up from school, Tess. I have work."

"Yes, yes," she drones. "I already know you're a *fancy* doctor."

"Hey, you're the one who's going to help open a *medical* center."

She scoffs. "I'm trying to make a difference in the world."

"And I'm helping kids, one virus and ear infection at a time." I clear my throat. "We're getting off track. What's this about three months?"

"I was hoping you would forget that part," Tess muttered. After a long moment, she continues talking. "My assignment in Africa is for three months. I know you work full-time, but you're my only option. Maybe Nadine can watch her after school at the reception desk? If it was summer, I would send Evie with Mom and Dad on their travels, but she's already started kindergarten and needs stability. And with Julian out of the picture—"

The second she mentions her ex, my protective mode kicks in. "I'll figure it out. You don't need to worry about Evie. Focus on your job, and I'll figure everything out."

Her sigh of relief travels through the phone. "You're the best."

"It's not a big deal. Are you okay with leaving Evie for that long? I don't think you've left her for more than a week."

The phone sounds muffled, as if Tess is trying to hide her emotion. "It's *because* of Evie that I'm willing to leave her for so long. My company is giving me a huge bonus for going at the last minute. It's the kind of money I need to set us up for the future, to feel a little more secure since Julian left."

"You know you never have to worry about money." I worked throughout my years of schooling and got every scholarship I could so that I'd be set up well when I started my career. But I'd give my sister and Evie every last penny in my bank account if it meant she didn't have to worry. "I can help—"

"You can stop right there." She cuts me off like she always does when I offer to help her financially. "I have to do this for myself. To prove to myself that I can take care of us." She sounds resolute, so I decide not to push the issue.

I wish I could do more for my sister, but I can worry about that later. "Evie and I will have a great time."

"I owe you big time. She'll be so excited. I'll pack all her favorite clothes and things, and we'll be there Sunday."

"Sunday?" I choke. "Like three days from now?"

"Did I forget to mention that?" She hums. "You're the best brother ever. Thank you, love you, byeee."

The call clicks. I sit in silence as I park in the spot in front of my house.

I shouldn't be surprised that she's springing this massive favor on me at the last minute. Tess knows I'd do anything for her. That doesn't mean I'm not freaking out, though. Thankfully, I know how to care for a five-year-old girl. I'm a pediatrician, after all. Plus, I've watched her for a weekend before, but I have a feeling three months will be a whole different ball game.

When I get out of the car, I'm relieved to see that my neighbor Kelsey's vehicle is gone. Normally, I can match Kelsey's obstinate personality and take her on in a battle of wits and words, but I'm not sure I can manage a run-in with her right now.

I have much bigger issues at hand than her dogs deciding to use my yard as their personal bathroom.

The second I get inside, I strip off my scrubs and throw both of today's soiled pairs in the washing machine, getting the load going with hot water and a decent amount of detergent. I go to my room and pull on a pair of athletic shorts before heading to my workout room. I usually just exercise in the morning, but I need another session today to rid my body of my pent-up stress from my phone call with Tess.

After putting on headphones and turning on my work-out playlist, I start by lifting weights and then go for a jog on my treadmill. But no matter what I seem to do, anxious thoughts cloud my mind.

Now that our parents are retired and traveling the world, I know I'm Tess's only option. Besides, family helps family, so of course I said yes. But I just haven't figured out how I'm going to be my five-year-old niece's guardian for three months with exactly zero notice when I work at Little Louisville Pediatrics every weekday from eight to five.

Who's supposed to pick Evie up from school and take care of her while I'm at work? And what foods does she like? I mostly eat a protein-based diet. Do kids nowadays even eat protein besides dinosaur-shaped chicken nuggets?

I groan as I power off the treadmill. I need more time to research and prepare, decorate my guest room with girly things, and go grocery shopping.

But first, I need to find a nanny for Evie.

# CHAPTER THREE
## KELSEY

FRIDAY HAS BEEN MY favorite day of the week since my besties and I began our sleepover tradition in sixth grade. Now that we live together, it's like a girls' night every night, but I still look forward to our weekly ritual. Especially now that I'm juggling four jobs, I'm exhausted by the end of the week, and that time with them is the light at the end of the tunnel.

I didn't realize how draining it would be to balance my time between so many places and still try to be a good friend. But I should only have to keep working all these jobs for another year before I have enough saved to open a dog rescue. It's scary to think those words in my head, let alone imagine saying them out loud to anyone.

Dogs have always been my favorite animal, and I've dreamed of helping them find their fur-ever home for as long as I can remember. Hopefully, by this time next year, I'll be able to make that dream a reality. Between all the money I've saved from my jobs in high school, college, and over the last two years, plus the money I inherited from my grandparents' passing last year, I think it's going to become a reality.

I gently tug on the leashes. "Let's get you cuties home." I walk Winston, Brutus, and Lilo three days a week for families who want their dogs to stay active but don't have the time or capacity to do it themselves.

After dropping Brutus and Lilo off at their homes, I walk a few streets down to where Winston lives. I knock on the light blue front door and his owner, Pamela, answers.

"Kelsey, do you have a minute to talk?" Her brow furrows, and my stomach drops. I can't think of anything I might've done to upset her.

"Of course." I pass Winston's leash over and step into her home. It's impossible not to notice the brown packing boxes littered throughout the entire first floor. "You're moving?"

She nods. "It's time for us to downsize, and we found the perfect retirement community in Florida."

"That's exciting." I try to sound encouraging even though I'll miss Winston. I mean, he's the cutest golden retriever ever. How could I not adore him?

"We're looking forward to it." Pamela's eyes dart to the floor, and I know there's a *but* coming. "The only downside is that the community only allows dogs under twenty pounds."

I reach out and offer her hand a reassuring squeeze. "I'm so sorry. You must be devastated."

Pamela pulls a tissue from her pocket and dabs it under her eyes. "We are."

"What are your plans for Winston? I'm happy to help you find a good family."

"That's what I wanted to talk to you about." She looks at her dog with so much love it makes me tear up. "Winston loves his walks with you. He's always waiting by the door like clockwork for you to pick him up. I don't know your living situation, but we wanted to see if you might be interested in adopting him before we try to rehome him." She sniffles.

I hold a hand to my chest. "I'm honored you would think of me. My lease allows one pet, but is it okay if I step outside and check with my roommates?"

"Of course. Whatever you need, dear."

She opens the back door for me, and I walk into their screened-in porch. After pulling my phone out of my pocket, I sit on the outdoor sofa and open the "Long Live Girlies" group text thread.

ME

What do y'all think about another roommate?

I attach a picture I took earlier this week of Winston smiling up at the camera and hit send. All their responses come in rapid succession.

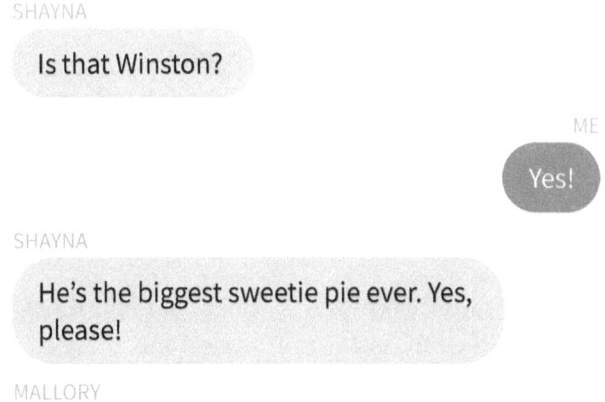

SHAYNA

Is that Winston?

ME

Yes!

SHAYNA

He's the biggest sweetie pie ever. Yes, please!

MALLORY

> Agreed. If I'm going to like any animal, it's him.

ALYSSA

> I love that floofball! I'm down.

My shoulders fall in relief that they're all in agreement. I've dreamed of owning a dog for so long that it's impossible to keep the bounce out of my step as I walk back inside. Winston runs over, his golden ears flopping in the breeze. I kneel and scratch his neck. "It looks like you're coming home with me, buddy."

Pamela comes out of the kitchen carrying a to-go cup, which she extends my way. "I know how much you love coffee."

"That's so sweet. Thank you." I pat Winston's head, stand, and accept the cup. "I heard back from my roommates, and they're happy to welcome Winston into our home."

Her mouth falls open, and she pulls me in for a hug. "Oh, thank you. I'm devastated he can't come with us, but I know you're going to take the best care of him."

I hug her tight. "I'll send you pictures and videos anytime you want."

Pamela pulls back and shakes her finger between us. "See, my gut always told me you were a good one, and it's never wrong."

"I've always loved Winston." I know you're not supposed to pick favorites, but he's always been mine.

"I'll let you go. Let me give you all the dog supplies." Pamela grabs a large reusable tote bag, filled to the brim, and starts dragging it over to me.

I hurry over and pick it up. It's heavier than expected. Inside, I spot a few gallon-sized baggies of dog food, dog bowls, a harness, a few toys, shampoo, and a brush. "This is great, thanks."

She clicks the leash back onto Winston's collar.

My eyes go wide. "You want me to take him right now?"

"Is that okay?" Pamela worries her bottom lip. "The movers are coming Monday."

I'm not sure my friends expected me to bring him home with me *today*, but it will make for a fun girls' night. I slip the tote onto my shoulder and accept the leash. "Yeah, of course." I walk out front, Winston following at my heels. "You have my number. Seriously, text me anytime you want a picture of him."

"I will." She leans down, hugs the dog, and kisses him on his head. When Pamela stands straight, her eyes glisten with unshed tears. "You better go before I become a blubbering mess."

I shoot her a sad smile before walking down her driveway. Once we hit the sidewalk, I wave goodbye. Then, with Winston by my side, I head home.

---

♡ ♡ ♡

---

"You're such a good boy. Yes, you are," Shayna coos as she scrunches up Winston's neck floof. If you look up the word "joy" in the dictionary, you'll find Shay's picture beside it. She's the epitome of sunshine—the eternal optimist. The friend you want on your side to pick you up when you're down.

"He doesn't understand English, Shay," Mallory deadpans.

"Do I need to say it in French, then? Spanish? Maybe Dutch?"

Mal throws a pillow at her.

"Even if he doesn't understand, he knows he's getting praise." Shayna turns back to Winston, her dark-brown hair swinging with the movement. She rubs his ears and turns her baby voice back on. "Isn't that right? You're the smartest boy in the whole wide world."

Alyssa walks in, carrying an armful of snacks. My mouth waters the second I spot the familiar packaging of Kizito cookies. They're a staple sweet treat in Louisville.

The pronunciation of our dear city is a controversial topic, even for locals. I pronounce it Looavul—like I have a mouthful of marshmallows. Some people might argue it's Looeyville, but heaven forbid someone pronounces it Lewisville. That's sacrilegious here. Regardless, it's the city that has our history and our hearts…and the most delicious cookies.

I grab a snickerdoodle. "What are we celebrating?" We only ever buy Kizito cookies for special occasions.

"Our new roommate, of course." Alyssa raises her cookie in the air.

I open the package and clink the cookie with my friends. "To Winston."

"To Winston," they echo back.

We laugh as he runs between us, tail wagging from hearing everyone cheer his name.

When our cookies are gone, we heat apple cider in the kitchen. The second we're all in our usual seats, mugs in hand, Alyssa starts talking. "Okay, happies and crappies for the week. You go first, Mal."

I set my mug on the coffee table and shake a bottle of burgundy nail polish. After twisting it open, I brush it on my nails as I listen.

"My crappy this week was parent-teacher conferences. They went until eight on Tuesday and are always draining." Mallory pulls her curly, light brown hair up into a messy bun. I think she calls it the pineapple method, but I have no clue what that means. "My happy is that our two-day fall break is getting closer by the minute."

"You're almost there, girlfriend." I toast my nail polish bottle toward her in solidarity.

Mal smiles. "What about you, Shay?"

Shayna sits on her hands as she bounces excitedly on the couch. "My boss at the flower shop told me she's planning on retiring soon." She's been working at Shirley's Florist for the past six years, saving up to open her own flower truck.

"I'm guessing that's good news?" I ask, unsure what Shirley's retirement might mean for her.

She nods, readjusting her knotted pearl headband. "Shirley doesn't have any kids, so she said she wants to leave the flower shop to me. It has a greenhouse and garden out back where I could grow enough flowers to keep running the shop and sell them from a mobile flower truck too."

I pull her in for a side hug. "We definitely needed Kizito cookies tonight, then. Congrats, Shay!"

Everyone else offers their congratulations before she turns back to me. "I don't have any crappies. Your turn, Kels."

I take a sip of my cider, savoring the notes of warm spices. "My happy is obviously that I'm now a dog mama." I lean down and ruffle Winston's fur. "My crappy is that I woke up to Tyler blaring hip-hop music *multiple* days this week before sunrise."

"Again?" Shayna leans over and squeezes my forearm. "I thought you started sleeping through it?"

"I do on occasion, but I think he switched up his playlist or something."

"Ugh, I'm sorry, girl." Alyssa gives me a sympathetic look. "I still can't believe none of us can hear it."

I shrug. "It must be because his workout room is right across from my window. I'm honestly glad none of you can hear it. At least some of us can get the beauty sleep we deserve."

"Do you want me to egg his house?" Mallory looks determined, like she's ready to go to battle for me. She's the kind of friend that would defend you to the grave, and we love her for it.

I laugh. "That's okay, but thank you." Dropping my gaze to my lap, I say, "I actually have another crappy this week. My mother texted me."

"No." Mallory looks like she could seriously injure my mother with her eye daggers.

"What did she want?" Alyssa pouts.

"She let me know she was moving in with her new boyfriend."

Mallory scoffs. "What number is this? Seventeen?"

I blow out a breath. "I've honestly lost count."

Shayna scoots closer to me, squeezing my arm. "Did she ask you for anything this time?"

I shake my head. "I guess the upside to her moving in with boyfriends is that she stops asking me for rent money."

"I'm sorry, Kels." Alyssa shoots me a sympathetic look.

"It's fine." I take another sip of my apple cider, trying to stave off the emotions that always rise to the surface when talking about my parents.

Let's just say that not many of my memories surrounding them are positive. After they divorced, they used me to keep tabs on the other. Then, when I became a legal adult, I fell out of touch with my father. The few times a year that I hear from my mother, she asks me for money or cries about her most recent breakup, reminding me that love never lasts.

I clear my throat and force a smile—this evening with my friends is supposed to be fun. "What are your happies and crappies, Lyss?"

She eyes me like she knows it's certainly *not* fine, but concedes to my wish to change the conversation. "My crappy is that I have to miss Austin's first playoff game tomorrow because I'm covering for someone on maternity leave at the salon."

Mallory, Shayna, and I share a knowing look. All of us think Alyssa's in love with her best guy friend, Austin Bradford. Yes, *that* Austin Bradford—the star shortstop for the Louisville Mustangs. Even though Alyssa swears she and Austin are only friends, she has yet to convince us that's true.

"And my happy is that I gave the best balayage of my life this week to one of the MLB players' girlfriends. Now she's referring all the other WAGs my way."

"WAGs?" Mallory raises an eyebrow.

"Wives and girlfriends of professional athletes."

"Oh, so you're going to be a WAG soon." Shayna smiles conspiratorially.

Alyssa rolls her eyes. "Like I've told y'all a million times, Austin and I are *just* friends."

"I don't believe you're *just* anything, but whatever you have to tell yourself to sleep at night." Mallory tilts her head, leaving no room for arguments.

Trying to bring the conversation back around, I smile at Alyssa. "Having all of them book with you has to be great for business."

"Yeah, my schedule is filling up fast."

"That's awesome, Lyss," Shayna says as I make another careful swipe of nail polish on my thumb.

"What movie—" Someone knocking on the front door cuts off my question.

"I'll get it." Shayna pops up from the couch and rounds the corner to our foyer. Winston chases after her.

I only hear the mumblings of conversation before Shayna reappears in the living room with Tyler behind her. When he spots all of us on the couch, he rubs the back of his neck, making the muscles in his arm ripple. I try not to stare, but I can't help it. Even if I can't stand the man, I can still appreciate good muscles. I mean, if he's waking me up at four-thirty every morning, he'd better have good muscles to show for it.

But his biceps don't tell me why he's standing in my living room right now, looking like he wishes he could run right back out the door and never return.

He points toward our front door. "I'm sorry, I should go. It looks like I'm interrupting."

"It's just girls' night," Alyssa says, always the one to ease the tension in any room.

"We have it every week," Shayna adds with a smile.

Mallory gives Tyler a once-over as he takes a step back. "You already came over and interrupted, so you may as well just say whatever you came over for."

There's the blunt bestie I know and love. If there's ever anyone I go to when I want them to tell it to me straight, Mal's my girl.

I can't help but admit that I'm curious why he came over, too. Even Winston is standing on guard behind our guest, assessing him.

Tyler has never knocked on our door in the two years we've been his next-door neighbors, so I can only imagine what's making him come to us now. Maybe he's baking and needs an egg or a cup of sugar. Maybe he has taken a second job as a pest control salesman and wants to sell us his service. Or, if I'm lucky, maybe he has finally learned the errors of his ways and is coming to apologize for all the early-morning workouts and promise to delete his hip-hop playlist forever.

After a longing glance toward our foyer, Tyler turns back to us with a sigh. "I know I haven't been the best neighbor, and I'm sorry for that, but I'm in a bit of a situation and was wondering if one of you might be able to help me out."

Mallory sits up taller, angling all her sass at him. "You're here asking for our help, but do you even know our names?"

"Alyssa, Mallory, Shayna, and Kelsey." Her eyebrows raise, and he laughs awkwardly, motioning to me. "Kelsey told me all your names when she dropped off my mail after y'all moved in. Although, I'm not entirely sure who's who."

Shayna smiles warmly beside him and shakes his hand. "I'm Shayna Monroe. Happy to finally make your acquaintance, Tyler."

"Alyssa Cartwright." She runs her fingers through her blonde waves. "Nice to finally meet you."

He offers them both a closed-lip smile in return before turning to Mal.

"Mallory Porter." She gives him an appraising look. "I don't like you."

"Noted." His jaw ticks like he's trying not to set her off with any kind of physical reaction.

When he turns to me expectantly, I shoot him an exasperated look. "You already know my name."

"Only Kelsey. You know my first *and* last name, so it's only fair I know yours."

I stare him down, unwilling to blink first. When his eyelids close for the briefest second, I smile in satisfaction, knowing that I won even if he didn't know what game we were playing.

Shayna looks back and forth between us, obviously uncomfortable and wanting to play peacemaker. "Tyler Reed, meet Kelsey Anderson."

"Anderson," he murmurs, like he's test-driving a car.

I don't like the sound of my last name coming out of his mouth one bit.

"All right, now that you know our names, what kind of situation are we talking about?" Mallory jumps right in, asking the question we all want the answer to—well, at least I do.

He runs his hand along his neck. "It turns out I need a nanny for a few months for my five-year-old niece. I called every babysitting service I could find earlier today, and they all laughed me off the phone or just hung up on me when I told them I needed someone to start Monday. Who knew nannies were booked up so far in advance?"

Tyler lets out a breathy laugh. "So, that's why I'm here. I know you all work, but I wanted to see if any of you have room in your schedule to pick up my niece from school and watch her until I get home from work. I know we're just neighbors, but you're the only people I know in this city aside from my sister and coworkers."

"I wish I could help." Alyssa frowns, obviously feeling bad for the predicament he's in. "I'm a hairdresser, and my schedule stays pretty booked, so I wouldn't be available every day."

"Me neither," Mallory says. "I'm a teacher, but I help with tutoring after school a few days a week."

Shayna sighs. "I work full-time at a flower shop, so I can't help either."

Everyone turns to me, and I can tell my friends are reining back smiles at the irony that Tyler Reed needs help, and I'm the only one who can give it.

"I already work four jobs," I say.

Alyssa shoots me a look and then whispers in my ear, "They're flexible, though."

Do I work four jobs? Yes.

But could I rearrange my schedule to help Tyler? Also yes.

"Plus, she was a nanny and dog sitter throughout college," Shayna adds. "So, she'd be perfect for the position."

Tyler's eyes narrow slightly like he's trying to get a read on me. "You work *four* jobs?"

"Yeah, but depending upon how much pay we're talking about here, I might be able to quit one or two of them."

"Kels." Alyssa nudges my arm.

"What? He always leaves the house in scrubs; we all know he's a doctor."

Mallory snorts.

Tyler covers his mouth to stifle the sound of surprised laughter, but I hear it, and I feel oddly satisfied that I was the reason for it. He rubs a hand across his jawline, drawing my gaze to the shadow of stubble covering it. I swallow hard and stare him down.

Shayna steps between us, offering a calming presence and a kind smile. "How about you two meet up in the morning? You can sleep on it and come together with fresh eyes and discuss what the job would entail."

Tyler nods and turns to me. "Wanna come by around eight? We can talk numbers and details then, but I'd make it worth your while. I know I'm asking a lot here, especially at the last minute."

"Works for me," I say.

"I'll see you then, Kelsey Anderson."

I narrow my gaze. "Not if I see you first, Tyler Reed."

Shayna walks him back to the front door, and Alyssa fans herself with a throw pillow. "Girl, I think we need to call the fire department from the sparks flying between you two."

"Oh, stop." I shake my head.

"No, seriously, you could cut the romantic tension with a knife."

I look at Mallory, wanting her to agree with me about how ridiculous Alyssa's comments are. She shrugs. "As much as I don't like him for how he wakes you up all the time, Lyss isn't wrong."

"There has never been and never will be *anything* between me and Tyler freaking Reed except loathing."

They look at each other with playful grins.

"I give it two months." Alyssa pulls up a streaming platform on the television and scrolls through the romantic comedy section.

"I give it three."

"You're on." Mallory and Alyssa shake hands as I watch in abject horror that they're betting that I'll fall for our jerk of a neighbor.

"What are we betting about?" Shayna eyes them as she takes a seat on the couch.

"How long it'll take for Tyler and Kelsey to fall in love," Mallory says matter-of-factly.

I grab a piece of popcorn from the bowl and throw it at her.

"Oooh," she squeals. "I give it a month."

I grab another popcorn kernel and throw it at her. "Do you all have such little faith in me?"

"It's just the law of attraction, Kels." Alyssa grabs the piece of popcorn that landed on Mallory's hot-pink sweatshirt and tosses it in her mouth.

Okay, sure, *objectively*, Tyler is handsome. Being a pediatrician might move him up a notch on the hotness scale too. But I'm not focused on romance when all my time and energy is going into saving to open my dog rescue. Even if I wasn't, I'd never date the man who has been a nuisance for the past two years.

"Let's up the ante a little bit, then." I lean in closer. "If any of you are correct, I'll buy a nice espresso maker and make you good coffee every day for a month straight. But if I don't fall in love with him—which I won't—y'all have to make me dinner for a month."

They smile at each other and rise from the couch. All four of us come together and cross our arms, making hand hearts with each other in a little circle. It's been our version of a pinky promise since middle school.

"You'd better start saving your pennies now, Kels," Mallory says as she falls back onto the couch.

As Alyssa puts on one of our favorite romcoms where the enemies become lovers, I smile because I know that will never be how my story ends with Tyler. I don't have to worry about spending the money on a fancy espresso machine because I know there's no way I could possibly lose this bet.

Right?

# CHAPTER FOUR

## TYLER

THERE'S NO EXPLANATION FOR what came over me last night.

I'm just going to say it was a desperate moment of exhaustion and defeat that led to me asking my female neighbors for help watching my niece. We're not even going to mention that Kelsey Anderson is coming over in five minutes to discuss the details of potentially hiring her.

I'm in a bind.

A big bind.

An I-don't-have-a-nanny-for-my-niece-and-need-one-to-start-in-two-days kind of bind.

When I went next door yesterday, I'd hoped one of Kelsey's three roommates would be able to help. But I hesitated when it came down to the only option being Kelsey. From my minimal encounters with her over the past two years, I'm not sure I can trust her. I mean, if she lets her dogs pee all over my lawn, what is she going to teach my niece?

Although, her roommate did say that Kelsey was a nanny in college, so at least she has some experience…but I wish there was any other option.

A knock sounds at my front door. I didn't even know a knock could sound annoyed, but if anyone's can, it makes sense that it's Kelsey's. How do I know it's her? It's 8:01. Of course she'd be one minute late to annoy me.

After double-checking that the coffee pot is still warm, I head to the front door. I'm greeted with Kelsey's unsmiling face. She steps past me without a word, entering my safe haven. I immediately regret this entire situation.

The only women who have been in my house are my female family members and my last serious girlfriend—but I try not to think about the woman who left me for being too dedicated to my work and my sister as she went through her divorce. It's strange to allow another woman into my space, especially one who doesn't like me.

Kelsey's eyes roam around my space like she's an appraiser trying to determine the value of my property. I rub the back of my neck as I wait for her to finish her thorough perusal.

After a minute, she turns to me and crosses her arms. "I guess I should've expected a doctor's house to be orderly. I'm pretty sure I could wipe my finger on your baseboards, and it would come back clean."

I just wiped down my baseboards last week, but I'm not about to tell her that. "I like a clean space." I gesture to the kitchen table and Kelsey walks past me again, hitting me with a whiff of floral perfume that is just the right amount to be pleasant but not overwhelming. "Do you want any coffee?"

"I never say no to coffee."

I pour her a cup and set it down in front of her, next to the bottle of organic vanilla creamer I already got out since I don't know how she takes her coffee. She adds a little of it to her mug, and I make a mental note and then scratch it out. There's no reason I need to memorize how Kelsey likes her coffee.

She takes a sip and grimaces.

"I take it back. I might say no to *your* coffee."

I swallow another gulp from my mug. "I thought it tasted fine."

"Coffee isn't supposed to be *fine*. It's supposed to be an engaging experience, a heavenly ambrosia."

I snort and she shoots me a glare.

"Good coffee involves all the senses. It's the perfect balance of complex flavors, bright and sweet and the slightest bit acidic."

"What are you, a coffee connoisseur?" My sarcasm hangs in the air.

"I'm a barista at Rise and Grind Café."

My lips press into a firm line. Of course, she is. "Let me guess, that's one of the jobs you might have to quit if you become my niece's nanny?"

She nods and starts to stand. "But I'm starting to think this wasn't the best idea."

I reach my hand across the table, grabbing hers to stop her from leaving. She immediately snatches her hand back, reminding me of an angry cat who hates physical touch. As much as I'd love to show her the door, I need to suck up to her big time if I want her to agree to be Evie's nanny. Just call me the world's biggest brown-noser.

"I'm sorry. Please, just have a conversation with me before you decide anything."

The way Kelsey's gaze narrows has me feeling like she has X-ray vision and can see right through me. Or maybe she's a psychic and can read my thoughts. Either way, it has sweat beading at my temples.

Thankfully, she sits back down. "Fine, you have ten minutes. Convince me, Doctor Evil."

I raise a brow. "Doctor Evil?"

"It's one of the many names I call you in my mind."

Lovely. Looks like we're off to a great start here.

"Well, uh, thanks for meeting me." I clear my throat. "You mentioned last night that you have four jobs?"

"Yep. Like I mentioned, I may be able to quit one or two of them depending upon how much you're offering."

"What does your work schedule look like with the jobs you want to keep?"

"I'd want to keep my dog-walking clients, but I could change up the times I walk them to be outside of my nannying hours." She fiddles with the sleeve of her maroon sweater. "I also would like to maintain my activities coordinator position at an assisted living facility. I coordinate all of our volunteers, so I should be able to do that outside of this position as well. There may be an occasional event on Thursday afternoons I need to attend, but Mallory already said she could have your niece hang out in her classroom while she tutors on those days."

"But you'd quit your barista job…and?" I ask, not knowing what her other job is.

"I'm a virtual assistant for an author, but I have a few friends in the business I could send her way to replace me."

I blow out a low whistle. "So you really have four jobs?"

"I'm many things, Tyler, but a liar isn't one of them," she bites back.

"I wasn't implying—" I start, then cut off my sentence since that was exactly what it sounded like I was implying. "I only meant that's a heavy schedule to balance."

"I manage." She brushes a strand of her caramel-brown hair behind her ear. "What would you expect from me as a nanny?"

"You'd have to pick Evie up from school every day and make her a snack. Help her with her homework. That kind of thing. Pickup is at two-twenty. I'd pay you starting at two for your drive to the school to cover your gas expenses. I should be home by five-thirty every day, except on Thursdays, it's closer to six-thirty."

Her face scrunches in concentration like she's doing math in her head. "So, you'd need me a little over eighteen hours a week." I nod, and her eyes move back to me. "What kind of pay are you offering with this position? I know you said you'd make it worth my while."

I swallow hard. I did say that, but I hope she doesn't try to drain my bank account. I got lucky with scholarships and worked an extra job throughout medical school, but I'm not a money tree. "That depends. What do you make at the two jobs you might quit?"

Kelsey gives me the number, and I sigh, knowing I need to give her an offer she can't refuse, even if I wish there was any other option than her. As much as I hate to admit it, I need Kelsey's help, and that might require some groveling.

"I'll double it if you can start this Monday."

Her eyes go wide. "You'll *double* what I make?"

I clench my teeth but nod.

She's quiet for a minute, and I start to bounce my knee under the table. If she says no, I don't have a backup plan. She *is* the backup plan.

"I'll do it." She stands and walks around to my side of the table, extending her hand.

*Now* she'll let me touch her? With her personality, I guess I shouldn't expect anything less than Kelsey needing everything to be on her terms.

I shake her hand, trying to ignore how soft her skin feels. Apparently, I've missed a feminine touch in my life more than I thought if I'm thinking about the feeling of Kelsey's fingers wrapped around mine.

I'm walking her to the door when she says, "Don't go getting any ideas that I'm doing this because I like you. I'm only doing this for your niece…and the money."

I roll my eyes. "I'm a doctor, not delusional."

Reluctantly, I hand Kelsey a key to my house. The thought of her being here when I'm not around makes me feel uneasy, but like I said, I don't have any other options.

"Thanks for agreeing to watch Evie," I mutter. It's the only gratitude I can offer when I feel like I'm making a big mistake.

"You won't regret this." Kelsey offers me a sly smile that does, indeed, have me regretting this.

At least one of my problems is solved: I have a nanny for Evie. But a new problem replaces it. I'm going to have to figure out how to muster enough patience to deal with Kelsey Anderson for the next three months.

———— ♡ ♡ ♡ ————

I still can't believe I hired Kelsey. Let alone the fact that I offered her *double* what she made as a barista and virtual assistant. I'm pretty sure I was swindled…or maybe blinded by my immediate need for help with Evie. We'll go with that.

Kelsey and I have gotten on each other's nerves since she and her friends moved in two years ago when I was still finishing up my residency. I was focused on reaching my career goal of becoming a pediatrician, and I know I wasn't the welcoming neighbor I should have been. Once I graduated from residency and became a licensed and board-certified pediatric doctor, it felt awkward to try and start a friendship with them.

I still regret not being kinder when they moved in. After all, we're the only people in the neighborhood under sixty. But then I think of how Kelsey lets her dogs pee all over my yard and glares at me every morning, and regret washes away like footprints on a beach when a giant wave hits the shore.

I need to stop letting Kelsey get in my head. Though, that may be difficult to do when she'll be at my house five days a week.

I huff in frustration and turn my focus to the website I pulled up on my laptop again. Evie. I need to figure out everything I need to do before Tess drops her off tomorrow.

After a few quick internet searches—and what I know from my pediatric medical training—I've determined three things.

One: Evie needs a routine. Although, this may be a bit more difficult since she's not used to living with me. But at least I can wake her up and put her to bed around the same time every day.

Two: I need to make sure she has time to play outside and use her imagination, which also means limiting screen time. I also need to make sure she has time with her friends to learn social skills and teach her other important things like cooperation and owning up to her mistakes.

Three: Kids eat *a lot*. Obviously, I knew I'd need to make breakfast, pack a lunch, and make her dinner. However, I didn't realize the amount of snacks I apparently should have on hand.

While I know a lot of this stuff from my research and work with kids, I have a feeling putting it all into practice will turn out differently than I expected.

Staring at my computer screen, I'm beginning to feel like a cup that's overflowing. It feels impossible to hold any more information, so I push up from my desk chair. After slipping on my shoes, I grab my keys and wallet and head out the front door to my car.

I give my sister a call on the way to my first stop.

"Please don't tell me you're changing your mind," she answers, her tone pleading.

"Hello to you too, sis."

"I'm dropping Evie off tomorrow. It's too late for you to back out now."

I hold up one of my hands before I realize she can't see me. "Relax, I'm not backing out."

"Oh, good." She blows out a relieved breath. "Then why'd you call?"

"I wanted to let you know that I found a reputable"—I shake my head at the thought of calling Kelsey *reputable*...but at least she's nannied before—"nanny for Evie who can pick her up from school and hang out with her until I get home from work."

"You didn't have to do that, but I trust your judgment."

"She deserves some normalcy. No kid wants to sit in a doctor's office for hours every day. But I'm also calling to see what Evie's favorite color is. I'm headed to Target to buy some decor to brighten up the guest room for her."

Her voice falls quiet. "You don't have to do that, Ty. You're already doing me a favor. She'll be fine."

There's no way I'm having my niece sleep in my decor-less guest room with a navy comforter.

"Just tell me her favorite color," I insist.

"It's pink right now, but don't hold me to it. I swear, it changes daily."

"Noted." I hover my thumb over the end call button on the steering wheel. "Thanks, see you tomorrow." I hang up as I hear her protesting again about me spoiling Evie. She's going to be living with me for a quarter of a year and is my only niece...of course I'm going to spoil her.

By the time I'm loading up at Target, I'm not sure I'll be able to fit groceries in my car. I might've gone a *little* overboard. My trunk is filled to the brim with everything girly. Pink curtains. A floral rug. A pink bedspread with a ruffle skirt and matching sheets. A plethora of throw pillows. Literally everything pink I could find.

I hope Tess will give me the essentials like a hairbrush, shampoo, and conditioner. I'm decent at styling my hair, but I wouldn't even begin to know what hair products a five-year-old girl needs.

Not wanting to take another trip into town, I decide to take a chance on everything fitting in my car. The next thing I know, I'm staring at the snack shelves in the grocery store, realizing I have no clue what Evie eats either.

"Does she like strawberry or apple cinnamon bars?" I mutter, looking back and forth between the boxes. I shrug and throw one of each into my shopping cart. *Guess I'm getting both.*

I continue walking through the aisles, adding healthy snacks to my cart, from clementines and baby carrots to yogurt bites. I make my way down an aisle to checkout when a box of protein pancake mix catches my attention. When I face forward again, it's too late to stop my forward momentum from crashing my cart straight into a brunette woman. She loses her grip on the shopping basket she's holding, and a mix of candy and other sugar-filled treats goes flying around us.

I rush around the cart and reach down to help her gather her food, if you can even call it that, with the amount of processed sugar in those items. I offer a hand to help her stand, but she rises on her own.

"I'm sorr—" My words cut off when I see who I ran into.

Standing before me, her cheeks burning red, is none other than Kelsey. I'm unsure if she's red with embarrassment or anger, but when her eyes narrow, I'm guessing it's the latter.

She places a hand on her hip. "Do you usually watch where you're going, or do you just bowl over anyone in your path? I need to know if I should get on the intercom and make a PSA to all the sweet old ladies in the store to steer clear if they see you coming their way."

I choose to ignore her snide remarks and grit my teeth. "I'm a little distracted today. I usually watch where I'm going."

I'm not sure if I'm seeing things, but I think her eyes soften the tiniest bit before taking on a more cunning gleam. "If you hurt me, does this count as worker's compensation?"

I shake my head. "I don't think it works that way."

"Well, it should." She rubs her lower back. "Now that I'm thinking about it, I do feel a little tweak."

I press my lips into a thin line. "If you go to the ER, you can send me the bill."

Kelsey peers into my cart. "Just looking at your food makes me sad. Where are the snacks?"

I lift up a box of protein bars. "These are snacks. Besides, most of this is for my niece."

"Isn't she five?"

I nod.

"Yeah, she's probably not going to eat half of this." Kelsey wrinkles her nose. "The fruit and some of the bars you can keep. But where's the kid-friendly food?"

"Kid-friendly?"

She looks unimpressed. Kelsey turns her head to the side, looking longingly at the self-checkout before turning back to me and placing her basket in my cart. She looks at the shelf beside us and adds a bottle of butter-flavored syrup to the cart.

"What're you doing?" I ask. "Do you need me to buy this for you?"

Kelsey let out an exasperated sigh like I couldn't be a bigger idiot. "What does it look like I'm doing? I'm helping you shop."

"I already shopped, but thanks."

"As her nanny, I think it's my civil duty to save Evie from her uncle's poor snack choices."

I cross my arms over my chest. She glances down at them, her cheeks flushing again. I bite back a smile. "Is that so?"

"Come on, Doolittle." She walks down the aisle.

"You know that's an animal doctor, right?" I call after her.

"Fine. Come on then, Frankenstein."

I take a deep breath, exhaling slowly through my nose. "That's even worse." And I don't know exactly why, but I follow her down the next aisle and the one after that, not saying a word as she throws in boxes of muffin mix, mac and cheese, and fruit snacks.

"Do these have *any* nutritious value?" I pick up the fruit snacks, and my eyes go wide when I read the sugar amount on the label.

Kelsey grabs it from my hands, throwing it back in the cart. "They're good for the soul."

I don't fight her, even though the thought of giving them to Evie makes me wince.

We make it out of the refrigerated and frozen aisles with bags of chicken nuggets, frozen pizzas, yogurt, and cheese sticks. Although everything Kelsey grabbed isn't what I would've picked, at least there's some protein and dairy in the mix.

Kelsey looks at the cart, places her hands on her hips, and a pleased smile covers her lips. "That oughta do it."

We reach the checkout line, and I start placing everything on the conveyor belt. I suppose I should thank Kelsey for her *help*, even though I didn't ask for it.

When we're waiting for the person in front of us to finish, I turn to her. "Thanks for your...insight."

She shrugs. "I've never been able to pass up helping a lost puppy when I see one."

I shake my head. Kelsey gets under my skin more than anyone else I've ever met. I know I asked her to be Evie's nanny out of desperation, but I have no clue how we're going to get through seeing each other every day for a few months without getting on each other's last nerve.

"How are we going to do this?" I ask.

"Do what?"

"Work together." I rub the back of my neck. "Be *cordial* to each other."

"It's simple, really." She leans against the side of the conveyor belt. "You just have to learn to be a respectful, civil neighbor who doesn't blast music at four in the morning, and then maybe I'll consider not letting the dogs pee in your yard."

"Yesterday, you didn't seem to mind the fact that I work out." I smirk, remembering how she'd blushed after looking at my arms. It looked similar to the blush covering her cheeks right now, except this one is more angry than ogling.

"I don't know what you *think* you saw, but you can erase it from your mind. I don't find you attractive." Her expression hardens, hiding all emotion.

I wipe a hand over my brow. "Whew, that's a relief. You should probably work on your staring-at-muscles problem then. And your blushing problem."

Kelsey shoves my chest. "You're right. Maybe we shouldn't work together. I wouldn't want to punch you in the face in front of your niece. Imagine how embarrassing that would be for you."

I take a step closer, smirking down at her. "I'd like to see you try."

The clearing of a throat has me dragging my gaze up to the cashier.

"Whenever y'all are finished with"—she motions to us with a raised brow—"whatever that is, I can get you rung up."

Kelsey's blush deepens. She grabs her shopping basket out of my cart and shoves past me, moving toward the self-checkout.

"I guess I'll see you at home," I call after her in a sarcastic tone, and Kelsey raises a hand in a sassy wave.

I push the cart up to the register and offer my best smile to the clerk. "Sorry about that."

"Not a problem." She begins scanning my items. "Trust me, I've seen my fair share of lover's quarrels. You wouldn't imagine how many arguments people get into over groceries."

"Oh, I'm not— We're not—" I stumble over my words.

The clerk grins. "Just give it time, sugar. There's a fine line between enemies and lovers."

I hold back a scoff. I know with *certainty* there isn't any love there. Kelsey and I will just have to see if we can put our grievances aside long enough to make it through these next three months in front of Evie.

Then we never have to speak to each other again.

# CHAPTER FIVE

## TYLER

SUNDAY AFTERNOON ARRIVES BEFORE I'm ready for it. Even though my situation is entirely different, I feel like I have the smallest glimpse into how new parents feel coming home from the hospital with a newborn. Except I'm being given a child who has opinions and can talk back.

I'm already feeling the whole lack of sleep thing after how late I stayed up getting Evie's room ready last night and childproofing my living room and kitchen. I stored all breakable decor away in closets and ensured everything in my fridge was kid-friendly. Even though I slept thirty minutes past my normal wake-up time to work out, I still only got about four hours of sleep, which doesn't seem like nearly enough to function.

I give props to all the new parents who run on little to no sleep. I'd give everyone their coffee of choice if I could. Instead of trying to solve the parenting population's need for caffeination, I find myself waving at Tess and Evie as their car slows to a stop in front of my house.

As soon as they park, Evie runs to me with a giant grin. "Uncle Ty!"

"I missed you, Eves." I crouch and catch her in a hug.

She's barely in my arms before she wiggles out of them and runs around me toward the front door.

My sister pulls me in for a hug. I wince as she yells after her daughter right by my ear. "Evie, your uncle says he missed you."

When I pull back, I can tell Tess is annoyed by the scrunch of her nose. That expression was aimed at me plenty of times growing up, and I'm glad I'm not the recipient of this one.

Evie stops in her tracks and huffs. "I want to see my new room."

My sister tilts her head and puts on a motherly tone. "Remember what we talked about."

"I *do* remember. You said he decorated a room just for me."

"And…" Tess's eyes take on a look that would persuade a child into spilling everything.

"To put on my listening ears."

"And…"

Her shoulders drop as she acquiesces. "To be nice to Uncle Ty."

Tess smiles, seemingly pleased with her daughter's response.

Evie runs back over and hugs my legs. "Sorry, Uncle Ty. I missed you too. Love you." She turns her head to look at her mom. "*Now* can I go see my room?"

I laugh. Tess glares at me. When her gaze moves back to her daughter, she sighs and waves her hand toward the door in defeat. "Go ahead."

As soon as Evie is out of sight, Tess smacks my arm. "Way to back me up there."

I hold my hands up innocently. "Hey, I'm just the funcle." I grimace as soon as the word is out.

She frowns. "Please don't ever say that again."

"Yeah, I don't plan on it."

"Good." She pats my arm. "Now, be a doll and go put your muscles to use." Tess throws me her car keys and heads inside, leaving me alone with her car full of bags.

I shake my head and unlock her car. There's not a chance I'd have let her carry a single bag inside anyway. It takes me a few minutes to get Evie's stuff inside. It practically fills my entire living room.

"Is she moving in forever?" I call out to my sister, knowing she's around here somewhere. There's no way all of this will fit in the guest room.

My sister pokes her head out from the built-in reading nook in the hallway between the living room and kitchen. I don't have much time to read, but Tess and Evie would kill me if I ever got rid of this hundred-year-old feature.

She shrugs. "I'm just preparing you for parenthood. But, oh wait, getting to that stage would require you to date someone."

"*Tess*," I draw out her name, the edge in my voice serving as a warning. If I let my sister, our great-aunt Darla, and my receptionist Nadine have their way, I would be out on blind dates every single night. "Like I've told you a million times, I don't want to be set up."

She joins me in the living room and gives me her best puppy eyes. "But Evie's teacher is sweet and single, and I showed her a picture of you. She thinks you're cute, so I really think you should reconsider." Tess pulls her phone out and shows me a picture of a pretty blonde who barely looks old enough to have graduated college.

"Tess," I growl, and she rolls her eyes.

"What is it this time?" She pokes my chest hard, and I wince. Is it possible to strengthen one's fingers? I feel like

I should know this as a doctor. "Are you not into blondes? Do you not appreciate teachers?"

I shoot my sister a look.

"Okay, fine. You're a big hotshot pediatrician, so you probably appreciate other occupations that work with children." She crosses her arms. "What is it, then? Why won't you let anyone set you up?" I open my mouth, but she cuts me off again. "And don't even think about lying because I know you've turned down Aunt Darla trying to set you up too. How you can tell that sweet old woman no is beyond me."

I wait a moment and then say, "Are you done now?"

She shakes her head. "Not unless you're going to tell me the real reason. Otherwise, I have a lot more fight left in me."

I barely refrain from rolling my eyes, knowing she'll tell me they'll get stuck that way and I'll end up cross-eyed. When we were kids, I was thoroughly convinced she was telling the truth. "It's stupid."

Tess settles on my plush gray sofa, cuddling one of my cream throw pillows on her lap. "Try me." I glance toward the stairs, and she waves her hand like she knows what I'm thinking. "Evie won't hear you. She's setting up all her stuffed animals just how she likes them, and that takes her forever."

With a sigh, I sit on my matching gray recliner. "Call me crazy, but I've always wanted to meet someone the old-fashioned way."

"That's perfect." Tess claps her hands together. "People were set up by their families often in the olden days."

No amount of restraint can stop my eyes from rolling this time.

"You know your eyes are going to get stuck that way," she quips.

"They haven't for thirty years, so I think I'm good," I bite back, falling into our easy sibling banter. I love Tess more than life itself, but she can get under my skin better than anyone else. Well, maybe anyone else *except* Kelsey.

"I'm not talking about being set up by family. I mean a run-in at the grocery store when we both reach for the same tomato. Or we're both at our favorite singer's concert, and our eyes meet across the crowd. Or we grab each other's coffee orders and exchange numbers by the time we leave the shop."

Her face pulls into a happy pout, and I know I'm in for an earful. "Aw, I never would've guessed you to be a hopeless romantic." Her mouth turns up into a scheming grin. "You go grocery shopping on Saturdays, right?"

"Yeah…" I stare her down, trying to figure out what she's getting at. "Why?"

She pulls out her phone and starts tapping quickly on the screen. "Oh, nothing."

"Tess, I swear if you're texting Evie's teacher to go to the grocery store next Saturday and meet me by the tomatoes, I will never speak to you again."

She stops typing to look up at me with a raised brow. "*Never?*"

"Never."

Tess tosses her phone onto the cushion beside her. "Ugh, fine, you win."

I let out an exasperated laugh. "You don't give up easy, do you?"

"You can't fault me for wanting my baby brother to find love and happiness and give Evie cousins to play with."

"Oh my gosh, get out of my house." I shake my head and point toward the front door.

She holds a hand to her chest and puts on a fake pout. "Is that how you're going to treat me before I leave for three months? I honestly don't know how you'll function without me."

"I think I'll manage."

Truth is, I'll miss Tess more than she realizes, but I'll never tell her that. Our great-aunt Darla is in an assisted living facility nearby, and I stop by and visit her once a week after work. But Tess is the family member who calls me a few times a week, texts me consistently, and has me over every Sunday for family dinner.

I know how badly Tess is going to miss her daughter, and I don't want to make her feel any worse for leaving, especially when this is such a great opportunity for her job.

She glances at her phone and sighs. "I really should get going. I need to drop my car off at home and call an Uber."

I stand and walk her to the door. "Are you sure you don't want us to drop you off?"

Tess nods. "It'll be harder to say bye to Evie there. At least I can cry in my Uber in peace." She swipes at a tear falling down her cheek.

I pull her to my chest and hug her tight. "Evie and I will be fine. I'll send you so many pictures you're going to get sick of it and put me on do not disturb."

Her laugh is shaky, like she's fighting off a flood of tears. "You better."

"Evie," I call upstairs. "Come say goodbye to your mom." Her little feet pounding on the old Victorian wood floors echoes throughout the house. I offer Tess one more reassuring squeeze. "You've got this."

When Evie reaches the bottom step, she flies into her mother's waiting arms.

"I'll give you all a minute to say goodbye." I start walking to the kitchen.

Tess thanks me again, and I offer her a smile before giving them privacy. I fiddle around with a pen on my kitchen island for a few minutes until I hear the front door click shut and a soft sniffling sound.

When I step back into the living room, I spot Evie looking out the front window, wiping her nose as she waves. I make my way over and kneel, opening my arms to her. She falls into them, and I hold her as she cries until her sniffles subside.

"You okay, Eves?" I hesitantly ask, not wanting to start another round of waterworks.

She wipes her eyes and nods. "What are we going to do now?"

"What do you think about going out for Sunday dinner? You can pick anywhere you want."

Evie's eyes go wide with excitement. "*Anywhere?*"

I nod even though I'm worried I made a mistake and she'll pick a kid's favorite, like greasy fast food or gas station pizza.

Her lips pull to the side as she thinks, and Evie's eyes are alight when she looks up at me. "I want Chipotle."

Relief floods through me. "That is an excellent choice." I open the front door and exaggeratedly motion for her to step outside. "After you, madame."

She giggles and curtsies before stepping out onto the porch. I lock the door behind us and help her get in the car, double-checking that her booster seat is still secure since the last time she used it.

When I get into the driver's seat, I take a deep breath, feeling more confident that I can parent Evie for the next three months. But nothing seems to calm my nerves knowing that I'll be coming home tomorrow to Kelsey Anderson in my house.

And suddenly, I've lost my appetite.

# CHAPTER SIX

## KELSEY

"Hɪ, Ms. Kᴇʟsᴇʏ!"

I search through the sea of children until I spot Evie running toward me, sporting a giant grin. I can't hold back the smile that pulls at my lips from seeing the joy on her face.

Tyler arranged for me to meet Evie briefly last night so we'd know each other when I picked her up from school today. She was shy then—nothing like the enthusiastic girl in front of me now.

"Hey, Evie." I kneel so I'm on her level. "Did you have a good day at school?"

"I finished writing the whole alphabet today," she says enthusiastically as I help her into the booster seat Tyler gave me, and she buckles herself in. "Most of my friends are still on 'm'."

"Wow, that's awesome."

I can't remember anything about kindergarten. Well, except that a boy named Owen was obsessed with me, chased me on the playground, and kissed my arm, leaving behind a ketchup stain on my favorite sweater. You know, the important things.

When I return to the driver's seat, I ask, "Do you like your classmates?"

She regales me with all the kindergarten drama for the rest of the drive home. By the time I'm helping her out of the booster seat and grabbing her backpack, I know about everyone in her class, from the kid who is a booger-picker and which of her friends always has the best food at lunch.

I stand in front of the door and hesitate. It feels weird entering Tyler's house without him there…like I'm breaking in even though I have a key. I'm half-worried that the cops will show up the minute I open his front door, but thankfully, instead of sirens, all I hear is the sound of Evie's little feet pounding against the hardwood floors as she runs past me into the house.

I lock it behind us and follow her into the kitchen, placing my purse on the counter. "Let's get you a snack."

Evie wrinkles her nose. "Uncle Ty has healthy snacks."

I hold up a box of fruit snacks like it's Simba from *The Lion King*. "Except when Ms. Kelsey helps him shop."

"You're the best." Her grin is the widest one I've seen yet.

I tear a pack of fruit snacks open and hand it to her with a cheese stick because I'm all about *balance*.

"Can I see what homework you need to get done?" I ask as she bites into the cheese. I've always been more of a tear-it-and-eat-it kind of girl, you know, since it's called *string* cheese, but I digress.

Evie pulls a blue folder from her backpack and slides it across the granite countertop. "Ms. Martinez puts new homework on one side and my graded work on the other for my mom to see."

"Mind if I look?"

Evie shakes her head, and I sift through the pile of graded homework. I blow out a low whistle. "There's a lot of A's in here. You should be proud of yourself."

She shrugs, popping another fruit snack in her mouth. "Kindergarten is easy."

Evie's words come out like she's saying *the sky is blue* or *Taylor Swift is the best pop star of our generation*—something that's an irrefutable fact.

I take out the single sheet of work on the other side. "This is all you have to do tonight?"

"Yep." She reaches over, takes it, and pulls a pencil out of her backpack. Evie makes quick work of her math sheet as she finishes her snack. After putting away her homework, she smiles up at me. "Want to see my room?"

"Sure."

I follow her up the stairs but quickly regret my decision when she opens the first door on the left.

"This is Uncle Ty's room."

I didn't want to walk in Tyler's front door, let alone see enemy territory—his bedroom. My hand pushes the door open a little further as if it has an independent brain controlling its actions.

*Well, since it's open, I may as well take a small look.* My eyes roam over the space, not surprised in the slightest at how tidy it is. His whole house looks clean enough to perform surgery in, but still homey at the same time with little touches of him.

There's a picture of Tyler with his parents, sister, and Evie on the nightstand, and a book propped open. He has the same navy blue throw pillows on a small couch and his bed, bringing a deeper tone to contrast with the house's white walls.

Beautiful pieces of abstract art are perfectly placed on the walls throughout the home. The only thing out of place is Evie's art on the fridge, filling the space with an array of colors it would otherwise be lacking.

Evie groans, grabbing my hand and pulling me down the hall. "His room is boring." She points to the next room on the left. "So is this one. I'm not allowed in there."

I know what's behind the door before I even open it. His workout room—the *real* enemy territory. The room where he blasts his hip-hop music and wakes me up every morning like the class-A jerk he is. I push the door open and find exactly what I expected: a treadmill, a weight bench, dumbbells, and the like. I have no idea what the weird fabric covering all the walls is, but I don't work out, so maybe that's a normal thing.

Through the open curtains, I can see the window to my bedroom. A shiver makes its way down my spine, and I quickly pull the door shut.

"*My* room is fun." Evie leads me to the other side of the hallway. With an air of drama, she throws open a door and flips the light switch. A queen bed sits on the opposite wall with a blush pink bedspread. The entire space is a pink haven, from the curtains and rug to the pom poms hanging from the ceiling.

Even though it may not seem like it from her personality, my roommate Mallory is obsessed with all things pink. But I think even she would be a little overwhelmed by its abundance.

Gesturing to the space, I say, "Your uncle did a great job decorating. You must love pink."

Evie shrugs. "It was my favorite color yesterday."

I smile at her honesty. "What is it today?"

"Yellow." She reaches a pinky out to me. "Don't tell Uncle Ty. I don't want him to be sad."

I wrap my pinky finger around her small one. "I promise."

He might've gone a little overboard, but even I can admit that it was sweet of Tyler to decorate for her.

"Let me introduce you to my stuffies." Evie leads me to her bed, and there's an entire lineup of stuffed animals on her mattress.

I smile politely through all the *introductions*, knowing I'll be lucky if I remember any of their names. Let's just say I lost count after thirty-seven.

After what feels like an eternity, Evie points to the final stuffed animal in her lineup. "And this one is Snuffykins." Evie hops up on the bed, looking tiny on the queen-sized mattress. "So, what do you think?"

"Snuffykins is the perfect name for a stuffed elephant."

She nods. "I thought so."

"What do you want to do until your uncle gets home from work?"

She looks thoughtful before a smile covers her face. "Maybe we could play a game and then make dinner for Uncle Ty."

I expected a suggestion like playing a game, but I would've never guessed she'd suggest we have a meal waiting for Tyler when he gets home.

I raise a brow. "You'd rather cook than go for a walk or ride your bike?"

Evie nods. "Mama said he was nice to let me stay with him. I'm only five, so I can't cook, but I figured you could. You have to be at least fifteen, right?"

I laugh. "Try twenty-four."

Her eyes go wide. "You're almost as old as Uncle Ty."

"Really?" I ask, running a hand through my hair. I've always been curious about how old he was...just because he's my neighbor, and I feel like I should know those things. No other reason. "How old is he?"

"Thirty. His last birthday party was called 'Death to My Twenties'. My mama put a bunch of fake tombstones and skeletons in our backyard. Isn't that scary?"

"Very spooky." I smirk. "Let's go find a game to play."

Evie jumps off the bed and runs out into the hall. Her feet pound down the stairs before I'm even out of her room.

When I reach the living room, Evie already has Trouble set up on the coffee table.

"Oh, I loved this game when I was your age."

Well, I certainly don't like it anymore. Or at least I'm not *good* at it anymore.

After Evie whips my booty three games in a row, we move to the kitchen to get started on dinner.

"You said your uncle likes healthy food?"

Evie nods. "But can you make something yummy?"

"We'll do both."

She comes over and gives me a high-five as I open the fridge and take a look at what Tyler has. I'm not at all surprised to find it stocked with a variety of vegetables and fresh proteins. When I spot fresh mozzarella pearls in the fridge and basil in a fruit bowl on the counter, I know exactly what I'll cook.

"We're going to make Caprese chicken with cheesy rice and broccoli." Evie eyes me warily, and I shoot her a reassuring smile. "I promise it will be good."

"If you say so."

I pull some seasonings out of a perfectly organized drawer. "Do you want to help me?"

She nods eagerly, so I search through Tyler's other drawers until I find measuring spoons and hand them to her. I read the measurements aloud from a recipe on my phone and help Evie add all the seasonings into a bowl.

"Why don't you tear off these basil leaves for me while I slice the chicken and other ingredients?" I suggest.

Evie sits on the barstool at the island and accepts the bundle of basil I hand her. I preheat the oven and search around the kitchen until I find a cutting board and knife. After slicing a chicken breast in half, I heat olive oil in a skillet and get the rice going before sprinkling the seasonings Evie measured over the chicken. Once the skillet is hot, I place the chicken in it and slice a tomato and the mozzarella pearls.

"Here you go," Evie says, giving me the basil leaves.

"Thank you." I quickly chiffon them and start to chop the broccoli. "So, are you in any sports or activities after school?"

"Dance. I'm going to be a ballerina when I grow up." Her smile falls.

"What's wrong?"

"I don't get to do dance while I'm here."

I toss the broccoli in some avocado oil, salt, and pepper before putting it in the oven. I turn to Evie, giving her my full attention. "Why not?"

"Mama said she didn't want to put too much on Uncle Ty's plate." Her brow furrows. "I don't get it, though. There weren't any plates around."

"That's just a saying." I laugh. "It means she didn't want to give him too many more things to do since he already has a lot of responsibilities."

"Then why didn't she just say that?"

"Sometimes adults make things complicated."

Evie huffs. "You can say that again."

I hide my smile behind my hand and move back to the stovetop, flipping the chicken while making a mental note to talk to Tyler about getting Evie back in her dance classes. She shouldn't have to give up her favorite activity for three months.

I grimace at the idea of calling me and Tyler a *we*. Let me be clear: we're only a *we* in the sense of watching after Evie—*not* a romantic *we*.

Once everything's ready, I dish rice and broccoli onto the plates and then put the chicken with some melted mozzarella pearls, a slice of tomato, and basil on top beside it. I top off the dish with balsamic drizzle, and it looks perfect.

I'm putting the two plates on the kitchen table when I hear the front door open. Evie runs past me and jumps into Tyler's waiting arms.

"Did you have a good day at school, Eves?"

"Yes," Evie exclaims before she proceeds to enthusiastically share every detail of her day. When she's done talking about school and how she destroyed me in Trouble, Evie points to the kitchen. "Then I helped Ms. Kelsey make you dinner."

Tyler's wide eyes move to me like he's shocked I would ever do something kind for him. Or maybe he thinks I poisoned his food.

I shrug. "I'm not a professional chef or anything, but I know my way around a kitchen."

His smile doesn't quite reach his eyes. "It smells great. Thank you."

I nod and move past him toward the front door.

"You're not going to eat with us?" Evie calls after me.

I turn to her and offer a warm smile. "I gotta get home, let my dog out, and make my own dinner, but I'll see you tomorrow."

"Okay, bye." She waves and heads to the kitchen.

When she's out of earshot, I look at Tyler and motion to the door. "Can we have a quick word outside?"

His face pales, but he follows me onto his porch. "Did Evie not listen? Are you going to quit? Because if you are, I need at least a week or two's notice to find someone else."

I hold my hands up. "There's no need to get yourself in a tizzy. I just wanted to talk to you about something."

Tyler clears his throat. "Sorry, what did you want to discuss?"

"Evie mentioned that she loves her dance classes."

His smile is genuine this time. "I've never missed one of her shows. She's great, and I'm not just saying that because I'm family."

If he's not a good neighbor, at least he's a good uncle. "Did you know that your sister pulled her out of dance for the time Evie's staying with you?"

"She did what?" he sputters. I think that flustered Tyler is my favorite version yet. It's nice to see the side of him that isn't completely put together. "I just assumed dance was a seasonal thing."

I shake my head. "Most dance schools run for the duration of the school year."

Tyler runs a hand through his hair. "Why would Tess pull her out?"

"Evie said her mom didn't want to put too much on your plate." I cross my arms, trying to stave off the chill from the early fall breeze. "I just wanted to let you know in case you wanted to reach out to her dance studio. I'm happy to drive her there after school if needed."

He nods. "Thanks for letting me know."

"I think this might be the most civil conversation we've ever had, Dr. Strange." I walk down his front steps and head toward my house.

"And you had to ruin it." I turn around just in time to catch Tyler's mock salute. "See you tomorrow, Crazy Dog Lady."

I glare at him. "That's Crazy Dog *Mom* to you."

He holds a hand to his chest. "Oh, excuse me."

"You're lucky I like Evie," I call back before continuing my quick walk home.

His low groan hits my ears, but I don't acknowledge it. If I'm going to have to put up with Tyler for the next three months, he's going to have to learn to put up with me too.

# CHAPTER SEVEN
## TYLER

KELSEY HAS BEEN MY nanny for three days and the world hasn't imploded, so I'd say we're doing pretty well. Or at least surviving. I'll take anything at the moment.

"You were right." Evie's eyes practically roll back in her head as she takes another bite of pizza. "This is the best pizza I've had in my *life*." Her emphasis on the word makes it sound like she's a pizza connoisseur.

I finish off my third slice, humming in agreement. Nothing can beat a good sourdough crust, in my opinion. Now, if we're talking about the best meals I've ever eaten…I still can't stop thinking about the Caprese chicken that Kelsey had waiting for me when I got home from work on Monday. Not that I'd ever admit that to *her*, but I wouldn't be mad if I found a plate of it at my kitchen table once a week.

I don't expect her to make me dinner, though. I didn't hire Kelsey to take care of anything other than my niece, and I told her as much yesterday when I got home from work to a pot roast dinner that was as delicious as the recipe my mom made growing up.

I shake my head and pull myself from thoughts of Kelsey.

"Auntie D told me to tell you hi and give you a big hug," I say.

Evie's nose wrinkles as she nibbles on her food. "She always squeezes me too tight, and her room smells like old people."

My sip of lemon water goes down the wrong pipe as I try to hide my laughter. I can't deny anything she just said when it's all true. After a few small coughs, I say, "She loves you though."

Every Thursday, I go to a local florist shop on my way home from work, buy a fresh bouquet, and stop by to give it to my aunt. Since my great-uncle passed and my parents are traveling the world, I try to make sure she's taken care of. It means I get home from work an hour later than usual on Thursdays, but I'm used to the routine now, and I typically enjoy my time with my great-aunt—except for when she's smothering me in one of her hugs or trying to set me up on a date.

When I got home today, a part of me hoped Kelsey might've made dinner again even though I told her it wasn't necessary, but instead of the smell of a home-cooked meal, I walked into my living room reeking of nail polish. I wasn't mad about it, because there's no way I'd have been able to paint Evie's nails half as well as Kelsey did.

There she is again, popping into my mind unbidden. It seems the more I've been around Kelsey, the more she appears in my thoughts like a nagging fly that won't leave you alone on a warm summer day.

It's not like I've even spent that much time with her. Kelsey leaves my house every day just as quickly as I arrive, as if she can't stand to be in the room with me for a second longer than necessary. I try not to let it get to my head. Besides, all my appointments ran over today, leaving me without a lunch break, so I was much too hungry to think about anything other than filling my growling stomach.

But now that my stomach is full of gooey cheese and pepperoni, the figurative fly is back taunting me.

I pay for the meal and grab the box of leftovers calling my name for tomorrow's lunch. As we park in front of the house, Kelsey is walking out of her front door with a dog on a leash. I glance in the rearview mirror and see Evie's whole face light up.

"Can we *please* walk Ms. Kelsey's dog with her?" she pleads, giving me her best puppy eyes expression. "Winston is so cute."

"Ms. Kelsey is home for the night, Eves. Just because we're her neighbors doesn't mean we—" Evie is out of the car, running toward her nanny before I can finish my sentence.

I unbuckle and grab the pizza box before chasing after her. When I reach them, Kelsey is kneeling, petting her dog while smiling kindly at my niece.

"I'd love for you to walk with us." Kelsey glances up at me. "That is, if it's all right with your uncle."

"You can go as long as she's sure she doesn't mind." I shoot Kelsey a meaningful look, trying to offer her an out.

She waves her hand like it's not a big deal. "I'd love to have her join. Besides, it looks like Winston has a new best friend."

"Okay, if you're sure, then y'all have fun." I'm heading to my house when Evie grabs my hand and pulls me to a stop.

"You have to come with us, Uncle Ty."

"I don't think—"

"Pleaseee." She cuts me off with the cutest puppy dog eyes. "It's getting dark. You wouldn't let Ms. Kelsey and me walk alone in the dark, right?"

Winston looks at her and then up at me with the same expression. These two are going to be trouble together.

"How can I say no to those faces?" I raise the pizza box. "Let me put this in the fridge, and we can head out." I jog to my house and hurry to unlock the front door, put the pizza away, and meet them back out front.

When I return, Kelsey is taking a picture of Evie and Winston, who both smile up at the camera. I'm a little freaked out by his facial expressions. Does Kelsey train all her dogs to smile? I don't know if that's even possible, but it's either that or this dog has a major personality.

As we start walking down the street, I can't remember the last time I took a walk for fun. It's refreshing, and the changing of the leaves to a beautiful array of yellow, orange, and red colors makes for a pleasant view.

When the silence between me and Kelsey becomes too much, I clear my throat.

"So, is this one of the dogs you walk?"

She nods. "He was, but he's my son now."

I bite back a laugh at her calling him her *son*.

"Oh, so I should expect him to use my lawn as his personal restroom every day now?"

"Unless you're ready to move your workout room to the other side of the house." She smirks.

"We already know you like to stare at my muscles." I flex. "So, I don't see what the problem is here."

"You're the one who keeps bringing up your muscles." Kelsey shoves my arm. "And I would suggest you stop saying things like that before you get punched in the face in front of your niece, like I promised."

"If you keep flirting with me, I'm going to think you like me."

We come to a stop while Winston sniffs some bushes.

Kelsey leans in closer and whispers, "Trust me, you wouldn't be able to handle me flirting with you."

"I'd like to see you try." My lips pull up into a sly grin. I'm not sure what game we're playing here, but whatever it is, I'm determined to win.

I hate saying that my sister is right... But right now, hiding in the family bathroom at Evie's dance studio, I'm beginning to understand her wisdom in pulling Evie from dance while she's staying with me.

Honestly, Tess was trying to do me a favor. I haven't been here more than five minutes, and I've already been approached by almost every mom here—at least all the *single* ones.

I feel like a sheep in a wolf's den, being attacked by the entire pack. Except I'm getting showered with flirtatious comments rather than bitten, although I'm sure some of these ladies would bite me if I let them. I shudder at the thought. I'd even prefer Kelsey's biting words to these ladies, and that's saying something.

After unlocking the door, I cautiously push it open and pop my head out, trying to see if the coast is clear. My gaze is instantly drawn to the group of single moms all standing together in the lobby a few yards away. I duck as I eavesdrop on their conversation.

"Did you hear he took Evie in last-minute to help his sister?"

"I love a man who steps up for his family."

"*And* he's a pediatrician."

"A hot children's doctor who looks like he could be on the cover of *Baywatch*? Yes, please."

"I'd let him give me an exam any time."

I look up as one of the blondes wiggles her eyebrows suggestively, and I think I've heard enough. Going back out there and braving the den of wolves is the last thing I want to do.

Turning the knob on the door, I close it as quietly as possible before locking it.

I've had the occasional woman flirt with me at the doctor's office, but I have a strict *no-dating-parents-of-patients* policy. This blatant, outright flirting is uncharted territory.

If I'm going to survive dance class pickups for the next three months, I need to figure out a way to survive the overzealous women here.

I pull out my phone but pause when I realize I don't have anyone to ask for help. My sister is out of the country, my parents are traveling, and I still don't have any friends here. As crazy as it sounds, I feel like the one person I can count on right now is Kelsey.

Before I can think better of it, I text the one person I thought I would never ask for advice.

ME

> I know we don't necessarily have a texting kind of relationship, but please just pretend we do for the next five minutes…

> Is there proper protocol I should follow when being cornered by single dance moms?

Her response is so immediate that the text vibration makes me jump.

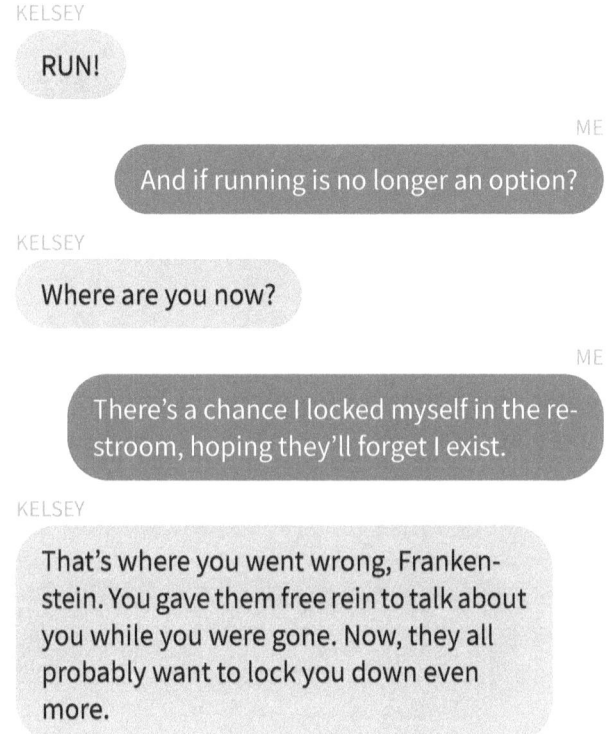

KELSEY

**RUN!**

ME

And if running is no longer an option?

KELSEY

Where are you now?

ME

There's a chance I locked myself in the restroom, hoping they'll forget I exist.

KELSEY

That's where you went wrong, Frankenstein. You gave them free rein to talk about you while you were gone. Now, they all probably want to lock you down even more.

I groan and then slap my hand over my mouth. Hopefully, none of the ladies heard me and took it as an invitation to join me.

My phone vibrates in my hand, pulling my attention back to our text conversation.

KELSEY

You may as well send me your last words to pass along to your family.

RIP *headstone emoji*

ME

You might want to cancel your comedy tour.

KELSEY

Is this how you treat the person you want to save you?

I'm not usually one for begging, but I'm willing to do just about anything to avoid the pack of amorous moms out there.

ME

Oh Great Crazy Dog Mom, what do you suggest I do to escape their flirtatious clutches?

KELSEY

What's in it for me?

I should've known she wouldn't just help me out of the kindness of her heart. I can't say I blame her, though. I'll do just about anything to escape these women. At this point, I'd give Kelsey my left kidney. Okay, not really. But basically anything besides that.

ME

Whatever you want. Name it, and it's yours.

KELSEY

Evie says you know a good sourdough pizza place.

ME

Correction: I know the BEST sourdough pizza joint.

KELSEY

Pizza delivery for me and my roommates tomorrow night could convince me to help you.

ME

I'll even throw in their cinnamon roll pizza for dessert.

KELSEY

You have yourself a deal, Doctor Evil.

Evie goes to Grace Dance Co., right?

ME

Yeah, why?

KELSEY

Stay put, I'm on my way.

I certainly wasn't planning on leaving anytime soon. A glance at the sticky floor tells me I'll be standing while I wait. I send up a silent prayer that no one needs to use the bathroom before Kelsey gets here to do…whatever it is she's planning.

My fingers tap my sides in anxious anticipation. Why did I think it was a good idea to involve Kelsey? Maybe she's not even coming and just told me she was so that I'd stay in here and make a fool of myself. Maybe she'll show up just to make fun of me and see me squirm. Or she's coming to conspire with the wolves out there, giving them my address and phone number so that I'll never know peace again.

A knock sounds at the bathroom door. I lift my foot to go to the door, and it makes a squelching sound as it rips off the tile. Gross.

Or maybe—hopefully—she's actually planning on helping me get out of this sticky situation.

In case it's not Kelsey out there, I try to throw my voice. "Occupied." It comes out sounding like a fake old lady. Just call me Mrs. Doubtfire.

A boisterous laugh I immediately recognize as Kelsey echoes from outside the door. I cringe knowing she's probably garnering attention out there.

"You can give up the act, Doofenshmirtz."

"Who the heck is Doofenshmirtz?"

"The evil guy in *Phineas and Ferb*."

I scoff. "The kid's show?"

"Precisely," she whisper-yells. "Are you going to let me in, or did you decide to move in there?"

I turn the lock and throw open the door, yanking Kelsey into the family-sized restroom with me and locking it again.

She salutes me with a cocky grin. "Good afternoon, this is your savior speaking."

"Did you just quote *Top Gun: Maverick?*" I whisper. Because there isn't possibly any way she could be quoting my favorite movie.

She smiles, and I'm momentarily stunned by how beautiful she is when she's not insulting me. "Just call me Hangman." Kelsey nudges my arm. "Get it? Because I'm not leaving you hanging." Her smile falls as she looks around the bathroom. "You couldn't have picked a better place to hide out?"

"Where do you suggest?" I ask, gesturing toward the door. "Behind the fake potted plant in the lobby? Or maybe underneath the waiting chairs? I'm sure they'd never see me there."

"Okay, okay, I get it." She reaches her hand out, and I stare at it blankly. Her expression turns teasing. "Have you never held hands with a girl before, Reed?"

I press my lips into a firm line and interlock our fingers. Her hand is slender and cold, making me shiver.

"Why are you acting so nervous?" Kelsey glances at me with a raised brow. "Have you really never done this before?"

"Of course I have." I huff. "Your hand is just freezing. Speaking of hands… Why exactly are we holding hands in the bathroom?"

She shakes her head like it's the most obvious thing in the world. "We're going to show all those single moms that their hot doctor fantasy is in the toilet because he's off the market."

"Please never use the phrase *hot doctor fantasy* again."

Kelsey opens the bathroom door and yanks my arm, leaving me trailing behind her like a lost puppy. When we reach the group of overzealous moms, she comes to a stop and turns, pushing her body against mine and running her hands through my hair.

Her fingernails graze my scalp, and I suddenly understand why the dogs she walks obey her. I would do just about anything she said too if I got a daily head scratch like this.

Every ounce of my body is on high alert as her fingers leave my hair and brush my jawline and down my arms. Even through my long-sleeve shirt, I can feel the ghost of her touch.

I shouldn't be enjoying this. I shouldn't be enjoying this *at all*. Heck, the reason she's even putting on a show is to stop the other women who were doing this to me twenty minutes ago, but for some reason, I don't mind now. I should care, though. This is *Kelsey Anderson* we're talking about, my obnoxious next-door neighbor. Although, she doesn't seem very obnoxious now, showing up on her day off to save me.

"You're supposed to look like you like me, Reed," she whispers in my ear, sending another shiver down my spine and causing goosebumps to cover my arms.

I wrap an arm around her waist, pull her closer, and trace my thumb along her bottom lip. She inhales a sharp breath. "I'm not sure you're prepared for me to pretend like I like you, Anderson."

Her eyes narrow. "You'd have to do a lot more than that to catch me off guard."

"Is that a dare?" I ask, my voice husky.

Kelsey's gaze flits to my mouth before returning to my eyes. "It's the truth." She turns to the entourage of onlookers staring at us with expressions ranging from gaping mouths to palpable envy. "Sorry, ladies. He's taken." She pats my chest like she's marking her territory.

The classroom door opens, and the moms disperse to find their kids after shooting glares at Kelsey and a longing look my way.

I slowly release my hold on Kelsey's waist, surprised to find I'm reluctant for her to leave my arms. I hitch a thumb toward the classroom. "I should go find Evie."

She smirks like she's completely unaffected by what just happened and takes another step back. "I've gotta run if I'm going to make my work shift. Tell her hi for me. And don't forget my pizzas tomorrow. A deal's a deal." Kelsey turns on her heels and hurries out the front door. I watch to make sure she makes it to her car safely before braving the sea of moms again to find Evie.

I'm pleasantly surprised that none of the ladies I pass tries to talk to me. Though, I'm unsure if it's because of what Kelsey said or because there are children around now. Either way, I'll take it as a win.

Evie bounds over to me and wraps her arms around my legs. "Thank you for letting me dance."

"You're welcome." I wrap my arm around her as we head to the car. I help her get into her booster seat, and she beams up at me.

"Ms. Ava said I should still be able to audition for a solo in our fall performance."

"That's awesome, Eves."

"You're the best uncle." She lets out a content sigh.

As I drive home, I can't help but be thankful that I'm doing something right with her. Then the thought pops into my brain that Kelsey was the one who suggested putting Evie back in dance classes, and that reminds me of everything that occurred in the dance studio.

Her hands in my hair. The way her lips felt under my fingertips. Her body pressed against mine.

And now I'm not sure I'm doing anything right after all. Because if I'm getting goosebumps from Kelsey Anderson, something must be seriously wrong.

# CHAPTER EIGHT

## KELSEY

TONIGHT IS MY FAVORITE activity that I plan for the residents at Sunrise Springs: dance lessons. Once a month, I have a pair of instructors come in to teach them a different ballroom-style dance. The residents love it, and I love *watching* it.

I mean, what's cuter than senior citizens waltzing with each other? Practically nothing. Although Winston is a worthy contender.

I need all the cute entertainment I can get today to distract me from my encounter with Tyler at Evie's dance studio. I was five minutes late to my activity coordinator shift because I had stupidly stopped there.

I'm not sure what possessed me to offer to help him. Well, I guess the pizza for me and my besties tomorrow…but I should've left him to manage the eager women himself. Instead, I found myself wrapped around him like cling wrap, running my hands through his hair—that's just as soft as it looks, by the way—pretending we're an item.

It almost seemed like Tyler was affected by me. Then he'd gone and traced his finger over my lips and… I shake my head. It isn't possible. There's no way Tyler Reed was *flirting* with me. Absolutely not. It was all fake—a show for the ladies.

Putting on a smile, I walk out of my office and into the activities room, where a dozen residents are waiting.

"Who's ready to dance?" I speak louder than usual, making sure they can hear me.

"I'm always ready to shake what my mama gave me." Darla shimmies, her white curly bob bouncing with the movement.

I hold a hand over my mouth to cover my laughter. I know I'm not supposed to have favorites, but Darla's my favorite resident for a reason.

"We don't shake our booties or"—Lorraine lowers her voice—"our chests in ballroom dance, Darla. We should be beautiful and elegant."

The female dance instructor claps her hands to get everyone's attention. "And today, we'll be learning the dance you've all been waiting for: the tango."

"Everybody, go ahead and grab a partner," the male dance instructor says.

Darla's smile widens. "Thank the heavens they're finally giving us a saucier dance. We're old, not dead." I press my lips together to hide my smile as she leans over to Lorraine and loudly whispers, "I might even be able to throw a booty pop in this one."

Lorraine tuts while Darla steps closer to me. "I'm going to ask Ed to be my partner. He's a hot commodity since he's the only man here with any hair left. I'm sure he can still get down and groovy."

I can't fight my smile anymore as she sashays across the room, calling, "Yoohoo, Ed."

When Darla sees another woman heading toward him, she practically sprints the remaining distance, wrapping her arm through Ed's and sticking her tongue out at the other woman as he escorts her onto the dance floor.

It's official. I want to be Darla when I grow up.

My cheeks hurt from smiling throughout the lesson. I watch all the residents get into the tango and attempt to hit each step with precision. It's adorable and the perfect reminder of why I love planning this activity each month. It's also just the distraction I need.

When the instructors are packing up, Darla joins me along the wall and pats my arm. "That was the best one yet, dear."

"The tango was made for you."

"Thanks for noticing." She beams. "I'll take any opportunity to strut my stuff." Darla taps her lips. "Now, if only I can get Ed to agree to go on a date with me. He thinks I'm too *enthusiastic* for him."

"He doesn't know what he's missing."

"That's what I'm saying." Darla fluffs her hair. "It's his loss."

I gently squeeze her arm. "It sure is."

"Escort me back to my room, dear?"

"Of course."

She loops her arm through mine as we walk out of the activity area toward her room. "You know what I'm most surprised by, though?"

"What?" I ask, ready for whatever outrageous thing might come out of Darla's mouth.

"That *you* haven't been snatched up yet."

I take it back. I guess I wasn't prepared for everything she might say—specifically, my non-existent love life. Most people are surprised to hear that I'd rather be single. I just value my independence, and there hasn't been a man I've met who's changed my mind otherwise. Plus, watching my parents' marriage implode didn't exactly leave me believing in the idea of true love.

I wave off her comment. "I have my whole future ahead of me. I'm young. There's still plenty of time to find someone."

"If you decide otherwise, I have a handsome nephew I can set you up with."

I don't even want to think about how much older her nephew might be than me. "Thank you. I'll keep that in mind."

"Do you know what dance they'll teach us next?" She nudges my hip with hers. "If they need some ideas, I've always wanted to learn how to twerk."

I giggle at the mental image, but it quickly turns into a nightmare of residents throwing out their backs. Clearing my throat, I say, "Maybe I can suggest another upbeat dance like the salsa."

Darla shrugs. "I guess that works too." When we stop in the hall in front of her room, she pulls me in for a hug. "Thanks for another wonderful activity."

"I only arranged the instructors." I push my hair behind my ear. It's always been difficult for me to accept compliments.

"You do so much more than that for me with your activities." She pats my arm and then winks at me. "You keep me young."

I shoot her my warmest smile. "You're the one who keeps *me* young, D."

"D." She holds a hand to her chest and grins. "No one besides family has called me that in years." Darla wags a finger at me. "You know, you really should take me up on my offer to set you up with my nephew. He's a looker, and he'll be here to visit me soon. He—"

I hold my hands up, not wanting to get her hopes up. "I'm happily single, but thank you."

Her sigh is fitting of an Oscar-winning actress. "Maybe one day the people I love will let me set them up." She opens her door and dramatically waves over her shoulder. "Toodles, dearie."

I feel lighter as I walk back to my office. Maybe a little Darla magic was all I needed to turn this day around.

I pull the slingshot back as far as I can before releasing it. An apple goes flying through the air and lands in the grass just to the right of the target. Another miss.

"Maybe if I pretend the target is Tyler's face, I'll have better luck," I mutter sarcastically under my breath.

When I turn and grab another apple, I make eye contact with Alyssa, who's looking at me like I'm one step away from losing it. Maybe I am… There's just something about Tyler that drives me crazy.

"Kels." She draws out my name and slowly steps toward me with her arms out in front of her like I'm a deer she doesn't want to scare away. "Put down the apple."

"Hilarious," I deadpan.

"Mal! Shay!" she yells over her shoulder.

I watch them shoot their final apple together at the station next to us before they head over.

Shayna's expression instantly turns from sunshine to a rain cloud when she looks at Alyssa. "What's wrong?"

I fold my arms across my chest. "Nothing's wrong."

"She's coding," Alyssa says at the same time.

Shay rocks on the balls of her feet. "Already?"

"I didn't think it would come to this." Mallory smooths down her wavy hair.

I look between all my besties and wait for them to explain what's happening. When they don't elaborate, I ask, "What do you mean?"

"It's hospital-speak here for when a patient is in critical condition and needs immediate attention." Mallory picks up my last apple, tosses it in the air, and catches it.

"Do I look gravely ill, and none of you told me?" I pinch my cheeks, trying to add some color to them.

"You look perfect." Shay wraps me in a hug. "That burgundy sweater really complements the green flecks in your eyes."

I flip my caramel-brown hair over my shoulder. "Thanks for noticing." Eyeing down my other roommates, I say, "Then what's the code thing for?"

Alyssa's eyes drop to the dirt. When Mallory looks like she's hit with the realization that no one else will answer, she sighs. "Isn't it obvious? It's a medical term for your new boss."

"Everything's fine with me and Dr. Evil."

Mallory snorts. At least someone thinks my nicknames are funny.

Alyssa gives me a sympathetic smile. "Kels, I heard you say you were going to pretend the targets were Tyler's face. If you classify that as *fine*, I'm scared to know your definition of bad."

I press my lips together, debating how much I want to tell my friends. I don't want them to feel bad for me or encourage me to quit because I'm still not ready to tell them why I need the money. I know they would support my dream, but I'm still terrified to talk about it when it may be unachievable.

Before I can think of something to say, Shayna jumps in. "I know we usually take the hayride to pick our pumpkins, but I think this information calls for the early arrival of our fall baking tradition to cheer up Kels."

"Do you mean…"

Shayna nods. "I think it's time we make our girl Taylor's chai cookies."

"You don't have to tell me twice." Alyssa grabs her belt bag off the ground, dusting off the dirt before putting it on. She's wearing the perfect fall outfit: a tan knit sweater tucked into a black jean miniskirt finished off with black thigh-high boots and a burnt-orange silk scarf tied around her half pony.

I feel casual in my burgundy sweater, leggings, and white platform sneakers, but I think anyone would feel dressed down when standing next to Alyssa. Even though she's always dressed to the nines, she's also one of the kindest people I know. Plus, I know that even though Alyssa almost always looks put-together, she can still rock an oversized t-shirt and shorts from her high school days. So, she's not that different from the rest of us.

Motioning to the slingshot, I say, "I just have one more thing I need to do." I take the final apple that Mallory hands me and place it in the slingshot. I pull it back until I can feel the muscles in my arms straining from the tension. Staring at the target, I imagine Tyler's smug grin right in the middle of it, and I release the slingshot.

The apple soars through the air, and my friends let out a collective gasp as we watch it near the target. The apple not only hits the target but is a perfect bullseye—or, in my mind, a shot straight to Tyler's nose.

I throw my arms into the air and cheer. All my friends shout with me and pull me into a group hug.

One of the farm employees walks over, letting out a low whistle. "It's not often we see a bullseye." He hands me a voucher for a free bag of apples or pumpkins of equal value. "Great job."

I thank him, and we walk to the main store. We each select a pumpkin for our front porch steps and then head to check out. Thanks to my sharp slinging skills, we only have to pay for one pumpkin.

We stop at the grocery store to get the ingredients we don't have for the cookies. Once we're home, we stagger the pumpkins along our front porch steps.

"Hold on, I know just what we need." Alyssa goes inside for a minute and comes back out with a pampas grass wreath. She replaces our usual eucalyptus wreath with the fall one, completing the whole look. After she joins us on the sidewalk, Alyssa gives her nod of approval. "It's officially fall."

"I don't know about y'all, but I'm ready to bake and sing my heart out." Shayna heads through our front door and waves for us to follow.

Once we're all in the kitchen, I move our turntable from the living room to our kitchen table and gently place the vinyl first disc of *Red (Taylor's Version)* on it. Anyone who says *Red* isn't an autumn album is sorely mistaken. I carefully lower the tonearm onto the record, and Taylor's beautiful voice fills our kitchen.

Alyssa holds a spatula like a microphone, mouthing the words to the first track while wiggling her hips. She tosses it to Mallory, who easily catches it and jumps right into lip-syncing the next verse, her muted pink cardigan sway-ing as she moves to the beat.

While they sing and dance around the kitchen, I preheat the oven. Shayna gets out the mixing bowls, all the measuring cups and spoons we need, and the handwritten version of the recipe we printed from Taylor's Tumblr account years ago.

As our other friends continue to dance, Shayna and I fall into a rhythm of our own. She reads me the recipe ingredients while I measure and pour them into the bowl. Once the cookie dough comes together, I put it in the fridge to chill for an hour.

I move to the sink and clean the dishes we've accumulated. I'm washing the beaters for the hand mixer as the opening music of "I Knew You Were Trouble (Taylor's Version)" starts playing. The song takes on a whole new meaning when I think about how it correlates to my situation with Tyler.

I've known he was trouble since the first day I met him. Okay, if I'm being honest, my first impression might've been that he was one of the most attractive men I'd ever seen…but that quickly faded when he didn't give me the time of day. Tyler equals trouble. Both words are synonymous in my mind, and I refuse to let anything he says let me think otherwise.

"I don't like that look in your eye." Shayna pulls the beaters from my hands and ushers me to the kitchen table.

"What look?" I take a seat, and everyone else sits in their usual spot.

"Like you're thinking of all the creative ways you can hurt Tyler with a hand mixer."

I tap my bottom lip. "I was thinking about how this song seems very fitting for him, but thanks for the idea." Shayna's eyes go wide, and I laugh. "I'm just messing with you, Shay."

"Good, because I totally wouldn't be able to lie to an officer if they asked me if I knew why you came at our neighbor with a hand mixer."

Everyone laughs.

"Oh, I know. I'd never trust you with a secret like that. I know you're too sweet to lie." I motion to Mallory. "I'd totally call Mal."

Mallory holds a hand to her chest. "I'm honored."

"Okay, but what's going on with you and Tyler? It can't be that bad when you only see him for a minute when he gets home from work, right?"

"For the most part, yes." I anxiously pick off my nail polish, knowing my friends are going to keep digging until they get answers.

"And for the other part?" Alyssa prods.

I sigh, knowing I should tell them about what happened at the dance studio, even if I'm not fully sure what went down yet. "When I accepted the nanny position, Tyler and I exchanged phone numbers just in case I ever had an emergency with Evie."

Mallory shrugs. "That's normal, like my emergency contacts for students at school."

"Right. I never heard from him…until yesterday."

My friends are quiet for a moment until realization dawns on Mallory's face. "But you had your work event yesterday. Evie hung out in my classroom while I tutored until I dropped her off at dance class. She said he would leave work early to pick her up."

Alyssa squeals like I'm about to tell them Tyler professed his love for me. "The suspense is killing me. What did he say?"

"He was hiding out in the bathroom at the dance studio because a bunch of the single moms were coming onto him."

"Was he trying to make you jealous?" Shay leans forward on her elbows, clearly invested.

"No. He wanted my advice on how to get them to stop."

When I don't say anything else, even Alyssa presses in closer. "Well, what did you say?"

"I didn't say anything." I pop my lips, dreading saying what I actually did out of fear my roommates will think they're winning our bet. They're nowhere close to winning. I simply was helping out the uncle of the sweet little girl I adore.

My sentence comes out rushed, sounding like one long gibberish word. "I stopped there on the way to Sunrise Springs and kind of pretended to be Tyler's girlfriend for a minute to get the other women to stay away from him."

All of their mouths fall open simultaneously as if they choreographed the action.

"Please tell me you made out with him." Alyssa covers her mouth with her hands like she's trying to contain her excitement.

I grimace. "Ew, no."

She sighs. "Oh, come on. You can't tell me you haven't dreamed about what it would feel like to have his muscular, hot doctor arms wrapped around you."

I don't have to dream about it, because I know how it feels now…the rippling muscles of his arms from all those morning workouts definitely did him favors. My face heats, and Alyssa points at me.

"Ha, I knew it. You've totally dreamed about him."

"I haven't *dreamed* about him. We just may have been wrapped up in each other's arms while pretending." I add the last sentence in a whisper. Maybe if I'm quiet enough, they'll just ignore that part.

"Shut. Up!" Shayna screams, grabbing my arm and squeezing as tight as a blood pressure cuff.

Ugh, there I go, thinking about more doctor-y things.

"So, what you're saying is you don't have to dream about his muscles because you already *know* what the planes of his abs and arms feel like." Alyssa grins as if she's about to win the bet.

"It didn't make me feel any type of way about him, if that's what you're implying." I'm lying through my teeth. It's hard not being fully transparent with my best friends, but I can't even understand whatever it was I felt yesterday, let alone vocalize it.

The doorbell rings, and I pop up, grateful for the excuse to get away for a minute and also because I know what's waiting at the door for us.

"Is it *Tyler*?" Shayna asks in a sing-song voice.

"No, it's the sourdough pizzas I got us in return for helping him yesterday."

"Even better. I need more than cookies to sustain me." Mallory leans back in her seat.

I head to the door, shaking my head. I may not be able to vocalize my thoughts from yesterday to my friends—or myself. All I know is that Tyler is trouble.

And as for the idea of letting myself ever fall in love…I think I'll stick to Taylor's love songs, pizza, and chai cookies.

# CHAPTER NINE
## TYLER

IT'S FINALLY SATURDAY, WHICH means I made it through the workweek. Although it was a little touch and go there for a minute, I also survived my first week with Kelsey as Evie's nanny. I think that's honestly more miraculous than the fact that I escaped this week unscathed from any children throwing up during their appointments. Trust me, that's a major feat in flu season.

"Are you ready for our day of fun?"

Evie bounces excitedly in front of me. "Yes! Will you *please* tell me what we're doing?"

I told her all week that I was planning a surprise day for her on Saturday so she had something to look forward to. Since Tess typically works from home, Evie is used to being around her family whenever she's not at school or dance. I feel awful that I only see her for dinner, a quick game or show, and bath time before she goes to bed. So, I've been talking up our first full day together all week.

Although she hasn't said as much to me, I've heard her crying softly a few nights. Nothing will ever be the same as her mom tucking her in. Three months is a long time to be apart from her, and even though we're only a week in, I can tell Evie's missing her mom.

Heck, I even miss my sister. We usually talk a few times a week and see each other every Sunday for family dinners. Since she dropped Evie off, I've only gotten a handful of texts checking in to make sure Evie's all right and voice messages for her daughter saying goodnight and that she loves her.

It's six hours later where Tess is, so it's hard to catch her since she's already asleep by the time I get home from work. But we have a video call date set with her this morning to start off our day of fun.

"I think you'll be very excited about the first surprise of the day." I pull out my laptop and set it on the kitchen table, gesturing for Evie to take the seat next to me. I hit the video call button next to my sister's name on the app and, after a few moments, Tess's smiling face pops up on the screen. She's tanner than usual, but aside from that, she still looks like my sister.

"Mama!" Evie's smile is wide but quickly turns into a chin-quivering frown. "I miss you."

"Oh, I miss you too, baby girl."

I can tell my sister is putting on a brave face but will likely blubber like a baby after we get off this call. It's hard to imagine how much I'd miss Evie if I didn't see her for three months. I can't imagine being apart from your own child for that long.

Tess puts on a smile I can tell is forced. "Are you having fun with Uncle Ty?"

"We're going to have a day of fun, but he won't tell me what we're doing." She pouts.

"That's the fun of surprises, sweet girl." Her smile turns genuine. "What did you do this week?"

"I had school and got to play and cook with Ms. Kelsey. I went on a walk with her and Winston and Uncle Ty, too." She looks down thoughtfully before facing the camera again with a wide smile. "Oh, I went to dance! Ms. Ava let me audition for a solo in our fall performance even though I missed a few classes."

Tess lifts her brows, and I know she's looking directly at me. "We'll come back to the whole Ms. Kelsey point." Her grin returns. "But first, I want to know about school. Are you doing all your homework?"

Evie nods. "Ms. Kelsey makes sure I do it every day and checks my work for me. She said you'd be proud of my A's. I can write the whole alphabet now too."

"That's my smart girl. And you're back in dance?"

"Dance is so much fun." Evie twirls the ends of her hair. "Are you mad that I have lessons again? Uncle Ty said he didn't mind taking me."

"I'm not mad. I know how much you love to dance. That's very nice of Uncle Ty to take you."

"Ms. Kelsey will take me most of the time. Ms. Mallory took me one day, but Uncle Ty picked me up."

After a few more minutes of them catching up, Evie proclaims she has to use the restroom and sprints away.

I feel my sister's attention hone in on me, and I rub the back of my neck. "How's the medical center coming along?"

"Oh no, you don't. You're not getting off that easy, brother." She gives me what I can only describe as an older sister look. It's similar to the look your mom gives you when she walks into the kitchen and catches you with your hand in the cookie jar. "We're not anywhere close to done talking about whoever Kelsey and Mallory are. Has my dear brother *finally* been going on dates?"

I huff out a laugh. "Kelsey is Evie's new nanny. I told you about her—she picks Evie up from school, watches her until

I get home from work, and occasionally takes her to dance lessons."

"Where did you meet her?"

"She's my next-door neighbor. She has three roommates, including Mallory."

"Oh, I love that trope!" she exclaims. I have no clue what that means, but I don't think I want to ask. "And are you spending time with Kelsey outside of her nanny hours?"

I grimace. "Definitely not."

"Oh, so she's out of your league then?"

"What?" My head rears back. "She's—" I don't know how to finish that sentence. Objectively speaking, Kelsey is beautiful. I would be lying if I said otherwise. Her hair is the color of warm caramel, and her hazel eyes take on a different shade depending upon whatever color her outfit is.

"She must be gorgeous to make you speechless." She interrupts my thoughts of Kelsey, which is probably for the best. Only now, I don't know how to respond to Tess without getting her hopes up that she has a new sister-in-law on the horizon.

I decide silence is the best route. My sister opens her mouth to speak again when Evie returns to the table. She smiles widely at her mom on the screen and proclaims, "I pooped."

Tess laughs. "Good job, Evie girl." She glances at her watch and frowns. "My lunch break is almost up, so I need to get going. I'm proud of how well you're doing in school, and I can't wait to find out if you get a solo in dance. Have fun with Uncle Ty today."

"I will. Love you, Mama. Are you having fun in Africa?"

"I am. You're sweet as sugar for asking." Tess discreetly wipes away a tear. "I love you more."

"I love you most."

I nudge my niece's arm. "Why don't you go get your shoes on."

"Okay, bye, Mama."

"I'll talk to you soon." The second Evie is out of the frame, tears stream down my sister's face.

My protective instincts kick in, making me wish I could reach through the screen and hug her. Do something—anything—to ease her pain. My sister has already gone through so much.

"She's doing fine, Tess. Really." I smile warmly, hoping my positivity will transfer through the screen and fill her too.

"I know. I just miss her so much it hurts, and we're not even a full week in." Tess lets her face fall into her hands.

Seeing her so distraught breaks my heart. I'll make it my mission to ensure she never has to leave Evie again. If I have to travel with Tess back to Africa to watch Evie, I'll take a sabbatical at work. I just can't bear to see her upset like this. She shouldn't have to deal with any of this alone. Julian, Evie's father and Tess's ex-husband, should be there taking care of them and providing for their needs.

I glance at Evie as she pulls on her light-up shoes. I'll never understand how that man gave up his parental rights like it was nothing and left my kind, caring sister for some woman who was barely twenty and only wanted him for his bank account.

"Please don't tell me you're thinking about punching Julian again."

My brows furrow. "How did you—"

"Your eyes take on this primal look whenever you think about him."

I blow out an exasperated breath. "How could I not after what he did to you?"

She sighs. "I've let it go, Tyler. Holding on to resentment and anger only would've hurt me. You need to let it go too."

"I can't make any promises." I run a hand through my hair. "Are you really okay out there? You look tired."

"The three words every woman wants to hear." She laughs. "I am tired, but it also feels like this is what I was created to do."

"You've always had a heart for helping others."

Tess's brow quirks. "Speaking of helping others…you should let me help you figure out what to say to get Kelsey to agree to go on a date with you. I'm sure she must find you obnoxious, especially since you're her neighbor. You have a lot of work to do, and I—"

I roll my eyes. "Bye, Tess."

Her laughter sounds like pure joy, and I'm happy she's leaving this conversation feeling a little lighter. "Love you, bye."

The call clicks off, and I meet Evie by the front door.

"*Now* can I know what we're doing?" she asks, tapping her foot impatiently.

"We're going to go for a hike and stop at the grilled cheese restaurant you love on the way home." I grab my backpack filled with the essentials like a first aid kit, snacks, and water, and we walk out the front door.

She pumps her fist in the air. "Yes! Can we go now?"

"Of course." I laugh.

"Can we get ice cream too?" she asks while I lock the front door behind us.

"We'll see." But I know I'd never be able to deny her the sweet treat. I try to take care of my body and be conscientious of what I put in it, but ice cream is a guilty pleasure.

I turn to walk to the car, and Evie is nowhere in sight. Frantically spinning around, I spot her over on Kelsey's front porch. *Splendid.*

I slowly walk toward them and overhear their conversation.

"I'm taking Winston on a hike," Kelsey explains as she clips on the dog's leash.

Evie gasps. "That's what Uncle Ty said we're doing."

Kelsey's gaze skirts to me, and the eye contact brings me back to the dance studio. I'm pulled back into the moment her hands are in my hair. Her body pressed up against mine.

I shove my hands in my jeans pockets and avert my gaze, needing to get a grip on my errant thoughts. "Since it rained earlier this week, I thought I'd take her to Hemlock Cliffs to see the waterfalls."

Kelsey lets out a breathy laugh. "That's where I'm going."

Evie wraps her arms around Winston's neck, hugging him close. "Ms. Kelsey and Winston should ride with us." She turns to Kelsey with an enthusiastic grin. "Uncle Ty said we could get grilled cheese after. You should come."

"I'm sure Ms. Kelsey has other plans today," I say, looking back at her, hoping she'll play along and give my niece some reason—any reason—that she can't spend the day with us.

She shrugs. "I actually don't have anything on my agenda besides having fun."

Evie jumps up and wraps her arms around Kelsey's legs. "We're having a day of fun! That means you *have* to come."

Kelsey bends and returns Evie's embrace. "I'm not sure. I've had a long work week."

Evie's chin trembles. "Please come. It won't be the same without you."

"What do you mean?" I ask.

She shrugs. "You're great and all, but I miss Mama." Evie sniffles, wiping her nose on her sleeve. "It's nice having another girl around, even if it's not the same."

Kelsey blows out a low breath. I mean, who could say no when this sweet girl puts it like that? Before any of my niece's tears can fall, Kelsey smooths her hands over Evie's hair. "I'll come if it means that much to you." She peers up at me, a question in her eyes. "As long as it's okay with Dr. Grey."

Evie wrinkles her nose. "Who's Dr. Grey?"

"She's the main doctor in a show called *Grey's Anatomy*," Kelsey explains.

I roll my eyes. "Oh, so I'm a girl now?"

"If the shoe fits."

I motion to my gray tennis shoes. "I mean they are gray, but they're also a size thirteen. I'd be astounded if you can find a woman who would fit in these."

"Thirteen?" Kelsey croaks.

"Mm-hmm." I head toward the car with the girls and Winston following behind. I make sure Evie gets buckled in okay, but once I close her door, I turn to Kelsey with a smirk. "You know what they say about big feet?"

Red blossoms across her cheeks, and my smirk grows at the fact that I'm the reason she's flustered.

"What?" she says apprehensively.

"It means I've got long legs. So, do your best to keep up on the trail."

Kelsey shakes her head. Her brown curls fall in front of her face and hide her blush. She opens the back door on the passenger side and lets Winston jump in. He quickly lays down beside Evie, resting his head in her lap.

When we're both in the car, she whispers, "It's nothing I haven't worked with before."

"What?" I sputter.

"Great Danes." She crosses her arms. "They have the longest legs I've ever seen on a dog, and I keep up just fine."

"Those dogs are *huge*," Evie says from the backseat with wide eyes. "I saw one with Mama that was even taller than me."

"Wow, that sure is big." I pull onto the road and try to keep a straight face. Kelsey laughs quietly in the passenger seat.

Evie lifts her hands like she's on a rollercoaster. "To the waterfalls we go!"

# CHAPTER TEN
## KELSEY

WE FINALLY ARRIVE AT Hemlock Cliffs, and I unbuckle my seatbelt before Tyler can put the car in park. I'm more than ready to be out of this confined space with him. As soon as the car rolls to a stop, I open the passenger door and all but jump out. If I thought holding each other for all of a minute in the dance studio was awful, sitting beside Tyler *freaking* Reed for an hour—which felt like four—was pure *torture*.

I had a front-row seat to his smug face and fresh sandalwood scent, reminiscent of the forest or a hot lumberjack. Not that I'm calling him hot. I'm purely stating a fact. When women smell something woodsy, I bet most of their minds immediately jump to hot lumberjack. It's a thing.

He also rolled up the sleeves of his quarter zip, showing off his rippling, veiny forearms. As if the thin, athletic material clinging to every contour of his arm muscles wasn't already enough. Not that I noticed... Again, purely stating the facts here. Tyler can have muscles without me finding him attractive. The two are mutually exclusive. Tyler equals muscular. Tyler does *not* equal attractive.

On the bright side, we didn't have to converse, thanks to Evie. She talked about school and dance and asked us questions the entire ride. Most of them wondering if we were there yet, but I'd take that any day over trying to converse with Tyler to pass the time.

"Come on, Winston," I call, opening the back door. He gives me a pitiful look, clearly stating he would rather cuddle with Evie the rest of the day than get in some exercise. When I call his name again, he reluctantly jumps out of the car, but I swear he rolls his eyes. I attach the leash to his collar and slide my backpack on.

As soon as Tyler lets Evie out, she runs over to us. Winston's tongue lolls, and his tail thumps against my leg as she pets him. I think he has a new favorite person, and I'm only a little bit offended that it's not me since I just adopted him. I can't blame him for loving the adorable five-year-old in front of us. It's impossible not to.

Tyler rounds the car. "Who's ready to hike?"

Evie bounces on her feet, shooting her hand in the air. "Me!"

He smiles at her, but his mouth falls when he moves his gaze to me. "You ready?"

"Whenever you are."

Tyler slings his backpack on and locks the car before walking toward the head of the trail. Tyler echoes Evie's earlier words: "To the waterfall we go."

A forest of lush green hemlock trees line the path. The earthy scent of the woods and the gentle autumn breeze make me feel alive. I tug my sweater sleeves down over my hands.

Tyler and Evie get a few yards ahead of us, with Winston stopping to sniff and mark his territory on every tree he passes.

Tyler turns around and calls out, "Better hurry up, slow poke." His mouth pulls up on one side, and I wish I could wipe the smug expression off his face.

I pick up the pace, pulling a begrudged Winston along. He doesn't seem upset about stopping his sniffing duty when he gets to walk alongside Evie, though. She points out everything to Winston as we walk, and his eyes eagerly follow her finger.

We walk down a long wooden staircase overlooking a beautiful valley with a creek visible up ahead. Upon reaching the bottom, there are two rock ledges with stone steps between them. The descent down looks steep, with only a small rope tied to a tree above to help hikers down the steps.

Tyler and Evie climb down with ease, and look back up waiting for me. I pass Winston's leash to Tyler, and he scrambles down the steps and sits dutifully at Evie's feet.

I glance back at Tyler, and his eyes tell me he'd love to see me attempt to come down myself, holding onto the rope for dear life. But the hand he extends my way says, *I'm a gentleman.*

I warily wrap my fingers around his. His hand is warm and strong around mine. And the way his thumb grazes my skin almost has me tripping anyway. I'm waiting for him to yank his hand back and run it through his hair, yelling *psych*, but he doesn't. He lets me grip his hand the whole way down.

When I slip on a slick area of the last step, his hand holding the leash comes up and settles on my waist, steadying me.

His normal, smug expression falters for a moment. "You good?"

I nod.

"Great." A smirk pulls at his lips. "Now try to keep up, Anderson."

Remembering how my touch caused goosebumps to erupt across his skin, I decide to get back at him the best way I can think of—with my feminine charm. I drag my fingertips along his arm, feeling every ridge of his muscles.

Maybe this was a bad idea, but it's too late to stop now. I move my fingers the rest of the way down until they wrap around the handle of the leash. I gently tug it off his wrist and wrap it around mine. "I think I can manage." My voice comes out slightly raspy, and I hope he doesn't notice.

He looks down at the path. "We—We should keep going."

His throaty tone shows he's just as affected by my touch as I was by his, so I count my mission a success.

We continue moving forward, and the sound of rushing water pulls my attention to the creek. The water is flowing at a steady pace from the rain the area got earlier in the week, filling me with excited anticipation that we're bound to see some beautiful waterfalls soon.

Evie runs over to me, reaching for Winston's leash. "Can I walk Winston by the water? I promise I'll be *so* careful."

I look to Tyler. "If it's okay with your uncle."

He nods. "Stay back from the water and in my sight, please."

She gives her word, eagerly takes the leash, and Winston prances at her side like a show horse as they walk to the creek. I smile at them, looking like two peas in a pod while Evie talks about something excitedly with animated gestures.

Tyler clears his throat beside me. "Have you hiked here before?" When I shake my head, he asks, "What do you think?"

"It would be a perfect, tranquil hike if not for the company." I look at him pointedly. "And by company, I mean you. Evie's welcome anytime."

He holds his hand to his back. "Ouch?"

"Did you pull something, Mr. Long Legs?"

"Mr. Long Legs?" He pulls his water bottle out of his pack and takes a sip.

"Well, I'm not about to call you Daddy."

He does a spit-take, spraying water onto the path before us. "Thanks to you, I'm never going to look at those spiders the same." He wipes his sleeve along his mouth. "And I was pulling something—the knife you stabbed me in the back with from your *company* comment."

I look him dead in the eyes, having to crane my neck to meet his gaze. "Trust me, if I was going to stab you with a knife, it would be in the front."

"Ah, I should've known your hot doctor fantasy would deal more with stabbing."

"Referring to yourself as a hot doctor is a little conceited. Don't you want to teach your niece humility?"

Tyler shoves his hands into his pockets, looking the picture of calm, even with our heated banter. "You're the one who said the phrase *hot doctor fantasy*."

I fist my hands on my hips. "And you're the one who told me never to mention it again, so why are you bringing it up?"

He groans and mutters something under his breath that sounds strangely close to *exasperating woman*. I don't know why he'd ever say that though. *He's* clearly the problem here.

"Fine, no more doctor talk."

Evie meets us back on the main path as we near the canyon. The canopy of trees overhead leaves me feeling the drop in temperature. I wrap my arms around myself, trying to conserve my body heat.

"What are these?" Evie looks around in awe at the rock formations.

"They're shelters, caves, and cliffs made of sandstone," Tyler says.

"It looks cool."

I take in my surroundings, just as awed as Evie. The sandstone is honeycombed from weathering over time, and it adds a beautiful effect to the rock shelters, outcrops, and cliffs it forms. Where we are in the canyon, there are several pocket caves in the stone, only big enough for a few people to fit in. I definitely wouldn't want to be trapped in one of those with Tyler.

Looking further ahead, I notice multiple waterfalls, and it's obvious Evie has spotted them too.

She squeals and runs ahead, still holding tightly to the leash. "Look, Winston!"

Tyler folds his arms across his chest and shakes his head. "I think I've been demoted."

"Same."

He takes another chug of water, and I watch his throat bob with the movement. "At least we can agree on something."

"Even if it's just that we're playing third and fourth wheel to Evie and Winston."

Tyler motions toward his niece. "We should go make sure they don't get hurt."

When we reach them, he walks over to Evie, but I can't help but stare at the waterfalls. You don't always have to travel far to see beautiful views. Sometimes beauty is only as far as your own backyard.

Tyler returns, handing me Winston's leash. "I'm going to take Evie a little closer to the falls. We'll be back soon." He walks away, and Winston whines at my feet.

"I know you want to be with her, buddy, but the mean man didn't offer to take you with him."

He groans, laying down with his legs up in the air like he's playing dead.

My overdramatic dog remains this way until Tyler and Evie rejoin us on the trail.

"What's wrong with him?" Tyler asks.

"I think it's his way of rebelling against the man who stole his best friend."

He rolls his eyes. "Your dog is a drama queen."

I cross my arms defensively. "You shouldn't judge someone for expressing their emotions."

"He's a dog."

I bend over and cover Winston's ears. "He can hear you."

"Like I said, he's a dog."

"What's that supposed to mean?" I grit my teeth.

He presses his lips into a firm line. "I don't know why you're making this out to be a big deal. All I said is that he's a drama queen. But he's also a dog. He might have emotions, but it's not like he understands everything we say. He'll be fine."

Tyler might think I have my dog-walking job as a quick way to earn cash. I couldn't expect him to know about my dream of opening a dog rescue because I've never vocalized that, but I'm sure even if he knew, he'd still say the same thing because my neighbor hasn't changed. He's still the uncivil jerk I've always thought him to be. Now, he's confirmed my thought was actually fact.

I'm quiet as we continue the loop back to the parking lot. Evie and Tyler talk in front of me while I grip Winston's leash like it's my last bit of willpower.

"Uncle Ty." Evie's sweet voice carries on the light breeze. "Since we drove Ms. Kelsey, does that mean she's getting grilled cheese with us?"

Well, butter my butt and call me a biscuit. In the time we were here, I forgot that we drove together.

Tyler glances over his shoulder at me, a steely look in his eyes that I can't quite decipher. "If Ms. Kelsey wants to. Otherwise, we'll drop her off, and you can get grilled cheese for dinner."

Oh, thank the heavens. There's the out I needed.

"I don't want to leave Winston in the car, so I think we'll take a raincheck this time."

Evie sighs and wraps her arms around Winston's neck.

Once in the car, I get on my phone and pull up a local Louisville newspaper. I follow the instructions necessary to take out an advertisement, letting all my frustration toward Tyler over the past years come out.

He'll regret every day he blasted his hip-hop music at four in the morning. I'll make sure of it.

I finish filling out the form, hit enter, and put my phone back in my bag. I'm not ashamed to admit that I feign sleep for the rest of the car ride home.

Sometimes, a girl just needs an hour of peace—and to pretend she's not currently in the car with her jerk of a next-door neighbor.

# CHAPTER ELEVEN

## KELSEY

Shayna walks into the activity room at Sunrise Springs, carrying a large box filled with flowers. I push the final chair into the long row of tables and move toward her.

"Need help?"

"I'm good." She grunts. "Just need to—" Shayna places the box on a table and sighs. "Set it down."

"Do you need to get anything else from your car?"

She shakes her head. "That's the last of it."

"Thank you again for doing this. The residents will be so excited to make flower arrangements."

She smiles. "I've always wanted to teach a flower arranging class, so you're the one doing me a favor."

On the long row of tablespace in front of us are clear vases in various shapes and sizes. Scattered around them are shears and floral tape ready for use.

We work together, staging the blooms Shayna brought from Shirley's Florist on an end table for the residents to select from. We arrange the flowers by color and place the multiple types of greenery beside them. The area smells like a floral haven when the residents enter the activity room.

"Aren't these prettier than a peach?" Darla walks over to the flowers and leans down to smell the blooms.

"At least there's a variety." Lorraine wrinkles her nose at the colorful array of flowers before running her fingers along the petals of the cream and tan ones with a satisfactory nod.

I walk around, handing out name tags to the residents so Shayna can easily identify them when answering questions or helping with their arrangements.

I move to the front of the room once everyone is seated. "All right, everyone. Today we have a special guest. My friend, Shayna, is here today from Shirley's Florist. Let's give her a warm welcome."

Soft claps fill the room, and I motion for Shayna to take the floor. She flashes a bright smile. "Thank you all for having me. Today, I'll be showing you how to create your own floral arrangements."

"Did she say *funeral* arrangements?" Hank, one of the older residents who uses hearing aids, yells, eliciting laughs from other seniors in the room.

"*Floral* arrangements. Flowers." Darla motions to the table they're sitting at.

"Oh good." He nods. "That's less morbid than funerals. Although, there are flowers at funerals."

I hold my hand over my mouth to hide my smile. This is the kind of commentary I've come to expect on the days when I host events here, and I love every entertaining second of it.

"There will be plenty of time for you to discuss funeral arrangements with your loved ones later." Shayna shifts on her feet, obviously uncomfortable about the direction the conversation went.

"Unless we die tomorrow," Darla adds. "I mean, I'm fit as a fiddle, but I can't say the same for everyone else."

Shayna shoots me a panicked look before lightly clearing her throat, trying to regain control of the senior citizens now talking about what kind of flowers they'd like at their funerals. "For now, what do you say we get back to these beautiful blooms?" Without waiting for an answer, she jumps right back into teacher mode. "You can select a vase of your choosing from the table in front of you and then make your way to the end table and select the flowers you'd like to include. I'd suggest a mix of flowers, greenery, and baby's breath to add texture. Then, we can discuss how to arrange your bouquets. Kelsey and I will be around if you have questions."

After everyone is back in their seats, Shayna walks around, instructing the residents on how to arrange the flowers and pointing out where some stems might need trimming. As the arrangements start to come together, compliments flow from my friend. Seeing the residents beam at the praise of the people coming in to teach them something new always does my heart good.

"That looks great, Darla," Shayna praises. "Your arrangement is so vibrant."

Her flowers are an explosion of rainbow that perfectly matches Darla's bright, spunky personality. Lorraine's arrangement is a dead ringer for her personality as well.

Shayna walks over to her. "Lorraine, I love what you did with the muted tones. Very sophisticated."

Lorraine sits taller at the praise while Darla snickers. Lorraine glares at her, and Darla's laughter grows louder. At first glance, someone might think they're enemies who enjoy poking fun at each other. But being around them long enough, I've come to realize they're more like frenemies. Yes, they mock each other constantly, but I always find them side by side at events, and it's clear they enjoy one another's company, even though they're complete op-posites. It's sweet and makes me appreciate my friends who show up for me even more.

The residents finish their floral arrangements and slowly filter out of the room, offering thanks to me and Shayna for the event.

I help Shayna pack up everything she needs to take back to Shirley's Florist when my boss, Kevin, pokes his head into the room.

"It's time," he exclaims. "They're ready to fly the roost."

"I'll be right there," I say.

Kevin scurries away as quickly as he arrived.

Shayna's head pops out around the box she's filling with the extra flowers. "What's that about?"

"I have to escort some ducks through the building."

Her eyes go wide. "Did you just say ducks?" I nod. "Is that some kind of code for something?"

"No, I'm talking about actual ducks."

"You have to escort *literal* ducks—the animals—through the building." She says the words slowly, eyeing me warily like something was lost in translation.

"Long story short, a bunch of ducks live around the pond in front of the facility. A few of them lay their eggs around it, but one specific mama duck flies into our courtyard every year at the start of fall to lay her eggs. I'm guessing it's because she finds it safe from other natural predators since it's an enclosed space."

"Don't most ducks typically breed in the spring?"

"Yeah, at least that's what the internet told me." I shrug. "I don't know why she lays so late in the year. But the staff has to march the mama duck and her ducklings out of the enclosed courtyard into the building and through the sliding doors back to the pond annually."

She's grinning at me like this is the most entertaining thing she's heard all week. "And management asked *you* to march them out of the building this time?"

"Yeah, once they found out I was a dog walker, I guess they assumed I should do it since I *work with animals*."

She laughs. "I can't wait to see this." With a glance at her phone, her smile drops. "Oh, sugar." Yes, Shayna's so sweet that the closest she gets to cursing is saying *sugar*. "I have to return to the shop so Shirley can make it in time for her book club. You have to tell me the play-by-play in elaborate detail when you get home."

"I will. Will you be okay getting everything to your car?"

"Yeah." She waves me on. "Go help the ducklings, you little animal hero."

"I expect a cape when I get home," I call over my shoulder. Shayna's laughter follows me into the hallway.

When I reach the courtyard, a crowd of residents and staff are waiting like spectators for a grand sporting event rather than marching ducks through the building.

"There's the woman of the hour." Kevin ushers me toward the ducks.

*Here goes nothing.*

I kneel in front of them. Even though I researched ducks, the internet didn't have much help to offer in terms of how to escort ducks through a building without incident, so I'm just spitballing here. "Come on, little duckies. Time to cross the proverbial road and enjoy all the pond life offers."

I turn and walk toward the sliding glass doors to enter the building, hoping with everything in me that the mama duck is following. As long as she follows me, her babies are sure to follow behind.

I glance over my shoulder and grin. The mama duck is waddling behind me, her ducklings trailing behind her.

Kevin shoots me a thumbs up as I walk past him before swiping his badge to open the doors. We enter the building with ease. I can't believe I'm doing this. I don't know where exactly I'd put it, but I feel like this deserves to be on my resume.

*Little Animal Hero. Escorted a mama duck and her eight ducklings through a building to find their place in this world.*

It seems like an important thing any future employers should know about. Although, hopefully, I won't have any more future employers if my plan for opening my own dog rescue goes according—

The flapping of wings causes me to duck and cover my head. I look to the left and watch as the mama duck abandons her babies and flies around the lobby, causing mayhem among all the residents simply trying to enjoy their Thursday afternoon.

I turn to Kevin, adrenaline coursing through my body. "Will you watch the ducklings? I'll go fix that situation." I gesture toward where the duck went.

"Of course," he says, though his face pales. Kevin gets on the ground, cooing at the ducklings. I know he needs help, but I have a much larger issue at hand.

I run through the seating area in the lobby where I last saw the duck go. When I pass Hank, who earlier asked if we were making funeral arrangements rather than flower ones, he sputters. "Was that a duck?"

I nod and skid to a stop. "Did you see where it went?"

He tsks and points to the hallway beside us. "Just when you think you've seen everything. Now people have ducks as pets."

"Thanks," I say, already running down the hall. A scream sounds from my right, and my heart rate picks up when I realize it came from Darla's room.

"D, are you okay?" I call out, running into her open door without waiting for a response.

The duck is in the air, its wings flapping against the window like it is trying to escape before it flies back toward me and out the door. Darla sits on her couch with popcorn all around her, clutching her chest, which is rising and falling in rapid succession. I rush over to her, placing my hand on her shoulder.

"Are you okay? Do you think you're having a heart attack?"

She reaches up and pats my hand. "I—I'm okay."

Relief floods my body. "Great, give me a few minutes."

I run back into the hall, where residents point toward the lobby with gaping mouths. When I'm back in the seating area, I quickly spot the duck. Thankfully, she's back on the ground, waddling back toward her ducklings as if nothing out of the ordinary happened. Kevin and I usher her and her babies out the next set of double doors with arms spread wide.

I stand back, watching with bated breath, until the doors slide shut. Only when they're closed do I allow my guard to fall. Kevin is slack-jawed when I turn to face him.

"She's never left her ducklings before. That's unusual behavior for a mama duck, but no one was harmed, right?"

I shake my head. "Not that I saw. Just a few scared residents. Speaking of which, I need to go make sure Darla's okay. The duck flew into her room."

"Lord have mercy." Kevin shakes his head. "I'll have someone write up a report." He crosses his arms. "Maybe next year we can create a barricade so the only path for the ducks is from one door to the other."

If only he'd thought of that bright idea before now or, you know, at *any point* in the last few years this has been happening.

"That's a great idea." I motion toward the lobby. "I'm going to check on Darla before I head home."

He nods before walking off. When I return to Darla's room, she's still sitting on the couch, reading a gardening magazine as if a duck didn't just fly into her room. I sit beside her, and she smiles at me.

"Well, I think that might be the most exhilarating thing that's happened to me since moving in here. Nothing exciting ever happens with these fuddy-duddies here. My only sources of entertainment are your events and that duck."

"I'm glad you enjoy my events." I place my hand on her arm. "Are you sure you're okay? We can have a doctor check you out."

She purses her lips. "I've watched enough *Grey's Anatomy* to know that I'm fine."

A grin pulls at my lips. "I don't think it works that way."

"I know plenty of doctors if I need to call one," Darla says with finality. "But something awful did happen." She points to the popcorn littered around us. "The duck startled me and sent my bowl of popcorn flying."

I walk into her small kitchen and pour some of the bagged popcorn on the countertop into another bowl. "Crisis averted."

"You're an angel. Truly." I hand the bowl to her, and she pops a piece into her mouth. "You know, I still think you'd be perfect for my nephew." Her eyes light up like the sun peeking out on a cloudy day. "He's single and has a good job. Handsome, too."

I nod at the vase of flowers perfectly arranged in the center of her coffee table. "Are those from him?"

Darla smiles. "He brings me a bouquet every Thursday after he gets off work. He'd probably do the same for whoever he was dating." She winks. "He left not even ten minutes ago, otherwise I could've introduced you. He's going to be sad he missed all the action. I'm not even sure he'll believe me when I tell him what happened."

"I'm not sure I can believe it, and I witnessed it with my own eyes," I tease. "And that's sweet of you, but I'm not looking to date right now. I already have enough going on between all my jobs."

"I thought you mentioned that you left two of your jobs."

"I did, but I started working for my next-door neighbor, which is a whole other job itself."

She lifts a brow. "You've been holding out on me, missie. Does said neighbor happen to be a hunky man?"

I grimace. I open my mouth to respond, but she raises her hand, cutting me off.

"Don't even bother lying. Your face says it all." Darla shimmies. "He must be the bee's knees to get that kind of reaction from you."

"It's not like that—"

"Well, if it's not like that, you shouldn't mind going on a date with my nephew." She throws another piece of popcorn into her mouth. "I could've just died. Would you really let me leave this earth without finding out if my nephew and my favorite activities lady could be each other's happily ever after?"

When she phrases it like that, there's no way I can tell Darla no. I wouldn't mind going on a single date, especially if it'll help get my mind off Tyler.

I hold up my pointer finger. "One. I will go on *one* date with him, D. But I'm not promising anything."

"All you need is one." Darla leans back into the cushion and sighs. "We'll be planning the wedding in no time."

I shake my head at her antics. "Don't get your hopes up."

"I don't need to. A woman knows these things. My gut never steers me wrong. Well, unless I eat five brownies because it told me one more wouldn't hurt." She finishes off the bowl of popcorn and hands me her phone. "Anywho, if you give me your number, I'll text you where and when your date will take place."

I add my info to her contacts. "You better know how much I like you. I wouldn't do this for just anyone." I hand Darla her phone, push up off the couch, and head to the door.

"That's what I was counting on." She cackles. "You'll hear from me soon. I can't wait to hear about your date."

"Bye, D." I step into the hall.

As I'm closing the door, I hear her humming, "Here Comes the Bride."

I press my lips together to hide both my laughter and horror. I have a gut feeling of my own that I have no idea what I've just gotten myself into.

# CHAPTER TWELVE
## TYLER

MY KNEE BOUNCES AS the phone rings. I'm on my lunch break and just noticed I missed four calls from my great-aunt this morning. My brain automatically jumps to the worst conclusions. She's in jail for doing something inappropriate in her independent living community and needs me to bail her out. She fell and is in the hospital with a broken hip.

"Hi, Tyler, dear."

Well, if she's answering her phone, at least she's not in jail.

"Is everything okay?" The words fly out of my mouth, panic in my tone.

"I'm alive and kicking."

When she doesn't say anything else, I press my lips together. "I saw a bunch of missed calls from you. I figured something was wrong."

"Oh, no. Nothing like that. I have a story to tell you."

I lean back in my desk chair, letting my panic dissipate. "Go ahead."

"So it was a normal Thursday except for this duck…"

Aunt Darla tells me the most outrageous story about a duck that flew into her room and the woman who saved her from said duck.

"You've always had some wild stories, but I think this one might top them all."

"That's what I'm saying," she agrees. "I'm not sure I'd believe it if I hadn't seen it with my own eyes. You should use it as Evie's bedtime story tonight."

"I just might." I laugh. "You're doing all right, though? No shortness of breath, chest pain, dizziness, or heartburn?"

"Nope, I'm healthy as a horse."

I shake my head. Aunt D always has random sayings up her sleeve. "I'm glad to hear it. Well, I—"

"I do have a request for you before you get back to work. I know you're opposed to being set up, but I told the woman who saved me that you would be a perfect match. So, I'm sending you on a blind date."

I groan. "And I don't have any say in this?"

"Nope. I know my favorite great-nephew wouldn't deny his loving aunt who almost *died* the pleasure of knowing he found true love. Plus, you need to thank the young woman who was so kind and attentive to me."

"That's laying it on a little thick for someone who just said they're healthy as a horse, don't you think?"

"Oh, pish posh. You'll do it because you love me."

She's right. I've said no to her before, just like I deny all attempts by my receptionist and sister whenever they try to set me up, but when Aunt Darla puts it like this, she doesn't leave me with an option.

"Fine," I concede. "But I'm not making any promises it'll go beyond this one date."

"Excellent," she yells, making me wince and pull the phone away from my ear.

I rub my temples. "When is this happening?"

"You'll meet her tomorrow night at six at that cute Italian place you like—you know, on the outskirts of downtown."

At least Aunt Darla listens when I tell her about my favorite restaurants.

"Do I get this girl's name or number?"

"So you can look her up or text her and cancel?" She tuts. "Oh, no. Just make sure you wear a white shirt with that dark blue jacket of yours. I'll tell her that's what you'll be wearing so she can find you in the restaurant."

"This is the truest definition of a real blind date then."

"It worked for your uncle and me."

I sigh. "Okay, as long as I can find someone to watch Evie tomorrow night, I'll be there."

"Perfect. Make sure you call me Sunday and let me know how it goes."

"Why not tomorrow night?"

I can practically see the wicked grin I know she's wearing. "I'm hoping you'll be out way past my bedtime, if you know what I mean."

I'd like to *not* know what she means. "I have to get back to work. Goodbye, Aunt D."

"Be a gentleman and always use—"

I shudder and end the call before she can finish her sentence. If I heard those words come out of her mouth, they'd repeatedly be in my nightmares. I hurry to finish my turkey wrap and carrots before my next appointment. With only a few minutes left on my break, I text Kelsey to see if she's free to babysit tomorrow. It's not ideal, but it is the easiest route since Evie already knows her.

> ME

> I know you have Saturdays off, but I had something come up tomorrow evening. Are you free to watch Evie?

> I'll pay extra for the week.

Her response comes before I can put my phone back in my pocket.

> KELSEY

> Well, hi to you too.

I roll my eyes. Kelsey always has a way of getting under my skin, even when I ask a simple question. My phone buzzes with new incoming texts.

> KELSEY

> I'd love to take your money!

> But I already have plans tomorrow night.

> ME

> Can you see if any of your roommates are free? I don't have their numbers.

> KELSEY

> Lucky them!

> I'll ask.

I want to send her the eye roll emoji, but I refrain.

One of the nurses knocks lightly on my office door.

"Your next patient is ready for you in Room 2."

I place my phone back on my desk and cross the room, opening the door and smiling at her. "Thanks."

The rest of my appointments go smoother than normal for a Friday afternoon.

"You heading out, Doc?" Nadine asks when I pass by the reception desk.

I nod. "Have a good weekend."

"I'm sure it won't be as good as yours, from what I hear." She shoots me a sly smile.

"Have you been talking to Darla about me again?"

"You hired me because we were friends. You can't expect us not to talk about your love life." She crosses her arms.

"That's exactly what I expect you *not* to do."

"No promises. You know us women like to talk."

"And just for that, I won't tell you how the date goes."

Nadine huffs. "Well, that's not fair. We only want you to find love and happiness. You can't blame us for that."

"Goodnight, Nadine." I make a quick escape out the front door so she doesn't see my smile. I'd rather her believe I won't tell her anything all weekend. It serves her and Darla right for always butting into my love life.

When I get to my car, I check my phone and sigh when I see Kelsey's response.

KELSEY

> Alyssa and Shayna said they don't mind having Evie over for a little girls' night while you're gone.

ME

Wonderful. Please tell them I'll drop her off at five-thirty.

KELSEY

*gif of Michelle Tanner saying, "You got it, dude."*

I'd secretly been hoping no one would be able to watch Evie, giving me a reason to tell Aunt Darla I couldn't go on this blind date.

"Maybe it won't be so bad," I mumble, putting the car in drive and heading home. I release a long breath through my nose. "Or maybe it'll be the worst mistake of my life."

Either way, it's only one night I have to get through to appease Aunt D. Then this mystery woman and I can both move on with our lives and never have to see each other again. Unless she's my soulmate—but the odds of that are highly unlikely.

———— ♡ ♡ ♡ ————

Evie finishes her bowl of macaroni and cheese with a contented sigh. While I normally try to feed her well-balanced meals, I caved tonight. But I did buy the most organic-looking box I could find.

"Eves, do you remember you're hanging out with some of Ms. Kelsey's friends next door tonight?"

Her eyes light up. "Do you think they'll paint my nails? My polish is almost gone from when Ms. Kelsey did them."

I shrug. "I'm sure they will."

She fist-pumps at her side. "Yes."

"I'll be home in time to put you to bed."

Evie slowly meets my gaze, her brow furrowing. "Where are you going?"

"I'm meeting up with…" I trail off. How exactly does one talk about going on a date with their five-year-old niece without telling them they're going on a date? "With a lady friend."

"Can I meet her later? I like your other friends, like Ms. Kelsey and Ms. Mallory."

I'm not about to tell Evie that said 'friends' have pretty much flat-out told me that they don't like me, let alone view me as their friend.

"Maybe, Eves." I rub the back of my neck. No wonder my sister hasn't been on a date since she divorced Julian.

"Okay." Evie leans forward and sniffs my jacket, wrinkling her nose. "Why do you smell like that?"

"It's cologne." I lean down and sniff the collar. "Do you think it's too strong?"

"How should I know?" Evie shrugs. "I'm five."

I laugh. "You sure are." I watch the microwave clock change to five-thirty. "All right, it's time to go."

She sprints out the front door while I put on my shoes and grab my car keys and wallet. I lock the door behind me and jog over to my neighbor's porch.

Alyssa and Shayna open the door together and raise their arms in the air. "Girls' night!"

They squeal, and I've never been more glad to be a man.

"Be good for Ms. Alyssa and Ms. Shayna," I call out as Evie runs inside, holding Alyssa's hand. "Thanks again for watching her."

"It's our pleasure." Shayna moves to close the front door, but I reach my hand out, holding it open.

"I have a really weird question." I clear my throat, embarrassed to be asking this.

She looks up at me with a kind smile. "Yeah?"

"Do you think I put on too much cologne? Evie mentioned something about it, but she's a kid."

Shayna laughs and steps forward, leaning into my personal space and inhaling a whiff. When she moves back, she doesn't look repulsed, so that's a good sign. "I think it's nice. It smells kind of like the forest, but in a good way, with a hint of vanilla."

"It's not too strong?"

"I think it's just right." She gives me a sympathetic look. "First date in a while?"

I nod. "It's that obvious?"

"Don't worry. You've got this." She pats my arm. "Just ask good questions, maintain eye contact, and don't be a creep. Then you'll be doing better than about ninety percent of the dates women go on nowadays."

I frown. "That seems like a low bar."

Shayna purses her lips. "The dating world is a scary place."

"Let's hope it's not tonight." I chuckle. "Thanks again for watching Evie. I'll be back between eight and nine."

"Stay out as late as you want. Good luck." She waves and turns to Alyssa. "Is it just me, or do you also find it strange that Kelsey is upstairs getting ready for—" Her words cut off as she shuts the door.

I guess I won't find out what Kelsey is upstairs getting ready for.

I walk to my car and grit my teeth when I realize how late it is. I don't even have time to stress about the evening ahead as I rush to the restaurant. Aunt D would kill me if she knew I was late. Luckily, I find a parking spot right by the door.

"I have a reservation for, uh, a blind date." I shove my hands in my pockets, feeling weird telling this to a complete stranger. "It might be under Darla or Tyler," I tell the hostess.

She glances down at her board and marks something before turning to me with an excited smile. "Great, we've been expecting you. Please, follow me." She leads me to a table with candles and a single rose in a small vase that none of the other tables have. I shouldn't have expected anything less from Aunt Darla.

I thank the hostess and look at my phone, noting I have about two minutes before my mystery date arrives if she's punctual. I can't stand it when people aren't on time. It may sound ironic coming from a doctor, but most of the time, if a patient is kept waiting, it's because someone was late for their appointment earlier in the day, creating a domino effect. I can only be in one place at a time.

I peruse the menu, trying to keep my nerves at bay even though I know my order here by heart. A few minutes later, I hear the hostess say to follow her. I glance at my phone. Six o'clock on the dot. Maybe it's my blind date. If it is, I respect her punctuality.

The hostess rounds the corner, her eyes lasered in on my table. She's tall, blocking my view of the woman behind her. I place my napkin on the table, prepared to stand and pull out my date's chair or shake her hand. Whatever feels right in the moment.

When the hostess steps to the side, my gaze collides with my date's, and I freeze mid-stand. No. There's no way. This must be a sick joke that everyone else is in on but me.

Standing beside the table, looking at me with wide, horror-filled eyes, is none other than Kelsey Anderson.

# CHAPTER THIRTEEN

## KELSEY

"Do you have a reservation?" the hostess asks.

"It's kind of embarrassing, but I'm here for a blind date." I peer around the guests seated nearby but don't see a man in a dark blue jacket.

She perks up. "I know just where you're going. Follow me." She waves and starts walking toward the back of the restaurant without a backward glance to see if I'm following. I hurry after her, doing a weird jog-step to keep up with her long gait.

My heart is racing—whether from the mini workout I just did or my nervous anticipation at who my date is, I don't know.

The hostess comes to a stop and steps aside. With a deep breath, I look up and…my eyes go wide.

Oh no.

It's impossible.

My blind date can't be with Tyler *freaking* Reed.

Except, he's wearing a deep blue jacket, just like Darla told me my date would. Tyler also asked me to babysit tonight because he said something came up, and Darla arranged this at the last minute. With the blank stare Tyler's giving me, it appears he didn't know who he was meeting here either.

I feel a plethora of emotions all at once—like all the emotions from *Inside Out* are in my head, battling for control of how I'm feeling. But I think disgust wins out.

Maybe it's not too late. Maybe I can turn around and bolt back to my car, and we can pretend none of this ever happened.

"Here's your blind date." The hostess grins, looking very invested in our *nonexistent* love story. She pulls out a slip of paper from her pocket. "Darla said she hopes you all have fun and don't do anything she wouldn't." The young hostess blushes. "Which she wanted us to say isn't very much."

Tyler is in an awkward half-sitting, half-standing position when he rasps, "What are you doing here, Kelsey?"

The hostess raises her eyebrows, looking like she'd much rather stay and hear all the drama play out than get back to work. I'm sure we look like a reality television show, one I *really* don't want to be the star of. She moves as slowly as a sloth away from our table until Tyler and I are left alone in awkward silence.

Tyler stands to his full height, waiting for an answer to his question. I shake my head, trying to clear my brain of the shockwave flooding through it. "What am *I* doing here? What are *you* doing here?"

"I'm meeting a blind date," he says.

"So am I." I place my hands on my hips, frustrated that I didn't run when I still had the chance. "Please don't tell me Darla's your aunt."

Tyler nods. He sits back down with a groan and reaches for a glass of water, chugging half of it in two large gulps. "My great-aunt."

"How? She's so fun and you're so…" I gesture to him. "You."

"You sure know how to boost a guy's ego."

"I think the ladies at the dance studio gave you your annual boost." I motion to the table. "You're welcome to invite one of them to meet you here instead. I'm sure they'd give you an evening you'd never forget."

He cringes. "Don't remind me. I've had nightmares about their comments."

I move to leave when I hear the scraping of chair legs on the wood floor.

"Wait," Tyler says. I glance back at him. "What am I supposed to tell Darla?"

"I don't know. Maybe not to set you up on a blind date with your neighbor and nanny."

"Okay, let's not look at it like a date."

I cross my arms around my middle, trying to sound more confident than I feel. "You think we should stay?"

He shrugs. "I already made Evie dinner. You'd be proud. It was macaroni and cheese—the boxed kind."

"Wow." I look up at the ceiling.

His eyes move upward, then back to me. "What're you doing?"

"Looking for the flying pigs."

"Hilarious." He rubs the back of his neck, and I remember when he did the same motion in my house and the way his muscles rippled—it must be his nervous tick.

My eyes move to his arm, which is covered by his jacket tonight, saving me from staring at his muscles again. I drag my gaze back to his face to find his smug grin.

"I can take the jacket off if you're missing the view." He stands and shrugs it off.

"Hard pass."

"As rock hard as my chest?" He smirks.

I stalk over to him, poking his chest, which does, in fact, feel more like stone than flesh. I yank my jammed finger back and hold it. "You hurt me."

"You're the one who decided to pick a fight with my muscles."

I take a step closer, unwilling to back down. "Stop talking about your muscles."

"I'll stop talking about them when you stop touching and staring at them." He folds his arms across his chest, making the rippling, veiny muscles return. My eyes move to them. "Ah, ah, ah. There you go again." He leans down and tips my chin up. "My eyes are up here, Anderson."

The sparks between us are enough to light up an entire fireworks show. And I don't mean the good, lovey-dovey, romantic-tension sparks. We're talking aggravating, you-get-under-my-skin, I-want-to-wipe-that-grin-off-your-smug-face level of sparks.

Tyler's pupils dilate as he looks down at me. He doesn't say anything else. He just removes his hand and sits down like nothing happened.

"What are you doing?" I sputter.

"I'm getting ready to order dinner." He extends a menu to me. "Are you going to eat or not?"

I grab it and take the seat across from him with a huff.

"You don't have to sound so pained to eat a meal with me. As you said, a lot of women would love to be in your shoes."

"You're lucky that I'm starving."

"Yeah, I've won the lottery tonight," he deadpans.

Sighing, I skim the menu, looking for the most expensive options. I mean, if Tyler's paying, I may as well indulge in something better than I'd normally buy for myself.

The waiter comes and takes our drink orders. He returns with my Diet Coke and more water for Tyler and takes our food orders.

"I'll have the lobster ravioli."

Tyler doesn't even look at the menu when he makes his selection. "And I'll do the salmon primavera."

I glance at the menu, wrinkling my nose at the sheer number of vegetables listed in his dish and that the base is quinoa rather than pasta. Who comes to an Italian restaurant and doesn't even order pasta? It's more expensive than my dish, but I can't imagine why anyone would want to pay more for quinoa than lobster.

Tyler hands our menus to the waiter and taps his fingers on the table, looking around the room.

When I can't stand the silence, I say, "I'm shocked that you don't seem surprised."

"By what?"

"You seem like the kind of guy that typically goes on dates with women who would order a side salad, eat one bite, and say they're full. Not someone who orders a rich pasta dish."

He shrugs. "Give me some credit. I know you well enough to know you'd never order a salad. I've seen your grocery recommendations, remember?" Tyler runs a hand through his hair, making me remember how it felt to run my hands through it—how soft and thick it was. "Besides, I'd rather date someone who eats balanced meals. You can't just eat bunny food."

I lean back in the chair, not at all worried about my posture and angles when I don't give a lick what Tyler thinks of me. "Have you seen those candy salads on social media? That's my kind of balanced diet. The perfect mix of sugar and sour deliciousness."

He winces. "Thank goodness I don't have to provide you with medical and dental insurance. I can't imagine the sheer amount of cavities you must have."

"I have perfect dental health, thank you very much." I pick up the rose from the vase in the middle of the table, spinning it between my fingers. "There's this invention called the toothbrush. Maybe you've heard of it? It might be a little above your medical pay grade, though."

Tyler lets a slow breath out through his nose. He shakes his head. "You know what surprises me?" I raise my eyebrows, signaling for him to continue. "For someone who likes fruit snacks, you've got an expensive taste in pasta. I thought you'd enjoy the *delicacy* of SpaghettiOs over lobster ravioli."

"Don't you dare insult my SpaghettiOs."

"I'm simply making an observation." He runs a hand through his hair, but one rogue curl still remains on his forehead. "I'm also surprised that Aunt D ever thought we'd be a good match."

I sigh, not wanting to argue with someone who can't recognize the brilliance of foods like SpaghettiOs and fruit snacks. "We can at least agree on one thing: Darla is crazy for thinking we could be each other's happily ever after." He stares blankly at me. "Her words, not mine."

He raises his glass of water toward me, and I clink my Diet Coke to it. "I'll drink to that."

We both sip our drinks and set them back on the table. Neither of us speaks, and once the silence becomes deafening, I can't stand it anymore. "So, do you come here often?" I laugh nervously. It's been a while since I've been on a first date. I chide myself. Not that this is a date. It's definitely *not* a date. Just a dinner between a boss and his employee. Two colleagues eating together.

"At least twice a month."

"Let me guess, you order the same thing every time?"

"I know what I like." He says it in a way that leaves much room for interpretation while looking directly at me. I blush as I notice his eyes for the first time. They're a beautiful shade of green, like the color of the buds at the beginning of spring bursting forth from the ground. Of course, he has the rarest eye color.

Brushing some hair behind my ear, I break eye contact.

"Do you usually eat out or at home? I know you can make a mean Caprese chicken, but I can't imagine you had much time to cook when you worked four jobs," Tyler says.

"Mostly at home. I have Taylor Swift to keep me company while I cook after a long day of work." I take a sip of my Diet Coke. "I sometimes grab food out on the way home if I didn't make it to the grocery store that week. Also, anytime I'm feeling sick or sad, I grab a Hot Brown sandwich. My mom always got me them growing up, and they became my ultimate comfort food." I laugh. "I know it's very Louisvillian of me."

"You know, I don't think I've ever had a Hot Brown."

I gasp. "How long have you lived here?"

"Four years." He leans back in his seat, looking more at ease with the flow of conversation. "But three of those were during my residency, so all I did was eat, sleep, and breathe work. Then one of my colleagues retired as the head pediatrician at Little Louisville Pediatrics, and I got the job. I jumped from one kind of busy to another, so there wasn't much time for exploring the area or trying new things. I tend to stick to what I already know I like since I don't have time for much else."

"Like ordering the same dish at an Italian restaurant every time you come and dropping off flowers to your great-aunt on Thursdays after work?"

"Exactly." As quickly as the word is out of his mouth, Tyler shoots me a quizzical look. "Wait, how did you know I get Aunt D flowers every week?"

"I saw them in her room when I helped her with the duck fiasco, and she told me about you. You know she's kind of your wingwoman, the way she talks you up."

"Don't encourage her." He laughs. "If Darla heard you call her that, I'd never be able to escape her matchmaking attempts."

"Then I should definitely tell her," I tease.

His eyes widen. "You wouldn't."

I shake my head. "Nah, I wouldn't stoop that low. Even for you."

"I'm touched."

The waiter returns with our food. I inhale the garlicky notes of the cream sauce, and my mouth waters. Tyler's plate looks exactly how I imagined it: healthy.

I take a bite of ravioli and hold back a moan.

"Good, right?" Tyler smiles at me. I'm not sure when we started being nice to each other, but I'll enjoy the civil conversation while it lasts.

"Delicious." I wipe my mouth with a cloth napkin, making sure I don't have any sauce on my lips. "So, where did you live before you moved here for your residency?" I dive back into my pasta while he talks.

"I grew up in a small town in Northern Alabama. I got my undergrad at The University of Alabama and went to medical school at The Ohio State University before landing at The University of Louisville for my residency. I originally planned on doing my residency at Johns Hopkins, but my sister lives here. When her ex-husband left them a few months before I was supposed to start my residency, I changed my plans to be near them so I could help as much as possible."

Anger stirs up in my stomach at the thought of someone leaving Evie. "I always wondered what happened to Evie's father, and now I'd love to meet up with him in a dark alley. Just to...talk, you know?"

Tyler laughs—actually *laughs*—at my words. "You have no idea how many times I've wished the same thing."

"Maybe there's one more thing we have in common." I smirk. "They're lucky to have you close by, though. Your family must mean a lot to you."

"I'd do anything for them."

"Are your parents still in Alabama?"

"No, they're in Florence right now. Once my dad retired, they decided to travel. They wanted to move here to be with Tess and Evie when everything went down, but I offered to do it." He moves around the vegetables on his plate absentmindedly with his fork. "They sacrificed so much for us growing up, and they shouldn't have to give up their dream of seeing the world now that he's finally retired and they have the time and means to do it. I'm sure they'll settle down here once they're done with their grand adventure."

"If I didn't know any better, I'd say you were kind for doing that."

The corner of his mouth pulls up in a crooked grin. "But you still think I'm the worst, huh?"

"Maybe not the *worst*." I do my best to keep a straight face. "What will your parents do if they settle down here?"

"My dad is a classic car fanatic, so I'm sure he'll buy one to cruise around in. And Mom will thrive being the doting mother and grandmother."

I shift in my seat, knowing my own mother will never be that. I shove another bite of ravioli in my mouth. "Do you like cars?"

Tyler nods. "I'd love to own a Corvette one day." He eats another bite of salmon and then grins at me. "Back to me not being *the worst*, though. Have you noticed anything different lately? Particularly in the mornings."

I purse my lips, trying to think of anything out of the ordinary. "I mean, I've been sleeping better, but what does that have to do with—" My mouth falls open. "You haven't been blaring your workout music."

"If I'd known it bothered you before," he says, his tone genuine, "I would've used headphones from the start. I soundproofed that room, so I didn't realize anyone could hear it. I can't believe it took you two years to say something. No wonder you hate me."

He says *hate me* in the present tense. For a while, I really did hate him, but knowing what I know now, it's kind of impossible to hate the guy. And if he didn't know I could hear his music and stopped immediately after I told him it bothered me a few weeks ago, then I'm not sure what else I can hold against him.

It's like the picture I'd created in my mind over the past two years is completely shattered, and I'm not sure what my thoughts are about him.

I move my fork through the remaining sauce on my plate. "I don't *hate* you."

"I wouldn't blame you if you did." He sighs, and I really feel for the man sitting in front of me. The one who gave up residency at one of the most prestigious medical institutions to be near his sister. The one who treats his niece like she's his whole world and gives up his routine and normalcy to be her guardian for three months—and pays me way more than he should to watch her while he's working. The one who visits his matchmaker of a great-aunt every week with a new bouquet of flowers to liven up her room. I still think said great-aunt is nuts for thinking we'd be a good couple, but I understand Tyler more.

"We just had our wires crossed from the beginning, but I know you a little better now."

He looks up at me. "So, you're not mad you stayed for dinner?"

I shake my head.

He smiles. "Good. Next time, you can tell me about your family. Sorry, I feel like I talked the whole time."

"Your sister is in Africa, your parents are in Florence, and you spend all your evenings listening to a five-year-old. I think that gives you a free pass to talk to someone about yourself."

"Well, thanks." He rubs the back of his neck with a shy smile.

The waiter comes and takes our plates. "Would y'all like to look at our dessert menu tonight?"

Tyler looks at me, and I shake my head. I've already extorted him enough tonight with the lobster ravioli. I'd feel bad making him spend any more money, especially after our conversation.

"Not tonight," he says. "We'll take the check, please."

The waiter returns a few minutes later and places the bill in the middle of the table.

Tyler pulls out his wallet. "You're not even going to offer to go Dutch?"

"Do you want Darla to find out you're an uncivil man who doesn't even pay for his date's dinner?"

He snatches the bill up, placing his credit card inside, and I snort. "I was going to pay," he mutters.

"I just like to see you sweat."

Once Tyler gets his card back, we head outside. He places his hand on the small of my back, ushering me through the parking lot. Even through my sweater, I can feel his strong and steady touch, and I shiver.

"Are you cold?" He starts shrugging off his jacket.

"Oh, I'm fine. My car's right there." I point at it and keep moving. He walks me to my car, and I unlock the door, fumbling with my keys.

Tyler places his hands in his jeans pockets, rocking on his heels. "Thanks for sticking around tonight. I know this wasn't the date you imagined."

"At least you're closer to my age. When Darla told me she wanted to set me up with her nephew, I was worried I'd walk in to find someone in their fifties."

He laughs and takes a step forward like he's considering hugging me. Panic floods my body, unsure whether I should lean in or push him away. I'm saved from having to do anything when he knocks his fist gently on my arm. Honestly, it feels even more awkward than if he'd hugged me.

"Drive safe." Tyler clenches his jaw, and he looks around, seeming unsure. He shakes his head and jogs to his car before I can respond.

I get in my own car, cranking the heat. During the ride home, I sit in silence, not even turning on Taylor Swift, which is how I know something is really wrong. But I don't want a random love song to come on and leave me questioning what just happened even more than I already am.

Tyler and I park in front of our houses simultaneously. I gather my purse and head up the sidewalk, locking my car door as I walk. Leaves crunch behind me, and I roll my eyes.

"What are you doing? I'm a grown woman. I think I can walk myself a few yards home," I say as Tyler follows me toward my house rather than his. "If you think you're going to get a goodnight kiss, you're—"

"I'm not trying to kiss you." He sounds more defensive than disgusted.

"You could only be so lucky." I place my hands on my hips. "I'm a great kisser."

"Kelsey." He steps in front of me and gently grabs my upper arms. I'd normally go all *Kung Fu Panda* on him. However, the firm but kind way he's looking at me has me holding back my ninja moves. "I'm not trying to walk you to your door to kiss or even hug you. I'm only trying to pick up Evie."

I press my lips together, cutting off my next retort. Embarrassment courses through me. He wasn't trying to walk his "date" to the door. He's just picking up his niece that *my* besties were watching.

"Right, sorry." I stay on the sidewalk while Tyler passes me, knocking on the front door.

Shayna opens the door, wearing a bright green face mask. "You have perfect timing. Evie just finished her facial."

Tyler awkwardly motions to his face. "You've got something."

She reaches up and touches the mask. "Oh, right. I should go wash this off." Shayna kneels and hugs Evie. "Thanks for coming to girls' night. We'll have to have another one soon."

Evie beams. "I had *so* much fun."

Shayna smiles and switches places with Alyssa as I walk up the steps to join Tyler. Winston pokes his head into the fray and whines excitedly when he sees me.

Evie looks between us, her eyes filled with joy. "Is Ms. Kelsey your lady friend?"

I turn on the heels of my white platform sneakers and glare at him. "You told her I'm your *lady friend*?"

"It's not like that." He holds his hands up.

Alyssa pops her lips. "We'll give y'all another minute to sort that out." She quietly shuts the door, leaving us standing outside.

The porch light flicks on, illuminating the blush covering Tyler's cheeks.

I cross my arms. "Explain."

"Evie asked where I was going tonight. Her mom doesn't date, and like I told you, her dad left them years ago. I didn't want to explain what dating is to my five-year-old niece—that's my sister's job—so I panicked and told Evie I was meeting up with a lady friend."

When he puts it that way, it sounds innocent enough.

"It's just crossed wires, remember?" He nudges my arm as his voice falls back into a playful tone. "I'm not like that. If I was, I would've gone out with one of the ladies from the dance studio."

"True." I open the door, hoping Alyssa and Evie didn't go far. "Sorry. Thanks for the dinner." I rush past Alyssa and Evie, saying, "See you Monday."

I round the corner into the living room and press my back against the wall, breathing heavily. I can still hear Tyler's low rumble of laughter as I slide down the wall to sit on the hardwood floor. Winston trots over to me, licking my face until I pet him.

After a few minutes, the door creaks shut and Alyssa joins me on the floor.

"Shay! Mal! Get your gorgeous booties down here." My other friends come downstairs in their pajamas and plop onto the couch. "Now that we're all here, do you want to tell us what all that was about?"

"It's nothing."

Alyssa shakes her head. "You got home at the same time as Tyler when you were supposed to be on a blind date. He mentioned something about a lady friend. And then you thanked him for dinner. You can't tell me that's nothing. I could feel the tension sizzling between y'all."

I take a second, scanning the room, waiting for someone to back me up. When nobody does, I sigh and mutter, "Tyler was my blind date."

They collectively gasp.

Winston runs around excitedly like we're playing a game with him. The only game I want to be playing is how long I can close my eyes in bed and pretend this night never happened.

"Can we talk about this in the morning?" I rub my temples. "I need to shower and sleep off the mortification."

"Fine," Alyssa concedes. "But tomorrow morning, you have to tell us every detail."

"I'll pick up our usual biscuit orders so we can stay in our pajamas," Shayna offers.

"You're an angel on earth." I hug her. On Sundays, those of us who are available eat brunch together at a biscuit-themed restaurant in town. It'll be nice to do something normal tomorrow because everything about tonight was far from it. "And maybe some bonuts?"

"It must be bad if you want the biscuit donuts." Mallory lets out a low whistle.

We usually reserve ordering bonuts for breakups, breakdowns, or to celebrate Mallory's breaks from school. But if I'm going to have to relive every shocking and confusing feeling from tonight again, I'm going to need all the sweet encouragement I can get.

# CHAPTER FOURTEEN
## KELSEY

AFTER A QUICK LOOK in the mirror, I head downstairs in my matching sweats set, ready for a morning with my favorite girls. Once Winston has finished his business outside, I make my way to the kitchen.

I get to work making our favorite fall-flavored drink with my cheap espresso maker. Step aside, pumpkin spice, maple lattes reign supreme in this house.

I pour the steamed milk into the mugs of espresso, not even attempting to make a maple leaf design with the foam. Trying to create designs on drinks without a stencil was my least favorite part of my barista gig.

"It smells like heaven in here." Alyssa gives me a side hug, already looking perfect in a burnt orange silk blouse and fall floral silk scarves tied into her space buns, and then reaches down to rub Winston's head.

"No talking before coffee." Mallory shuffles in behind her. I place a mug in her extended hand. Even though she's usually teaching before the rest of us are awake, she's a gremlin in the mornings without her caffeine. She sits at her usual spot at the kitchen table and takes a sip.

"Better?" Alyssa laughs as I hand her a latte.

"Much." Mallory closes her eyes and sighs contentedly.

I hear the front door open and shut, and then Shayna walks into the kitchen wearing a cute white floral set. Her dark-brown hair is pulled up in a messy ponytail, and her signature knotted pearl headband sits perfectly in place. She sets two brown to-go bags on the kitchen table.

"Mmm." She inhales deeply, and her eyes light up. "Maple lattes?" I nod. "I love you," she coos.

Shayna grabs the yellow mug, and I take the remaining one to the table for myself.

Winston lays dutifully at my feet under the table as Alyssa pulls the food out of the bags and passes out everyone's orders. "Thanks for grabbing breakfast, Shay."

Mallory and I hum our thanks while digging in. I'd like to personally thank whoever thought to put hot honey, fried chicken, and pickles together on a biscuit for their ingenious creation. The biscuit makes it a breakfast food, okay?

"I can't wait any longer. I'm dying to hear about your blind date with *Tyler*," Shayna says in a sing-song voice.

I take a sip of my latte, savoring the sweet maple notes. I carefully place the mug back on the white-painted table and then jump into storytelling mode.

Once I've finished regaling them with the events of last night, my friends sit in stunned silence, the last bits of their lattes and sandwiches long forgotten. I grab a bonut and dip it in the berry compote before devouring it in a single bite.

"I can't believe that Darla is his great-aunt." Shayna grabs a bonut and clinks it with the next one I grab.

"Do you think she knew?" Alyssa gets up and adds some ice to her latte.

"Knew what?"

"That you're Evie's nanny and Tyler's neighbor."

I shake my head and then pause, wondering if it's possible. I do remember telling Darla about my annoying next-door neighbor...but I never mentioned his name. "No, I don't think she knew. Although, I'm sure she would have put the puzzle pieces together by now if Tyler told her who I am."

"It's so romantic how he started using headphones for his morning workouts." Shayna tilts her head to the side with a dreamy sigh. "Don't you think, ladies?"

My friends nod like bobbleheads.

"I'm going to be winning that bet in no time." Alyssa grins.

Shayna eats another bonut. "Not if I beat you to it."

I scoff. "There's no way *any* of you are winning that bet because I'm not going to fall in love with Tyler Reed."

"We'll see about that." Mallory gets up and microwaves her latte. It kills me a little, knowing it will likely make the coffee taste more bitter from the rapid heating.

"Why are y'all so set on the idea that we'll fall in love?" I ask.

"Point number one: You're beautiful, and he's handsome." Alyssa shrugs like this is all common knowledge.

Mallory pulls her mug from the microwave and walks back to the table. "Point number two: There are literal sparks between you and Tyler. All it will take is the tiniest amount of fuel to turn those sparks into a roaring inferno."

I shake my head at how ridiculous it all sounds.

"It's true." Shayna pats my arm. "And point number three: He's different than you originally thought. He brings his aunt flowers and takes in his niece for three months at the drop of a hat. Not to mention the headphones thing. Since he's not the jerk you thought he was, there's nothing to hold you back from falling now."

Hearing my friends speak my thoughts from last night into existence is slightly terrifying.

"Fine, I'll say it." I groan, and all my friends press in, leaning forward on their elbows. "Tyler's hot. Like hotter-than-the-average-human-should-be *hot*. But it doesn't mean I'm going to fall for him."

"We've still got time." Shayna fist bumps Alyssa.

Mallory nods. "But boy, does Tyler have his work cut out for him."

Alyssa raises her mug in the air. "To Kelsey falling in love, buying a nice espresso maker, and making us lattes for a month."

"Hear, hear." Mallory and Shayna raise their mugs to meet hers.

I grab the rest of the bonuts and berry compote from the middle of the table. "Just for that, I'm not sharing the rest of these."

"So, are you going to make out with him when he gets home from work on Monday?" Mallory crosses her legs, looking like she's thoroughly enjoying all this. "Get it out of your system?"

"That's a definite no. Honestly, I don't know how I'll get through the next two months nannying for him. I feel like it's going to be awkward after our non-date."

"Why don't you just quit?"

I bite my bottom lip. There are two reasons I couldn't quit. One: I would never want to do that to Evie. She's already dealing with her mom being out of the country and living in a new house. She needs some stability right now. Two: I need the generous paychecks.

Shayna takes a sip of her latte. "What are you not telling us?"

I bite my lip. "There might be something I've been saving up for a while now."

"You mean the real reason you had four jobs?" Alyssa raises a perfectly manicured brow. "Well, two now. But one of which pays you extremely generously."

"How did you know?"

She shrugs. "I sort all our mail, and you haven't gotten any about your student loans lately, so I can only assume you paid them off."

"Sooo," Mallory draws out the word. "What are you working all these jobs for?"

"This wasn't really how I planned on telling y'all." I wring my hands together in my lap. "I want to open a dog rescue," I blurt out, scared that if I don't say the words quickly, I never will.

"That's amazing." Shayna smiles.

"If I could ever pick a perfect job for you, that would be it." Alyssa reaches across the table, squeezing my hand.

"What they said," Mallory echoes.

I feel like I can fully breathe, knowing they're not mad at me for not telling them. "I'm sorry I didn't tell y'all. I think it's just scary to voice my dream out loud to anyone, even my best friends."

"You don't have to apologize." Shayna gets up and wraps her arms around me from behind. "You told us when you were ready."

"And now you have us to help you achieve your dream. Whatever we can do to help, we're here." Alyssa joins the hug before waving for Mallory.

"Oh, all right."

Soon enough, I'm wrapped up in all three of my besties' arms. Their support fills me with hope that I'll be able to achieve my dream with them by my side.

I swipe my thumb under my eyes. "Okay, enough of this."

Shayna wiggles her eyebrows. "If you're not going to kiss Tyler tomorrow, then what are you going to say when you see him?"

Tomorrow. Monday. Oh, crap.

"Oh my gosh." I jump, grabbing my phone as a thought crosses my mind. I scroll through my emails until I find the one I'm looking for. I scan through it, searching for the last date I can cancel.

I groan when I notice the cancellation deadline was Friday.

"What did you do?" Alyssa searches my eyes like she'll find the answer there.

I press my lips together, wishing I could turn back time. "I might have put out an ad in the newspaper."

"For what?" Mallory asks.

I hand her my phone so she can read it. Mallory bursts out laughing, clutching her stomach. When she's calmed down, she reads it aloud. "*Doctor for hire. In-home visits only. Here to help with your every need.* And there's a photo of Tyler in his scrubs above his phone number."

Shayna's mouth falls open while Alyssa laughs so hard that tears begin streaming down her cheeks.

"I have two questions," Alyssa says when she's composed herself. "When and why?"

"I sent it in last weekend on the car ride back from Hemlock Cliffs." I play with the ends of my hair. "I was so fed up with him that day and wanted to do something to get back at him."

"And your first reaction was to have his phone blown up by overeager women?" Alyssa raises a perfectly manicured brow.

"It sounds a lot worse when you say it like that." I facepalm. "Obviously, if I knew then what I know now about him, I would've never done it."

"Did you put his work phone number or cell?" Shayna asks.

I hang my head. "His cell."

"He's going to have to change his number." She clenches her teeth, looking like the grimacing emoji.

"Or leave the country. At least he could join his sister in Africa." Mallory steals one of the bonuts from me and pops it in her mouth.

I feel too awful to even care. "It goes out tomorrow morning. What am I supposed to do?"

Mallory dabs her mouth with a paper napkin. "You can't tell him."

"Of course, she needs to tell him." Alyssa throws a hash-brown at Mallory. "He needs to be prepared for all the calls he's about to get."

"What do you think, Shay?" I always trust her opinion.

"I mean, it's funny, but it's also his business. This could impact his reputation with patients and colleagues. I think you need to tell him tomorrow."

My stomach drops. I never even thought about the implications this could have for Tyler workwise. After last night, I thought we could move past our rivalry and maybe even move toward being friends. I wasn't trying to start a neighbor war, but I just might be getting one.

I can only hope that Tyler's in a forgiving mood, and we can both laugh about this tomorrow when he discovers what I did.

# CHAPTER FIFTEEN
## TYLER

"Wait!" Nadine calls after me. "How did your blind date go?"

"Since you love talking to Aunt D about my love life so much, you can ask her," I say.

"She said you didn't give her the deets yet."

I face my receptionist, shooting her a wry grin. "Maybe this will teach you two to mind your own business from now on."

She harrumphs and mumbles something about it being unfair and not being able to enjoy her daydreams without the details. I don't think I want to know what that's about.

"See you tomorrow." I narrowly escape out the front door before she can stop me.

As I drive home, I think about what Nadine said. If I don't call Darla soon, she'll probably find a way to hitchhike to my house and demand all the details. Although I'd love to make her wait it out for setting me up with my neighbor, I don't want Sunrise Springs calling to tell me my great-aunt snuck out.

I click her name on the touchscreen of my dashboard.

"Oh, so you *do* know how to use a phone," Darla answers with all the sass of a strong Southern woman.

"Is that how you treat your great-nephew who has information you desperately want to know?"

She's quiet for a moment, a rarity. "I'll keep my trap shut for the next minute."

I smile, knowing how difficult it is for her not to say what she's thinking. "First, I want to know how you're doing. Still no shortness of breath, chest pain, dizziness, or heartburn?"

"You quit your worrying. I've been given a clean bill of health. Sunrise Springs made me fill out paperwork because of the duck incident, and part of it required a medical professional to check me out. A strapping young EMT came flying up in an ambulance just for me. All the ladies were jealous. Maybe I'll even get a date with Ed out of it..." She trails off. "Anyway, he took my blood pressure and listened to my heart and everything. Now that's what I call a public service."

I shake my head. "You know there's such a thing as oversharing, right?"

"Not when it comes to family, dear," Darla tuts. "Now, I'm going to shut my trap, and you can tell me everything. I want all the details."

"Did you know that she's Evie's nanny?"

"Who?"

"Kelsey."

"Kelsey works here at Sunrise Springs." Darla sounds confused. Maybe she didn't know after all.

"She's also Evie's nanny, a dog walker, and my next-door neighbor."

"*You're* the hunky man that she works for next door?" Aunt D squeals like a schoolgirl. "Oh, this is too good. Just like the telenovelas."

"She called me hunky?" I can't hide the incredulity in my voice.

"Not in so many words. It was in what she *didn't* say. You have to read between the lines."

"I'm not sure what to believe with Kelsey. I'm pretty sure she hated me until the date."

"But now?"

The question hangs in the air, the answer just out of reach. "I don't think she despises me anymore, but that doesn't mean she wants anything more with me."

"Do you want more with her?"

That question might be even more difficult to answer. I've never denied Kelsey's beauty, but I did stuff down every ounce of attraction I felt toward her for the last two years. It was easy to do when she always let her dogs in my yard and glared at me every time she saw me.

But the more I've been around her, the more I appreciate our banter. I give her an A for effort with the list of fictional doctors she calls me. When I push aside my pride at being referred to as evil villains or monsters, I can admit it's actually hilarious. She's witty and beautiful, and when I watched her walls fall the slightest bit Saturday night, it left me wondering what it would take to make the rest of them come crumbling down.

If they fell completely, I'm not even sure what I'd do, but I hope she lets me stick around long enough to find out.

"I'm not sure what I want," I say, "but I have time to figure it out."

"The clock's ticking. I want more great-great nieces or nephews."

I huff out a laugh. "Let's just start with dating first."

"Are you at least ready to admit that I'm a wonderful matchmaker?"

"It's not that I didn't think you'd be good at it, I just wanted to meet someone the old-fashioned way."

"Technically, you met Kelsey when she moved in next door. There's your good old-fashioned love story. Problem solved."

"It's not that easy, Aunt D." I pull up in front of my house and put the car in park.

"Love is easy. It's people who make it hard."

"Some of us more so than others, right?"

I can hear the smile in her voice. "Congratulations, you're learning to read between the lines."

"I should get going. I just got home."

"Tell Evie and Kelsey hello for me."

Once we hang up, I grab my phone and walk toward the porch when I notice how many missed calls and voicemails I have. Twenty-seven. It was a hectic day in the office, so I didn't get a chance to check my phone. I scroll through them.

That's weird. They're all from random numbers in the area. I'm about to play the most recent voicemail when an incoming call pops up.

I accept the call. "Hello?"

The lady on the phone explains why she's calling. My eyes go wide at her *descriptive* word choices. Words that certainly aren't worth repeating.

"I'm not available for any of the"—I drop my voice to a whisper—"*services* you're mentioning. Please don't call this number again."

I shake my head. *Weirdest prank call of my life.* I press play on the next voicemail as I unlock the front door.

A woman's voice comes through the speaker as I step inside. "Hey there, gorgeous. I'm calling about your ad. I'm in need of an in-home exam, but only if you show up in your scrubs and nothing el—"

My face heats. I rush to exit out of the voicemail as Evie runs over to me. I drop my things and catch her in my arms. I know there will come a day when she's not as excited to see me, so I never take times like this for granted.

"How was your day?" I ask.

"The best." She spins, her arms spread wide. "I got an A-plus on my spelling sheet."

"You know what that calls for?" I smile, knowing I'll take her wherever she wants to go.

"Pizza?" Her eyes are wide as she bounces in excitement.

"You got it. Make sure you use the restroom and grab your coat. It's a little chilly tonight."

"Aye, aye, captain." Evie salutes me and runs upstairs.

Kelsey steps into the room, and I turn to her. "You wouldn't believe the number of calls I received today."

"Oh?" She picks at her nails.

"There's no other word to describe the voicemails besides *disturbing*."

Kelsey wrings her hands. "I tried to stop it, I swear."

"Wait." I hold up my phone. "You had something to do with this?"

"Isn't that why you're talking to me about it?"

"I just wanted to talk to another adult about it." I point upstairs and lower my voice. "Evie doesn't need to hear what these women are saying." I press play on the most recent voicemail and hand Kelsey my phone. She blushes and her eyes go wide with horror about halfway through.

"I think I've heard plenty." Kelsey steps closer, peering up at me with her soft hazel eyes flooded with guilt. "I'm so sorry. I did something stupid when I was upset. I remembered about it too late to take it back."

"What did you do?" I groan.

She pulls her phone out of her back pocket and scrolls for a minute before handing it to me.

My eyes gape at the screen as I look at an advertisement with my face and phone number. *Doctor for hire. In-home visits only. Here to help with your every need.*

It takes everything in me to stifle my laughter and keep a stone-cold expression. I thought she was funny before, but this takes it to a new level. I can't laugh yet, though. She needs to sweat it out a little longer.

"I called the newspaper, and they're going to put a redaction out, but you might want to change your phone number in the meantime." Kelsey places her hand on my arm. "I'm really sorry. If I could go back in time and never send the email, I would."

She bites her lower lip, waiting to see how I'm going to react. I've never seen her look this vulnerable. I'm sure she already felt awful the past few days, so I let out all the laughter I've been holding in until I can hardly breathe. Her expression morphs from scared to confused as she watches me.

"You're...not...mad?" She pauses between each word like she's tentatively testing the waters to see if I'm about to let out a roaring wave of anger.

"It's hilarious." I point at her phone again and chuckle. "Who even thinks of putting out an ad like that?"

"I was worried it might impact your business. If it does, you can dock it out of my pay."

"I mean, it may not be the best for business, but if you're already having the newspaper put a redaction out, there's not much else you can do. Besides, maybe some of my twenty-seven callers have children they can bring into my office." I smirk.

"This is *not* the reaction I was expecting."

I step closer to her, our chests almost touching. "Game on, Anderson."

"What?" Her voice is breathy.

My smile grows knowing that my nearness made her breathless. Maybe she doesn't hate me as much as I thought. Or maybe that grocery store clerk was right about there being a fine line between enemies and lovers.

"You heard me." I reach down, cupping her chin and tilting her head up to meet my gaze. "You just started a war." I let go of her face and step back, crossing my arms and flexing my muscles in a way I know will have her staring. "Don't worry. I won't play dirty." I wink. I don't think I've ever winked at anyone in my entire life, but Kelsey Anderson has a way of making me react in ways that surprise even me.

She sighs, dragging her eyes from my arms back to meet my gaze. "I'm never going to live this down, am I?"

"Not if I can help it."

Once Evie is fast asleep, I research prank ideas online until I find the perfect one for Kelsey. I order everything without a second thought, not caring that I'm throwing money out the window. It will be worth it when I see the look on her face.

"You have someone here to see you, boss," Nadine says.

"I'll be right up." I rack my brain trying to figure out who could be here to see me. Tess stops by sometimes when she's in the area, but she's in Africa.

The last person I expect to see standing there is Kelsey. She's in another one of her sweaters today—cream with a tiny black bow print. She starts rocking on her feet, and my heart drops into my stomach.

I rush over to her. "Is Evie okay? Did the school call you?" I pull out my phone but don't have any missed calls from the school—or otherwise, thanks to my new cell number.

Kelsey grasps my forearms, "She's fine. Sorry, I should've been clearer about why I'm here." Her gaze drops to the floor. "I still feel awful about the ad."

"That was you?" Nadine jumps out of her seat like she's twenty rather than going on seventy. "Honey, don't feel bad about that. You gave me the best laugh of my life." Nadine smacks the desk with a chuckle. "I clipped the ad and put it on my fridge."

I shoot a look at her. "I never took you for a traitor."

"I'm team this girl here after you never told me about your date. I only know what Darla told me," she harrumphs. "But that Kelsey must be pretty amazing for you to be tight-lipped all week."

I feel the blush climbing my cheeks, silently begging Nadine to shut up. "Nadine, have you met Kelsey?" I gesture to her, and Nadine's grin rivals the Joker's.

"Well, I'll be darned." Her eyes move between us like a ball bouncing back and forth in a pinball machine. "She's even more beautiful than I imagined." She blows out a low breath. "She's definitely out of your league, but she must like you to be stopping by so soon after the date."

"Please stop talking." I rub my temple before turning to face Kelsey, who looks highly amused. "If you aren't here because of Evie…"

"Right." She bends and grabs a bag off the floor. She hands me a food container. "I hope bringing you lunch makes up for the ad."

I open the lid and my mouth waters. It's the same Caprese chicken she made for me on her first day of nannying. "You didn't have to do this."

"I wanted to." She passes me a fork along with a fancy bottled water.

"This meal is one of the best things I've ever eaten, so thank you."

Kelsey smiles, extending another container to Nadine. "I'm Kelsey. It's nice to meet you…"

"Nadine," my receptionist says, still smiling widely. "Thank you so much for the lunch, sugar." Nadine waggles a finger at Kelsey. "I knew I liked you." She points to me. "Maybe even more than Doc here right now."

"Why didn't I think of that one?" Kelsey tuts.

"One what?" I ask around a mouthful of chicken.

"Your nickname. I could've called you Doc." I stare at her blankly and she rolls her eyes. "You know, like one of the seven dwarves."

"I don't think he's a real doctor."

She shakes her head. "You're no fun."

"After our date, maybe you should start calling me Mc-Steamy."

Kelsey places a hand on her hip. "I thought you said it wasn't a date?"

"Uh—" I was just trying to joke around, and now I feel backed into a corner, unsure of a way out.

"Relax, Doofenshmirtz. It's called a *joke*. Maybe you can learn how to make them one day." She turns and reaches a hand out to Nadine, but she waves it off, rounding the counter and squeezing Kelsey in a warm hug.

"You come back anytime you want. I like seeing Doc all flustered."

"I'll make sure to do that." Kelsey smiles. She offers me a quick wave. "See you later."

Before I can wave back, she's already gone.

Nadine is back in her seat, grinning at me when I face her. She points her forkful of chicken toward the door. "I like that one. Don't mess it up."

I'm not sure what *it* even is right now. A hatemance? A flirtationship? A deep-seated attraction?

But whatever *it* is, I'll do everything I can not to mess it up.

# CHAPTER SIXTEEN
## KELSEY

"WHAT ARE YOU MAKING?" Alyssa asks from behind me before leaning against the counter.

I startle, holding a hand to my heart. I've been jumpier since Tyler told me I'd started a war. I'm not sure when or how he'll prank me, hence the jumpiness.

Once I've composed myself, I hold up the empty bag. "A teenage classic: pizza rolls."

"It never ceases to amaze me how you can eat like that every day and still look that good." She gestures to my body.

I strike a pose. "Why, thank you."

Alyssa grabs my phone off the counter. "You've got a text." She makes a kissy face. "It's from *Tyler*."

I grab my phone from her. "You're making something out of nothing."

"Mm-hmm, sure. Tell me that in another month."

I sigh. There's no use in arguing with her about this.

"Well, what does it say?" she asks.

TYLER

I'm not sure what your plans are tonight, but Evie has an art show at the school in thirty minutes.

I know it's last minute, but having you there would mean a lot to her.

ME

I'll be there.

TYLER

Great, see you then.

"He wanted to invite me to Evie's art show tonight."

"Did you say yes?"

I nod. The air fryer beeps, and I use a spatula to scoop the pizza rolls from the tray onto my plate. "Evie deserves to have as many people supporting her as possible, especially since her mom isn't here."

I bite into a pizza roll, burning the roof of my mouth with the molten filling inside. I cover my mouth with my hand and blow out the heat.

"Is there some kind of science behind why they're always lava hot or cold?" I'm like Goldilocks; I want it just right.

"You did shove it in your mouth right out of the air fryer, but you're not wrong. With those, you have to pick a painful death for the roof of your mouth or a cold filling."

"I would usually let it cool a little, but I have to leave in ten minutes, and I need to put on a little bit of makeup." I eat another one, biting the corner off this time to let the steam escape before eating the filling.

"You need to put on makeup for a kindergarten art show?" Alyssa doesn't even bother trying to hide her smile.

"I'm not putting on makeup for Tyler if that's what you're implying." I swat her arm. "I already wiped off my makeup when I got home from watching Evie. I'm only putting a little back on."

"Keep telling yourself that." Alyssa smiles before grabbing her purse from the kitchen table.

"Where are you going on a Wednesday night?"

"I have a date."

"With who?"

She tightens the cream-colored silk scarves around her space buns. "Peter," she mumbles.

"You're going out with *him* again?"

"I thought I'd give him another shot. See if he's changed." She shrugs nonchalantly.

I wrinkle my nose. "I thought you said he never wanted to get married. A leopard doesn't change its spots."

"It's just dinner. I'll be fine." Alyssa glances at the time. "I have to leave now if I'm going to make it." She wiggles her fingers in a small wave. "Have fun with the hot doctor."

I finish my remaining pizza rolls, which are now, of course, cold. I head upstairs, swipe mascara on my lashes, and add a little bit of blush to my cheeks before heading to my car. Even though I don't have extra time, I still pull up my social media and send a DM to Austin Bradford, Alyssa's *friend*. He has over a million followers, but we've messaged on here before, so hopefully he'll see my text.

ME

> Hey Austin. Lyss is on another date with Peter. *eye roll emoji* If you're free later, she might need you.

Alyssa is beautiful and has the biggest heart...but she's terrible at choosing men. There have been multiple times I've messaged Austin in the past, under similar circumstances, to cheer her up in a way only he seems to be able to. It's like his kind, steady presence gives her hope that there are still good men out there in the world.

I'm still waiting for the day they stop avoiding the inevitable and kiss already. But for now, at least Austin can cheer up one of my besties in a way my other roomies and I are unable to.

Arriving at the school in the nick of time, I lock my car and hurry into the building. I walk through the rows of artwork until I finally spot Tyler's tall, muscular stature among the crowd. When I reach him, I see Evie's name under the art on the wall.

"Oh, this is lovely." I stare at the painting, trying to figure out what it is. The background is painted a deep blue, and there are white, oddly shaped squiggle lines and a white circle on it.

"Ms. Kelsey, you came!" Evie wraps her arms around my legs. "It's the night sky. I worked so hard on the stars." She points at the squiggles. "Do you like them?"

"I do." I smile, kneeling to hug her. "They look so life-like that you almost made me think I was outside."

Evie giggles. "Do you think I'll win a ribbon?"

"I'm not sure, but what's important is that you submitted your art and did your very best."

"I did try my best, but I'll be sad if I don't win." Her chin quivers, tugging at my heartstrings.

"You're allowed to be sad." I squeeze her shoulders. "We don't always win everything we want, but putting yourself out there, knowing that you may not win, is very brave."

She falls into my arms, squeezing me tight. I glance at Tyler as I hug her back. He mouths *thank you*, and I offer him a soft smile in return.

Evie wraps her small hand around my fingers. "Come see my friends' paintings." She escorts me and Tyler around the show, pointing out all the artwork from the other kids in her class.

When we come back around to her painting, a white ribbon hangs from the corner.

Evie runs over and points to it. "What does it say, Uncle Ty?"

"You won third place, Eves." He picks her up and spins her around while she squeals in delight. Tyler pulls her against his chest. "I'm so proud of you, and I know your mom will be too."

If my view of Tyler wasn't completely altered at dinner this past weekend, it is now. I feel the switch flip in my brain. It's staggering, like being in a dark room that suddenly shines with the brightest floodlights. All of the harsh things I thought about him, now illuminated by all the positive things I've seen him do for Evie and Darla...and even for me.

But that doesn't mean my view of what I want in the future has changed. I still don't plan on getting married or settling down. So, maybe the best thing for Tyler and me right now is some distance, because if I keep watching him be all cute with his niece, I'm not sure how long I'll be able to resist getting to know the man behind all those muscles.

----------- ♡ ♡ ♡ -----------

Tyler told me that I had started a war on Monday, so the fact that I've made it to Friday unscathed has me feeling unnerved. After the coffee is done brewing, I grab my favorite mug. I'm about to pour the liquid joy into my mug, but something at the bottom of it catches my eye.

"What the—"

I flip the mug over, catching a miniature rubber duck in my palm.

"How did you get there, little guy?" I place him on the kitchen table and finish making my coffee.

Throughout the rest of my day, I find more miniature ducks everywhere. In my makeup bag. In my favorite pair of white platform sneakers. On the handle of the leashes for my dog-walking gig. In my sunglasses case. On my car seat. In the drink holder in my car.

By the time I pick Evie up from school, I've found at least twenty of them. She gets into my car, and I help buckle her into the booster seat. Evie giggles when she sees multiple ducks on my dashboard.

"You wouldn't happen to know where these came from, would you?" I raise an eyebrow at her in the rearview mirror.

Her giggling intensifies until she's full-on belly laughing. She reaches into her backpack and grabs a handful of the little ducks.

"*You* hid them all?"

"No, I helped Uncle Ty do it."

"How do you feel about helping me get back at your uncle?"

"We can do something that will make him laugh?" Her eyes are wide with excitement.

"Yeah," I say. We'll go with that. It's not like a five-year-old is going to understand what a prank war is.

"Yes!" she exclaims. "Can we do it when we get home?"

"*After* homework."

Evie sighs. "Fine. I'll be really fast. Like faster than recess."

I smirk at her reflection in the mirror. We park in front of my house, and the second I unlock Tyler's front door, Evie sprints to the kitchen table, whips out her homework folder, and gets straight to work.

While she's distracted, I pull out my phone to do a little bit of sleuthing of my own.

ME

Any idea why I've found an entire flamboyance* of little ducks?

*parliament

*murder

*unkindness

What is a group of ducks called, anyway?

TYLER

How do you know the words for a group of flamingos, owls, crows, and ravens but not ducks?

ME

I remember all the funny ones.

TYLER

Of course you do.

> I think the word you're looking for is flock.

ME

> ...and the answer to my first question?

TYLER

> I already told you. Game on, Anderson.

If Tyler thinks he can prank me without any retaliation, he's sorely mistaken. I glance around the kitchen, trying to think of a prank I can easily pull. When I spot his old-school kitchen sink with a separate water spray feature, I can't suppress my smile. Target acquired.

"Done." Evie runs over to me, handing me a sheet of paper. I read over her work.

"Great job, girl." I give her a high-five. "Now, are you ready to learn a classic trick?"

She nods, grinning wide.

I lead her back into Tyler's kitchen and lift her up, propping her on my knee. "All we have to do is tie this"—I hand her the hair tie off my wrist—"around the water sprayer." Evie pulls herself off my leg to sit on the counter, wrapping the hair tie around the sprayer twice. I wrap it around once more before helping Evie get down.

"What will it do?" she asks.

"When your Uncle Ty gets home from work and wants to wash his hands or his dinner plate, the water will come out of the sprayer aimed right at him, showering him in a watery surprise."

She beams. "I can't wait."

"Me either." I smile. There's no way Tyler will be expecting me to retaliate this quickly.

Game on, indeed.

# CHAPTER SEVENTEEN
## TYLER

An evening away from the house is just what the doctor ordered.

It's me, hi. I'm the doctor, it's me.

Even though I don't know much about Taylor Swift, I'd have to live under a rock not to have heard that song—well, with the original lyrics.

Honestly, I just need a Kelsey-free zone for one night. I get home from work tonight ready for just that.

"Have a good weekend." Kelsey hugs Evie and shoots me a soft smile and wave before heading out the front door.

"I'll be right down, Eves." I run upstairs, taking the steps two at a time. I throw my scrubs straight into the laundry bin and pull on my favorite pair of jeans and a black, long-sleeve shirt. After I swipe on more deodorant, I head to the kitchen.

"What are we eating tonight?" She's sitting at the kitchen table, looking at me like she's hoping I'm going to say I'm making boxed macaroni and cheese again.

"We're eating some leftover spaghetti tonight so that we can make it to your surprise."

Her face falls when I mention leftovers, but she perks up again at the mention of a surprise. "Where are we going?"

"You'll have to wait and see." Once I split the remaining noodles between our bowls, I add the leftover meat sauce and get her meal in the microwave.

I move to the sink to wash the empty glass containers. However, when I turn the faucet on, instead of cleaning my bowl, I'm greeted by a thorough spraying of water...straight to the crotch. I hold back the curse word that wants to come out for the sake of the young ears in the room. I attempt to block the stream of water with my hands as I scramble to turn off the faucet.

I place my hands on the counter, breathing hard. What in the world just happened?

Evie bursts into laughter, pointing at me. "It looks like you peed your pants."

I glance down. She's not wrong. I'll have to change my pants—and probably my shirt—before we leave.

I lean down, glancing at the spout, trying to figure out where it's broken. That's when I notice the black hair tie wrapped tightly around the sprayer.

I pull off the offender, holding it up in the air. "How did this get here?" Evie laughs again, and I turn to face her. "Did *you* do this?"

She giggles. "I helped Ms. Kelsey."

I'm starting to think the prank war was a bad idea because it's only given me more reasons for Kelsey to live rent-free in my thoughts.

I put the hair tie on the kitchen table. "You did?" Taking slow steps toward Evie, I hold my hands up like a monster. "You know what that means."

"No," she squeals. "Not the tickle monster." Evie runs around the table, and I catch her in my arms, tickling her sides before lifting her in the air. Her laughter fills the space, making me wonder if I'll ever hear my own children's laughter floating through my house.

I shake my head, unsure where that thought came from. I've always wanted a family, but I have a few steps to take before getting to that point. You know, like dating.

*You already went on a date with Kelsey*, I remind myself. Or maybe a non-date. Either way, I enjoyed our non-date way more than the real ones in my twenties.

Even the two years I spent with my last girlfriend weren't as enjoyable as the short time I've spent with Kelsey. But I guess I shouldn't be surprised. My ex wasn't exactly *marriage material*. After all, I could never end up with someone who thought I spent too much time taking care of Evie and Tess after my sister went through her divorce.

"Uncle Ty, you're getting my shirt wet." She wiggles in my arms.

I put Evie back on her feet. "Sorry, kiddo." The microwave beeps, and I drop to my knees. "Dinner or new clothes first?"

She pinches her wet shirt. "New clothes."

I help her find a sweater that should keep her warm since we'll be outside after dusk for the surprise I have in store. I leave her alone to change and head to my room, throwing my pants into my laundry hamper and putting on a pair of khakis. After looking at myself in the mirror, I change out of my black long-sleeve into a maroon one.

We meet back in the kitchen to eat dinner. Evie tops her bowl of spaghetti with an obscene amount of Parmesan cheese that probably takes away all the nutritional value of this meal, but she's a growing girl, so I don't say anything.

I put our used bowls in the sink. Even though it kills me to leave dirty dishes out, I don't want to risk missing our entry time for tonight's event.

"Put your shoes on, please." I pull on my duck boots and grab her coat from the closet. "To the car," I say, throwing Evie over my shoulder. She playfully hits my back. "Hmm, this sack of potatoes sure is wiggly. Maybe it needs a quality check." I put her down and hold up an imaginary magnifying glass, moving it up and down her arms.

Evie shakes her head, but the grin she's wearing is worth all the gold in the world. "It's *me*, Uncle Ty."

"Well, thank goodness. Otherwise, you would miss the Pumpkin Spectacular."

She gasps. "I heard people talking about that at school." Evie wraps her little arms around my neck. "Thank you."

"You're welcome." I smile, glad to feel like I'm at least doing one thing right. While it's hard to process all my muddled feelings toward Kelsey, at least I can sleep at night knowing Evie is loved and cared for while her mom is gone.

We park and walk to a local amphitheater, getting in line behind a large group of people waiting to be let in for our time slot. Evie and I talk about her day at school and play games together on my phone until the sun sets. After dusk, the volunteers begin letting people in. The second we pass under the arch and enter the trail for the park, Evie looks around like it's Christmas morning.

We walk along the paved path between a forest of trees. Pumpkins surround us on both sides, all exquisitely carved. There are so many little details that you could walk around for hours and still need more time to look at them all.

Evie's hands ball into little fists as she excitedly takes everything in.

"Can you guess how many pumpkins there are?"

"A hundred?" she asks with awe.

"More than five thousand."

Evie's jaw drops. "That's way higher than I can count."

"Maybe it will be good math practice."

"No." She groans. "We're here for *fun*, Uncle Ty. Not school." Evie points ahead. "It's Elsa!" She drags me to a section featuring characters from *Frozen*, where baby-blue lights illuminate the pumpkins and the chorus of "Let It Go" plays.

Evie finally lets us continue walking once I've heard the song at least three times. "Is Ms. Kelsey coming?"

"No, I thought we'd have fun tonight, just the two of us."

She scrunches her nose. "Then why is she here?"

I glance up and see Kelsey and her roommates looking at the rest of the Disney-themed designs.

"Ms. Kelsey!" Evie shouts, letting go of my hand and running to her nanny.

Kelsey turns our way, her surprise morphing into a giant grin as she hugs my niece.

*So much for my Kelsey-free night.* There's not a chance Evie will let me pull her away from Kelsey and her friends now.

I walk over and suddenly have no idea what to do with my hands. Do I hug Kelsey? Or maybe go for a firm handshake? A little wave? I'm way out of my depth here.

Before I can do something stupid, I shove them in my jeans pockets. "Fancy seeing you here."

She raises a brow. "Are you following me, Frankenstein?"

"You wish, Anderson." I really need to come up with a better nickname to irk her. Trying to avoid a conversation with Kelsey, I turn to her friends. "Which pumpkins are your favorite so far?"

Shayna sighs dreamily. "Definitely the one of Rapunzel and Flynn Rider."

"I'm partial to Jack Sparrow." Mallory kicks at a pebble on the path.

"And you?" I look at Alyssa.

"There's only one real answer to that question: Taylor Swift."

"That one was so pretty." Evie pops up between Alyssa and Shayna, grabbing each of their hands. They must've really bonded for her to feel this comfortable around them.

"Which one was your favorite, Evie?" Shayna swings their joined hands.

"Elsa!"

Alyssa smiles down at my niece. "It was cool that the 'Let It Go' track was playing in the background there."

"It wasn't a track. Elsa was singing it." Evie shoots us all a *duh* expression.

"Right, silly me." Alyssa thunks her forehead with her palm, making a goofy face and pulling a laugh out of Evie.

Evie continues forward, talking animatedly with Shayna, Alyssa, and Mallory, leaving me behind to walk beside Kelsey. I can't help but wonder if this was planned.

I clear my throat. "You know, I had to change my pants before coming here."

She stifles a laugh. "Why is that?"

I turn on my heels. "I think you know why."

"What did you do?" Mallory turns around and nudges Kelsey's arm, looking amused.

Well, at least I know her friends are listening and that this walking situation was definitely planned. Whether it was forced on Kelsey like it was on me has yet to be determined.

Kelsey shrugs. "I was just continuing what he started."

"I think you mean what *you* started," I correct.

"Then you pranked me." She points an accusatory finger my way. "I was only returning the favor."

"Or you could've done nothing and accepted defeat."

Kelsey smirks, looking like the thought of crowning me the victor is ridiculous. "Never."

Mallory clears her throat. "Do we need to leave you two alone? Or…"

"No," Kelsey and I say simultaneously.

Her lips pull up into a sly smile. "Just say the word if you change your mind."

Once Mallory is a few steps ahead, I nudge Kelsey's elbow with mine. "Sounds like we've added another matchmaker to our list."

She scoffs. "Seriously. You'd think Darla and your receptionist would be enough." She motions to her friends. "Now we've added three more to the list." Kelsey looks at the pumpkins to our right and smirks. "On a different note, someone really captured your likeness in that one."

I follow her finger to see Frankenstein's head. "Don't you think you've overused that?"

"That joke will *never* go out of style."

I rub my hand over my mouth to hide my smile. It's refreshing how she always sticks to her guns. "You know what else doesn't go out of style? Making you sweat while you wait to see how I'm going to pay you back."

She crosses her arms. "I'm not nervous."

"Yeah, keep telling yourself that."

Kelsey comes to a stop, playfully whacking my arm. "You don't scare me, Tyler Reed."

My lips tilt up into a playful grin. "Good to know, Kelsey Anderson."

We're staring at each other in the ultimate showdown, waiting to see who will back down first. Spoiler alert: it won't be me.

Mallory's voice breaks our staring competition. "Looks like you two have to kiss."

Kelsey whips around, sending a wave of her sweet shampoo scent my way. I can't see whatever face she sends her friends, but Mallory only lifts an eyebrow in response.

"Don't blame me." She points up. "Blame the mistletoe."

"Mistletoe?" Kelsey laughs. "It's October, not December."

Yet I look up and find mistletoe carved into a pumpkin hanging from a tree branch above us. I'm unsure whether I want to thank or punch whoever did this.

I told myself this was going to be a Kelsey-free night. But I would be lying if I hadn't been thinking about how beautiful she was with her wind-blown hair and gray sweater.

Without thinking about the ramifications of my actions, I wrap my hands around Kelsey's back and dip her. She gasps, and I wish I could bottle up the sound as physical evidence of the effect I have on her.

I press my mouth to the corner of her lips, and she inhales sharply. That little sound makes goosebumps erupt across my skin, and I question for a second if I should actually kiss her or not.

No, if we kiss, I want it to be real. Not because we're standing under some fake mistletoe and especially not when we have an audience.

If I'm going to kiss Kelsey Anderson, it's going to be just for us.

That doesn't mean I can't tease her, though.

I move my lips slightly, grazing the corner of her mouth. "I'd say we should put on a show for our wannabe matchmakers." I keep one of my hands around her back and cradle her cheek with the other, blocking our lips from the view of her friends and Evie. "But if I ever kiss you, it'll be because it's real."

Pulling back, I look into her hazel eyes, ignoring the wolf whistles around us and her friends' gaping mouths. Her eyes search mine like she might find the answer there. I don't have any answers, though. I've only got questions myself.

Up until now, I wasn't sure if Kelsey would ever be interested in something more with me than the banter we effortlessly toss around. But the fact that she didn't pull away makes me believe that a shred of hope might be there.

With the way her pupils are dilated and move to stare at my lips, I'm starting to allow myself to wonder how they might taste pressed to mine.

# CHAPTER EIGHTEEN
## TYLER

"What's up with your face?" Tess leans forward and sniffs the camera. "Yep, just what I thought."

My brows furrow. "What are you talking about? And why are you sniffing the camera?"

"My baby brother reeks of *love.*"

"If you were here right now, I'd flick you."

Tess rubs her head as if it actually happened. "Good thing I'm an eighteen-hour flight away."

"And, by the way, I'm not in love."

She lets out a dramatic sigh. "How am I supposed to live through your romance stories if you don't have any to share?"

"Like the blind date I let Aunt D set me up on?"

"Shut. Up." Tess emphasizes each word. "You let her set you up on a date before me?" She pouts and crosses her arms. "I'm offended."

"I don't let anyone set me up on dates, but I made an exception this time." I laugh. "Let me tell you a tale I like to call *Darla and the Duck.*"

My sister smiles and moves closer to the screen. "Tell me *everything.*"

I dive into the story, sharing what I learned from Darla's and Kelsey's perspectives. Once I finish telling her all the crazy details, I sigh. "That's why I agreed to let her set me up. How could I not after everything she went through?"

The mischievous smile on Tess's lips lets me know she's about to tell me exactly how she feels. "You, dear brother, have been hoodwinked."

"Aunt D didn't trick me. She was legit scared."

"Yeah." She snorts. "Scared of dying before you get married and give her more great-great nieces or nephews to spoil."

The more that I think about it, I wouldn't put it past my matchmaking great-aunt to swindle me into going on a date. Darla's words from that day flood back to the front of my mind. I rub the back of my neck. "She might've mentioned something about a ticking clock."

Tess brandishes her fist like it's a judge's gavel, banging it on the table in front of her. "I find the defendant guilty as charged." She steeples her hands under her chin. "Now, are you going to tell me about your date? I'm not above begging."

I resist the urge to roll my eyes. "What's with women wanting to know every little detail?"

"I already told you. I'm living vicariously through you."

"Why can't you just go on dates yourself?"

She waves off my comment. "Evie's my priority. I don't have the time to invest in getting to know someone right now."

My heart breaks for my sister. I know she's doing what she thinks is right for Evie, but I also know how much love my sister has to give. She deserves to have someone to share that love with and be loved by in return.

Tess snaps her fingers. "Stop trying to change the subject and tell me about your date."

"You're gonna love this." I laugh nervously. I know there's no turning back once I tell my nosy sister about this—about who I went on a date with and my potential *feelings* for said person. "I'm sitting at the restaurant, waiting for my date to show up, and in walks none other than..."

"Oh, spill it already."

"Kelsey."

Tess's mouth falls open. "Your neighbor and the woman watching Evie? *That* Kelsey?" I nod. "How juicy." She wiggles her eyebrows. "Did Aunt D know?"

"I don't think so. She seemed surprised when I brought it up."

"Maybe it's a happy coincidence."

"There's one thing it is—confusing."

"So, I guess the date didn't go well?"

"It wasn't really a date."

"But?"

I may as well tell her the whole truth and nothing but the truth before her fist-gavel makes a reappearance. "I can't stop thinking about it. About *her*."

"Aha! I knew it." She points an accusatory finger at the screen. "I *knew* you liked her."

I shake my head. "Not before. Kelsey kind of hated me, and I wasn't too fond of her either. But we talked things through at dinner, and now I can't seem to get her out of my head."

"Every great love story has to start somewhere." Tess holds a hand to her heart. "What are you going to do to win her over?"

"Nothing."

"Oh, come on. Every girl wants a love declaration or grand gesture."

"I'm not going to declare my love to someone I'm not in love with."

Tess huffs. "You're no fun. What will you do when you *do* love her—or someone else?"

"I don't know." I shrug. "Tell her?"

She tuts. "That won't do. What are her interests?"

"From what I know, I'd say she likes dogs, sweaters, coffee, and Taylor Swift."

"That's perfect. You can get treats or toys for her dog. Recite Taylor's lyrics to her as your text responses. Bring her coffee just the way she likes it. Heck, maybe you could even buy matching sweaters for her and the dog." She sighs dreamily. "When you tell her you love her, you totally need to do it in a way related to Taylor."

"How do you declare love in a way related to Taylor Swift?"

Tess hangs her head. "How are we even related? I have so much to teach you, little brother. Just call me when you need help winning her over. I've got your back."

"You know who doesn't have my back? Your daughter."

Her brow furrows. "What did she do?"

"Kelsey and I are in a bit of a prank war right now, and your daughter helped the enemy."

"What did you do to that poor girl?"

"*Me?*" I scoff. "She started it."

Tess leans back and kicks up her feet. "In that case, I need the details, stat."

"She put out an advertisement in the newspaper with my face and phone number that said I was a doctor available for *in-home visits* to help with anyone's needs."

My sister laughs uncontrollably. All I can do is sit there and wait while she gets all her giggles out at my expense. Once she's finally gotten control of herself, Tess says, "That's hilarious. I only wish I'd thought of it first." She wipes the tears from her eyes. "Did anyone call for your *services?*"

I nod. "I had so many women blowing up my phone. Kelsey had the newspaper put a redaction out, but I still had to change my number because of the obscene amount of calls I got."

"I'd wondered why you texted me that you got a new number. It all makes sense now." She chuckles. "Please tell me you still have some voicemails I can listen to when I get back home."

"Those were all deleted immediately. I just imagined Evie opening my phone and accidentally playing one of them." I grimace. "There was no way I was about to let that happen."

"As much as I would've loved to hear them, thank you for preserving my daughter's innocence." She laughs again. "I can't wait to meet Kelsey. I have a feeling we'd be great friends."

I have no doubt that Tess and Kelsey would be two peas in a pod, teasing and pranking me for the rest of my life. My heart pounds in my chest at the thought. They would make a terrifying pair, but also the thought of Kelsey being part of the rest of my life doesn't sound quite so bad.

"What did you do to retaliate?" she asks.

"Evie and I got one of her roommates to let us in, and we hid a bunch of miniature rubber ducks in her house and car."

"Because of the duck situation at Sunrise Springs?" I nod. "That's gold. I'm impressed with your creativity."

With a compliment like that, there's no way I'm telling her the inspiration for the idea came from the internet. "Thanks." I smile. "Then I was welcomed home yesterday with a lovely spray of water to the crotch."

She presses her lips together, trying to hold back her laughter. "I think I need more of an explanation than that."

I tell her about the hair tie around the sprayer and how I had to change before taking Evie to see the pumpkins last night. When I'm finished talking, Tess smirks knowingly.

"What?"

"She has to like you too. No one goes through this much effort for someone they don't like."

"What about for someone they loathe?"

Tess shakes her head. "You said you talked stuff through at the dinner and how she had the newspaper retract the ad."

"I guess you're right." I mull over the idea of Kelsey potentially liking me. "She also brought me lunch at work this week because she felt awful about it all."

"See? It's a thing. I know it." She grins.

"Do you have any prank ideas? I'm not sure what to do next."

"Remember that annoying little cricket-chirping thing you hid in my house a few years ago? That's good if you want to make her dig through her entire house or car for a day trying to find a non-existent cricket."

"Have I ever told you that you're my favorite sister?"

She presses her cheek to her shoulder and looks up, fluttering her eyelashes. "Please, tell me more."

"You're so weird."

"No. I'm your *favorite*." Tess grins.

It does my heart good to see her so happy. I know she misses Evie—and maybe even me—something fierce, but she's also great at what she does. I know she must be thriving in an environment where she gets to shine all day long, doing what she loves.

At least, I think she loves her job. She doesn't talk about it much. Tess teases me about everything, but when it comes to trying to ask her questions about her own life, she gives me vague answers, deflects questions, or brings up Evie as her excuse. I make a mental note to get her to open up more when she's back home. There's little point trying to do it now when we have limited time and she could easily hang up on me.

"Don't make me change my mind," I say.

"How could you after I just gave you the best prank?"

"Did I mention how humble you are, too?"

She sticks her tongue out at me, then glances at her watch. "I should get back to work."

"I know you already talked to Evie, but do you want me to grab her so you can say goodbye again?"

My sister dabs at her eyes with the sleeve of her t-shirt. "No, it's hard enough to say goodbye once. I'm not sure I can do it again right now."

I shoot her a pitying look. "You only have a little under two months to go. You've got this, sis."

"Give Evie a big hug for me?" Her voice is shaky, riddled with emotion.

"I'll squeeze her extra tight. Love you."

"Love you too."

When we hang up, my heart physically hurts for my sister. I wish I could do more for her, but that's a little hard with her on the other side of the globe. I make another mental note to be more intentional when she's back home. With our parents away and her single parenting, I feel like it's my responsibility to make sure she and Evie have everything they need.

I get up from the kitchen table and dig through my junk drawer until I find what I'm looking for—the small sound device that makes annoying cricket sounds at random intervals. When I bought it, some of the reviews said the battery life could last for up to three years.

With help from my little sidekick, this is the perfect prank to pull on Kelsey.

"Hey, Eves?"

Her footsteps come bounding down the stairs. She skids to a stop in the entryway to the kitchen. "Yeah?"

"This is from your mom." I bend down, picking her up and squeezing her tight.

"Uncle Ty," she croaks. "You're squishing me to death."

I set her down. "To make up for squeezing you to death, do you want to help me with my next prank on Ms. Kelsey?"

She twirls in delight. "Yes."

"Perfect." I smile. "So here's what I need you to do…"

# CHAPTER NINETEEN

## KELSEY

"You're finally back. I was starting to think you may never return." Darla moves a checker across the board, taking her opponent's final two pieces. "Ha! Better luck next time, Ed."

He gets up from the table. "You can never take the throne from the queen." He winks at her before walking away.

"Um, do you care to explain why Ed just winked at you, Ms. Queen?" I take his empty seat and shoot her a saucy grin.

"Oh, he's just flirting with me now that I'm playing hard to get."

"I thought you said you liked him because he was the only man who still has hair that comes to events?"

She places all the checkers back on the board. "He is, but I'm still going to make him chase me."

"As he should."

"Enough about me. I've been waiting *weeks* to see you and hear all the details." Darla huffs.

I wasn't actively avoiding Darla. I just didn't have any events at Sunrise Springs that were on my normal working days. Though, I'm sure she would never believe that.

"Details about what?" I try to sound as serious as possible, even though I'm biting back a smile.

"Don't play coy with me, dear." She wiggles her finger at me. "Hearing the story from a man's perspective isn't enough. They leave all the good stuff out." She pouts.

"I'm sorry to disappoint you, but there's nothing to miss out on."

"There has to be *something*. All Tyler told me was that y'all are neighbors and that he thought you hated him until the date. He was evasive when I asked him if he wanted anything more with you."

"Evasive?" Consider my interest piqued. "What do you mean?"

"It means he wants more than a neighbor-nanny relationship with you. But those are my words, not his."

I don't know whether to take Darla seriously or not. She's known for her flare for the dramatics, but the no-nonsense look on her face right now makes it seem like she's telling the truth. Well, at least *her* version of the truth.

Darla leans back and crosses her arms. "Now, please tell me your side of the story so I can finally put all the pieces of this puzzle together."

"He's...*kinder* than I first thought."

"Right, because you told me that you worked for your hunky neighbor and that it was a lot of work living next to him." Darla fills in the blanks in my story.

"Yeah, except I don't think I've ever called him hunky."

"Your eyes said it all, dear."

I press my lips together and blow a slow breath out through my nose. "Fine, he's not bad to look at, but I'm not looking for a relationship. I don't know if I ever want to get married."

She holds a hand to her chest. "Why not?"

"I have dreams I want to accomplish, and I don't need any distractions."

"Why can't you have the man of your dreams by your side?"

"I don't want anyone holding me back." I pick at my plum nail polish.

Darla purses her lips. "If they're your dream man, they should support and encourage you while you achieve that dream together, not hold you back."

I sigh. I don't like talking about my parents often, but I feel like my answers don't make sense without bringing them up. "My parents divorced when I was young and never remarried. I guess I've never seen a lasting love—one that sticks around when things get hard and aren't picture-perfect anymore. They never supported each other or encouraged the other to chase their dreams. All they did was argue. Even through the divorce process, they continued to fight for custody of me."

"I'm so sorry. No child should have to endure that." She reaches her hand across the table, gently patting mine. "Do you still see them?"

I shake my head. "Whenever I do, they just ask about what the other person is up to." I don't bother mentioning how my mother typically asks me for money and that I haven't heard from my father in years. "It's exhausting."

"That's horrible. You're a wonderful young woman despite everything you dealt with growing up. That's a true testament to your character." Darla squeezes my hand. "And I'm so sorry you've never had an example of true, sacrificial love to look up to, but that doesn't mean it doesn't exist."

I'm not sure if I'm more surprised that Darla is having a deep conversation with me or because of the fact she thinks true love exists. I mean, she's the lady who asked me if I could bring in a dance instructor to teach a twerking lesson. Either way, I feel like I need to hear what she has to say, so I try to keep an open heart.

Darla gets a dreamy, far-off look in her eyes. "When you're with the right person, they should make everything in your life easier. You know you have someone who always has your back and is willing to fight all your battles with you and for you. They should encourage you in your dreams and help you make them a reality. Don't swear off love quite yet. Keep your heart open to the possibility. Love might find you, even if you aren't looking for it."

I fight back the tears dangerously close to streaming down my cheeks. Just like Rome wasn't built in a day, years of pain and avoidance can't all be fixed in one conversation. But I do feel like Darla's words helped heal a small part of me. Or maybe she just awakened a small ounce of hope for a future I never dreamed of having from deep within my childhood fairytale-believing heart.

I swallow down my emotion and offer her as much of a smile as I can muster. "Thank you. I'm not promising anything, but I'll try my best."

Darla pats my hand. "That's all you're expected to do, dear." She clears her throat. "Now, can we get back to the juicy details? There has to be at least a steamy front porch kiss you can tell me about."

She slips from deep conversation back into her saucy attitude so effortlessly that I can't help but laugh.

"I'm sorry to disappoint. There wasn't a front porch kiss." I smirk. "But there was some pumpkin mistletoe."

She leans in, grinning devilishly. "Tell. Me. Everything."

———— ◦ ♡ ◦ ————

Earlier this week, Evie confided to me that she was missing her mom, so I wanted to do something special for her today while she's out of school for fall break.

We're lucky to find a close spot in the packed parking lot. I open the back door for her and motion to the large welcome sign. "Ta-da! What do you think?"

"I love the zoo." She smiles and grabs my hand, pulling me toward the entrance. "I need to see the giraffes."

"You know what's even better than seeing the giraffes?" Evie shakes her head. "Getting to feed them."

"A giraffe will eat from my hand?" Her eyes are wide, her voice filled with unbridled excitement. I nod. "This is the best day *ever*," she exclaims with a twirl.

I give our tickets to the attendant at the entrance, and we walk inside. After looking at the map, we head to the left. The zoo has multiple zones based on different regions of the world, and I brought Evie here today with one sole purpose in mind: taking her to the zone dedicated to animals from Africa.

"I know it's not the same thing as actually seeing your mom, but I thought we could see some animals from Africa," I say as we approach the lemur exhibit. When I planned this field trip for Evie, my only hope was for her to leave today feeling more connected to her mom. "You could tell her about them the next time you talk to her. Maybe she's seen some of the animals out in the wild."

Evie squeezes my hand. "I can't wait to tell her."

Her words make my heart overflow. I know she's not my family, but over the last month and a half, I've come to love her like she is, and seeing her so joyful after a hard week fills my soul.

We reach the first set of animal exhibits, seeing lemurs, warthogs, and rhinos. Evie never wants to leave the animals, so I have her say goodbye to each one so we can move on to the next exhibit.

By the time we approach the giraffe house, she's bouncing with excitement. I'm not keeping track of the time, but we have to be standing here for at least thirty minutes just staring at the animals and listening to the zookeepers share facts about them. Evie's captivated by every little bit of information about her favorite animal.

I pat her shoulder. "We should go see the other animals." When she pouts, I say, "We'll come back and see them later for the feeding."

Evie sighs, but she waves goodbye to the closest giraffe. "Don't worry, I'll feed you soon, buddy."

We visit the elephants next, but they aren't super active, so Evie quickly says goodbye and dances down the path.

"Are you still enjoying your dance classes?"

She nods and squeezes my hand. "I got the solo in our recital."

I stop walking and hold both hands up for a double high-five. She jumps, hitting my hands with hers.

"I'm so proud of you. I can't wait to see it."

"You'll come?" The grin she's wearing is contagious.

"I wouldn't miss it." We continue on the path until we reach another enclosure. "They have a petting zoo. Do you want to pet the goats?"

She nods, wide-eyed like a kid in a candy store.

A teenage worker lets us in, pointing out the food for the animals along with the hand-washing station. Evie grabs a cup of food and heads off to feed a baby goat. I follow behind, staying close but not enough to make her feel smothered.

A goat walks over to me with a swagger I didn't know goats could have. He's very obviously male from the way his *unmentionables* sway with each over-the-top step, like he's trying to show off how dominant he is. While I love dogs, I'm not sure goats are really my thing, especially after this little display, but I squat and pat the goat's back anyway, not wanting to offend his masculinity.

One minute, I'm petting the goat while keeping an eye on Evie. The next, I feel his horn in my pocket.

I panic.

The goat bleats.

He stomps his little hooves anxiously, trying to free himself. I carefully attempt to get his horn loose, not wanting to hurt him or myself. When the goat deems my attempts not good enough or fast enough, he pulls away. Hard.

I hear a ripping sound and pinch my eyes shut, not wanting to see whatever this stupid goat just tore open for all to see. When I work up the courage to look down, I gasp, horrified.

The goat didn't just rip a little hole in my pants...he ripped my pants *off*. I glance around until I find him prancing around the enclosed space with my tan fabric pants attached to his horn, flowing in the breeze behind him like a flag declaring him king of the petting zoo.

This is what I get for wearing loose-fitting fabric pants instead of my tried-and-true leggings. I don't want any stupid pockets where a goat can put its horn in and rip my outfit right off my body.

It's like my childhood nightmare come to life of being in front of my class and realizing I don't have pants on. Except, I'm a grown woman in her underwear in the middle of a children's petting zoo. I'm not sure which is worse, but since this is my only pants-less occurrence in front of a crowd, I'm gonna go with this one.

I stand, pulling my sweater down, attempting to cover as much of myself as possible. With as much dignity as I can have under the circumstances, I rush over to Evie.

She's looking past me as she says, "Ms. Kelsey."

"Yeah?"

"Why is that goat wearing your pants?" She points at the devious little pants burglar.

"His horn got caught in them when I was petting him."

"Did he ask before he took them away?"

I bite back a laugh, shaking my head. "Goats can't talk, unfortunately." Although, I'm not sure I'd want to hear what he's saying now as he prances around triumphantly gloating.

He's probably a very *baaa-d* boy.

Evie frowns. "Mama and Uncle Ty always tell me to share. That's not very nice if he can't even ask if he can borrow them." She's quiet for a moment, her brows furrowed in concentration. "Goats don't even wear pants."

"You're one hundred percent right, Evie girl." I try my best to smile at her despite my current situation. "What do you say we get me some new pants so you can feed the giraffes?"

She nods enthusiastically. I do a weird waddle-slash-speed walk back to the entrance, where the teenage worker stares at me in horror. She glances over my shoulder, covering her mouth when she sees the goat still wearing my ripped pants as his badge of honor.

She holds up a finger. "Let me run to the gift shop and see if I can find you some…" She gulps. "New pants." The angel of a worker returns a few minutes later, but with a frown. "Unfortunately, they only sell pajama bottoms." She hands me cheetah print pajama bottoms, which I gratefully accept and immediately pull on.

Placing my hands on my hips, I say, "It's a lot better than walking around with nothing. Thank you. How much do I owe you?"

She waves me off. "Nothing. Once I told the cashier your situation, they threw them at me and told me to hurry."

I laugh. "So this isn't something you see every day, then?"

The worker shakes her head, wearing a teasing smile. "Definitely not. Although, Snowball has always been a bit of a ladies man, always peacocking around."

"Someone needs to tell Snowball that's not the way to a lady's heart." I snort. "Thanks again." We wave goodbye and head to the next area, looking at the meerkats and naked mole rats.

"Why are those called naked? Aren't all animals naked?"

I squeeze Evie's hand. "You know what, that's a great question. You should ask your uncle when we get home."

"Okay." She shrugs.

We move onto the pygmy hippo and gorilla exhibits before making our way to the lions and camels.

After she's said goodbye to them, we walk to the giraffe feeding area. I purchase our tickets, and we walk in right at the allotted time.

A zookeeper greets us and kneels in front of Evie. "What's your name?"

"Evie. I *love* giraffes."

The zookeeper laughs. "It's a pleasure to meet you, Evie. Can I let you in on a little secret?" Evie nods. "I love giraffes, too." They giggle together. "Are you ready to feed one?"

She lets go of my hand and nods, bouncing on the balls of her feet like she can barely contain her excitement.

The zookeeper leads us in and introduces us to the giraffes.

When we get to the final one, Evie squeals. "I saw him earlier today."

She smiles. "This is Jabali. His name means 'strong as a rock' in Swahili." The zookeeper hands Evie a small bowl of food and motions for me to join them. "You can hold her now and feed Jabali."

I extend my phone her way. "Do you mind taking a video?"

"Of course." She takes it, holding it up, ready to record the moment.

I lift Evie onto my hip, and she raises the food to Jabali. He leans his head toward us, and his abnormally long tongue comes down, bringing the food from the bowl to his mouth. Evie laughs when part of his tongue grazes along her hand, leaving behind a trail of slobber. When all the food is gone, I set her back down.

The zookeeper hands back my phone before smiling at Evie. "You did a great job. He must like you."

"I love him." Evie hugs my leg and looks up at me with the sweetest eyes. "Can we get a mini Jabali to take home?"

"Sure." Before we leave the zoo, I buy her a stuffed giraffe because I could never say no to a face as cute as Evie's. We stop by Chipotle on the way home, grabbing dinner to-go for us and Tyler because I'm in a generous mood after my conversation with Darla yesterday.

By the time we make it back, Tyler is getting out of his car, likely having just gotten home from work. I would be lying if I didn't admit how good he looks in his scrubs.

"Uncle Ty, look at what Ms. Kelsey got me." Evie gets out of the car and runs to him, holding her newest prized possession up in the air.

"Wow, that's cute. What's its name?"

"Jabali. Just like the giraffe I fed at the zoo."

He raises an eyebrow, turning at me. "She got to feed one?"

I nod. "I got it on video so you can send it to Tess."

His whole demeanor softens. "That was really thoughtful."

Evie tugs on the bottom of his scrubs top. "I got to see *all* the animals in Africa. I can't wait to talk to Mom and see if she's seen any of them in the wild."

Tyler looks at me while Evie hugs his pant leg. He mouths *thank you*. I know he's thanking me for more than taking her to the zoo. If she was off around me all week, missing her mama, I'm sure she was even more sad around her uncle.

When Evie pulls back, he glances down like he's just now seeing my outfit. "Why are you wearing"—Tyler stares at my bottoms—"pajama pants?"

"A goat stole her pants without asking." Evie sighs. "It wasn't very nice."

His mouth falls open. "A—A goat?" He rubs the back of his neck. "Do I even want to know how that happened?"

My face heats. "It's a story for another day. But know that if you ever meet a goat named Snowball…just run."

"Noted." He laughs. Tyler picks up Evie and hugs her. "I guess we should figure out what we're doing for dinner."

"Ms. Kelsey got us Chipotle."

I grab the brown bag from the car and lock the doors. "Here." I pull out my bowl and chips, handing him the rest of the bag.

He pulls out his wallet. "How much do I—"

"Don't worry about it." I reach up and squeeze Evie's arm. "I had fun today. I'll see you next week."

She giggles. "Me too."

I walk toward my house, ready to put on some real pants.

When I reach my porch, I hear Evie ask Tyler, "Uncle Ty, why are all animals naked?"

I press my lips together to suppress my laughter. This day just got even better.

The following day, I drive to pick up a breakfast burrito since I'm too lazy to make breakfast on a Saturday morning.

I'm jamming to my current favorite Taylor Swift song on the way home when I hear a weird chirping noise.

What the heck?

I turn my car speakers down and listen closely for a few minutes, but I don't hear it again. "I'm going crazy," I mutter.

Cranking the volume back up, I get back to my car solo. It's a sold-out show. Crowd of one.

The next song in the album starts to play, and I hear the random chirping again. I turn down the music and scratch my head. Maybe a cricket jumped into my car to escape the cooling temperatures yesterday when Evie and I went to the zoo.

When I get home, I eat my breakfast burrito and make a maple latte. Once I've finished, I return to my car with a cordless vacuum, ready to find whatever chirping thing is hiding in my car.

I search for *hours*. I move the car seats all the way up and back, grimacing at the number of crumbs, coins, and other odd objects I find underneath them. I vacuum under the seats, but there's still no cricket in sight.

I remove everything from the glove box and center console, again cleaning out a lot of random things as I go, but still not finding whatever insect is making all the noise in my car. The chirping happens multiple times as I clean, so I know I'm not going crazy. But the little dude is good at playing hide-and-seek.

With a shudder, I even check in the zone where things go to be lost forever—my trunk. I pull out an array of items from a first aid kit to dirty towels used to wipe off muddy dog paws, and my favorite sweater that I've been missing since last winter. When I can finally see the bottom of the trunk again, I vacuum, but I still can't find the source of the sound.

The only other place I can think to look is the pocket on the back of my passenger seat, so I climb into the car and send up a prayer for whatever my fingers might come into contact with. The first thing to hit my hand is cold metal, and I yank my fingers out. Carefully, I reach back in and pull out a little metal strip that can't be bigger than two inches. I flip it over and see an on/off switch. I turn it off and then back on, and I immediately hear the chirp sound again.

That little—

I stalk over to Tyler's front door and pound on it. "Tyler!" When he doesn't answer, I knock even louder. "Your car is here; I know you're in there."

He opens the door, and I shove the little device straight into Tyler's chest.

His very *bare* chest.

My eyes trail down of their own accord, stopping to peer at his six—no, eight—pack. It's unfair how good he looks. A crime against society that anyone can wake up looking this good. Though, I suppose he works out every morning and eats super healthy. But I'd much rather eat cookies than have abs.

Under my fingertips, I feel every contour of his muscles and his racing heart.

*No.*

We're mad at Tyler.

No muscles or hearts allowed.

I double down on my angry face, hoping I don't look absolutely ridiculous.

He places his hand around mine, and my breath catches as the warmth of his strong, masculine hand warms my own. Tyler turns my hand around, and I'm wondering if he's about to interlock our fingers or pull me closer. Nope. He only takes the sound device from my palm.

His lips tilt up in a cocky grin when my eyes shoot up to his. "Do you like what you see?"

"No, I just destroyed my car looking for a nonexistent cricket."

"You say it's destroyed; I say it's the cleanest it's ever been."

I roll my eyes. "I hope you're happy now. Because you won't be when I get you back."

He steps closer, forcing me to look up at him, my chest nearly touching his abs. "I'd like to see you try, Anderson."

I stalk back to my car, shutting the doors and my trunk.

"What? You're not going to wish me a wonderful day?" he yells from his porch.

"I would, but my mom told me it's not nice to lie."

His laughter is the last thing I hear before his door clicks shut.

"You know what this calls for?" I whisper to myself. "Double or nothing."

I walk back into my house, smiling like a fool.

# CHAPTER TWENTY

## TYLER

PULLING UP TO MY house after work, I have to do a double take that I'm in the right place. I rub my eyes after putting the car in park, making sure I'm seeing clearly. Yep, my eyes still work.

Covering my entire front yard are *dozens* of flamingo lawn ornaments. I don't even have to wonder how they got here. It brings me back to our text conversation when she mentioned the names of different groups of birds. There's only one possible explanation for the *flamboyance* in my yard—Kelsey Anderson.

I hear giggles as I near the house and spot Kelsey and Evie staring out the front window at me. Before I can step inside, Evie runs onto the covered porch, pointing at me and laughing. "We got you."

"You sure did." My gaze moves to Kelsey. "I hope you didn't spend too much on this prank." With how much she works, it's obvious she's saving for something. A part of me hopes she'll open up to me about it soon, and another part realizes how unlikely that is. Either way, I'd hate for her to have spent a small fortune on our prank war.

Kelsey crosses her arms, wearing a satisfied smile. "I got them from an estate sale for free. The family was more than happy to get them off their hands."

"I can't imagine why," I deadpan.

"It's one of life's greatest mysteries."

"They're so cute." Evie tugs on my arm. "Can I name them all?"

I press my lips together to hide my amusement. "Sure, Eves."

When she's outside, Kelsey turns to me with an incredulous expression. "Does literally *nothing* bother you?"

"What? That?" I gesture with my thumb toward the yard. "It's hilarious. I only wish I'd thought of the idea first."

She smirks. "My doom scrolling on social media finally came in handy." Her smile softens as she looks at Evie running through the yard, tapping each flamingo and dubbing them with a name. "Did you have a good day at work?"

"Yeah, it wasn't too bad. I'm just seeing a lot of flu patients. It's really going around this year."

Kelsey wrinkles her nose. "The flu is the worst. You must have an immune system of steel."

"I got sick often during residency, but my body is much better at fighting everything off now. I honestly can't remember the last time I was sick."

"That's not a bad thing." She playfully nudges my arm, a soft smile on her lips.

Since the shift I felt between us when we almost kissed under the mistletoe pumpkin, every little touch with Kelsey drives me insane. Something as innocent as her elbow touching my arm has my eyes dragging down to her lips. I would pull her into my arms and kiss her right now, but I can't kiss her the way I want to—the way she deserves—with Evie around. I don't even know if Kelsey wants me to kiss her. So, instead, I shove down my attraction—pour water on the romantic tension sizzling between us, making it fizzle out.

I clear my throat, ready to ask about her day, but she steps toward her house. "I should get home. Also, Evie hasn't started her homework yet." She grimaces. "Sorry, I meant to have her do it, but I underestimated how long it would take us to set up all the flamingos."

"Don't worry about it. Have a good night, Kels."

I like the sound of her nickname on my lips. I'm sure it would only be rivaled by the feel of her lips pressed against mine.

I'm guilty as charged for watching her walk a whopping ten feet to her front porch. She turns and shoots me a mischievous grin. That little minx knew I was watching. Maybe she even *wanted* me to watch.

She slips inside, leaving me wanting so much more.

The verdict is in. I need to ask Kelsey on a real date as soon as possible. *This week*, I internally declare. Once we have the opportunity to talk, I hope all of our feelings will be laid out in the open. And maybe then I can finally find out what her perfect lips taste like.

Now that it's Friday, I'm filled with equal parts excitement and dread. I always look forward to the weekend, especially now when I get to spend more time with Evie. But I'm also dreading today because of the promise I made to myself to ask Kelsey on a real date by the end of the week. Since it's the last day I'm guaranteed to see her after work, it looks like today is the chosen one.

"Are you finished with your breakfast?" I ask Evie, motioning to her plate of mostly eaten eggs and toast.

"Yeah." She hands it to me. I rinse it in the sink and put it in the dishwasher when there's a knock at the door. "Who's that?"

I shrug. It's seven in the morning, so Evie's guess is as good as mine. I dry my hands on the kitchen towel and move to answer the door. I open it to find one of the last people I expect to be standing there: Kelsey's roommate, Alyssa.

My heart rate immediately picks up speed. "Is everything okay?"

Her eyes fill with pity. "Kelsey wasn't feeling the best last night and went to bed early. I woke up in the middle of the night hearing her vomiting. I'm going to take her to the doctor as soon as they open, but I'm pretty sure she has the flu or a stomach bug."

I frown, hating the idea of her not feeling well. As a doctor, I know that the flu strain going around right now is awful. I told Kelsey that myself. "Is she feeling any better this morning?"

Alyssa shakes her head. "She's back and forth between the bathroom and sleeping. I just wanted to let you know that she obviously won't be able to pick up Evie from school today. Mallory already said she could hang out in her classroom, though."

I nod. "Thanks for taking care of Evie."

"It was Kelsey's idea." Alyssa smiles softly. "She needed to make sure Evie had someone to watch her."

Kelsey shouldn't have to worry about Evie when she's this sick, but it means the world to me that she did. "That's very kind of her. Is someone able to check on Kelsey today? Does she need anything?"

"I wish we could, but Mallory will be at school, and Shayna is working a full shift at Shirley's Florist. My first appointment for the day canceled, so I'm able to take her to the doctor, but then I have a full day at the salon."

"She doesn't have any family nearby?" For all the time I've spent with Kelsey, I know next to nothing about her family.

Alyssa grimaces. "It's not my story to tell, but let's just say we're pretty much all Kels has."

My heart breaks for her. I don't know what I'd do without Tess, Evie, and Aunt D. Even though my parents are off living their dream right now, I've never questioned if they love me. I wish Kelsey had a family that made her feel the same way.

"I'm sorry to hear that." I shift uncomfortably. "I feel bad that she'll be home alone all day."

Alyssa pats my arm. "Me too, but she's been taking care of herself for a long time."

*But she shouldn't have to*, I respond internally. "Let me know if you think of anything I can do," I say instead.

"I will." Alyssa indicates her house. "I should make sure she's getting around okay so I can get her to the doctor. I'll see ya around."

I'm still thinking about Kelsey as I drop Evie off at school...and when I meet with my patients for the day...and as I take my lunch break. Especially since Alyssa texted me this morning letting me know the doctor confirmed that she had the nasty stomach bug going around.

I pop the last bite of my chicken salad sandwich into my mouth when there's a knock on my office door. "Come on in," I say around my mouthful.

Nadine steps into my office and shuts the door. "What in tarnation is wrong with you today?"

I take a sip of water. "I'm not sure what you're talking about."

She places her arms on her lips. "Don't make me out to be stupid, boy." The look she gives me hits me like Category 5 hurricane winds.

There aren't many people I'd let call me *boy*, but I know better than to talk back to a strong Southern woman like Nadine or Aunt D.

"Okay, maybe I've been a little *distracted*."

"Distracted?" She scoffs. "I heard you tried to look inside a patient's ear with the little flashlight thing rather than an otoscope."

Rats. The nurses sold me out.

"Fine." I huff. "I found out that Kelsey is sick this morning."

"What's wrong with her?"

"She caught a stomach bug."

"Oh, that poor dear." Nadine tuts. "She's being taken care of, right?"

I shake my head. "She doesn't have family nearby, and her friends had to work today."

"You mean to tell me that sweet-as-pie girl is alone? She could be lying on the cold, hard ground as we speak, and we'd be none the wiser." Nadine leaves my office with a dramatic flourish.

I hurry after her, finding her at the reception desk, typing on her computer. "What are you doing?" I ask incredulously, surprised at how spry she still is for her age.

"All but one of your appointments this afternoon canceled. Apparently, the kids are feeling better as the week's gone on. The only patient coming in needs a strep test. Marcie can handle them and write a prescription, if need be."

I don't like to make a habit of giving my physician's assistant my patients when she already has appointments of her own, but maybe I could make an exception today...

Nadine throws a pen at my head.

"Ow." I rub my temple. "What was that for?"

"You looked like you needed some sense knocked into ya." She throws a pad of Post-it notes at me, and I dodge them. A paper cut to the face doesn't sound like fun.

She grabs a stapler and holds it back like she's about to throw it too. "You better get over there before I hit ya where the good Lord split ya."

I hold my hands up like I'm trying to talk down someone about to murder me rather than my overzealous receptionist. "Nadine, put down the stapler. I'll go, all right?"

"Well, it took you long enough." She puts the stapler back where it belongs and reaches a hand out. "Be a dear and pick up my favorite pen and paper."

"You mean the ones you threw at my head?"

Nadine at least has the decency to blush. "You know what, on second thought, I'll grab them myself." She looks down bashfully. "Doc."

I keep my laughter at bay until I'm back in my office. This is what happens when you have a bunch of headstrong women in your life...but I wouldn't have it any other way.

Once I pack up my lunchbox, I grab my jacket and head back to the lobby.

"You go take care of our girl," Nadine calls after me.

I'm not sure when Kelsey became *our* girl. All I know is that she's started to wiggle her way into my heart, and I have this innate need to take care of her because of my growing affection.

If I can't ask her on a date today, I can at least show up for her when it matters most.

# CHAPTER TWENTY-ONE
## KELSEY

ACHES.

Nausea.

Pounding.

I moan, squeezing my eyes shut. My head is throbbing as if I stood in the front row of a rock concert, my eardrums muffled and full of pressure. Everything sounds like I'm underwater.

Except, the only sound I've heard today is my vomit entering the toilet. The pounding happens again, and I curl up under my sheets, dramatically pleading with the universe about what I'll do in exchange to make it stop.

I'll give all my cash away the next time I see the people out collecting money with their red buckets and bells ringing.

I'll let people check out before me at the cash register, even when I'm in a rush.

I'll even tell Tyler that I hid a candle called *Swamp Tush* above his fridge with the lid off, letting the stinky butt odor permeate throughout his kitchen.

I will literally do *anything* to stop the throbbing and vomiting.

The pounding worsens again, and Winston nudges my arm with his nose. This time, a manly voice calling my name precedes the pounding.

"Tyler?" The single word makes my throat feel like I'm rubbing sandpaper on it. Am I hearing things? Dreaming up a strong, handsome doctor to take care of me?

It takes every ounce of energy I have to push up from my bed, wrap a fuzzy blanket around myself, and crawl downstairs. Winston follows dutifully behind, at my heels. I hide my face from the bright sunlight as I open the front door.

Okay, maybe I wasn't hearing things. Standing before me, in the flesh, is Tyler Reed, holding a bunch of bags. Winston moves in front of me, standing guard. There's no love lost between those two. But Tyler shocks me even more when he pulls a giant duck toy out of one of the bags and extends it like a peace offering to my dog.

Winston's tail slowly starts to wag, like he's trying not to give in. But when he can't take it anymore, he jumps up, snatching the toy from Tyler's hand and running past me to play with his new friend.

Tyler's face softens as he takes me in. I'm sure my hair looks *wonderful*, up in my messy bun and dried in crazy ways from my fevered, sweaty state. Honestly, I might even have vomit somewhere on my face or my shirt. I've been too exhausted to bother to look in the mirror.

I make a move toward him, wanting to help him carry his bags inside. But exhaustion takes over, and I crumple to the ground.

The next thing I know, strong arms are around my back and under my legs, and I'm floating up the stairs.

"Maybe I am dreaming," I murmur.

"What?" He laughs.

"You're at work, so I'm either dreaming or hallucinating." I grab my throat, whimpering. "Ouch."

"Shhh." He sets me down in bed, tucking me in under the sweat-soaked covers.

The whole room smells like vomit, so I'm really glad he's not actually here and I'm only dreaming.

Dreamy Tyler smooths my sweaty hair back from my forehead. "Don't try to talk, sweetheart. Just go back to sleep. I'll be here when you wake up."

Yeah, this is definitely a dream. There's no way Tyler would call me *sweetheart*.

I snuggle deeper into my blanket cocoon, and sleep finds me once again.

I don't know what time it is when I startle awake. My hand flies to my mouth, and I rush to my shared bathroom with Alyssa. I barely make it to the toilet before I hurl again. One second, I'm getting sick, using all my strength to hold onto the toilet seat that really needs a deep cleaning after the day I've had, and the next, someone's hands are tenderly rubbing my back as I vomit.

When I've emptied my stomach yet again, I turn to find Tyler *freaking* Reed crouching behind me with a pitying but kind look in his eyes. He hands me a water bottle. I pour some into my mouth and swish the liquid around before spitting it into the toilet. Then I take the toilet paper he's extending my way and wipe my eyes and mouth before flushing.

"How—" I start to ask how he got into my house, but he cuts me off.

"Do you feel strong enough to shower? It might help you feel better."

"Is that your way of telling me I stink?" I cross my arms, trying to hold in the terrible stench.

"Just trying to help, Anderson." He brushes a stray clump of hair that escaped my bun behind my ear.

The way his knuckles graze my cheekbone with the movement causes my breath to hitch. I clearly must be delusional right now if I'm feeling some type of way because of *him*. "A shower sounds great."

"I'll grab you some clean clothes."

I get the water heating up, and Tyler returns a minute later with a fresh pair of pajama pants, one of my oversized shirts, and a pair of underwear. I'm too drained to be embarrassed that he went into my underwear drawer.

"Thanks," I mutter. "I won't be long."

"Take however long you need." He motions to the laundry room on the other side of the hall. "I'm going to get your sheets and blankets in the wash. Which detergent is yours?"

"The blue bottle."

"Great, thanks." He disappears back into my bedroom. I'm not sure what alternate reality I'm living in right now—or maybe I'm hallucinating everything. But wherever I am, a nice, warm shower is calling my name.

I feel a little better when I step out of the tub. My worn tee and pajama pants are soft against my clean skin. I brush my tangled hair, apply some moisturizer to my face, and brush my teeth before dropping off my dirty clothes in my hamper in the laundry room.

I attempt to walk downstairs to get a glass of water and maybe something to eat, but my body still feels exhausted, and I slump down on a step halfway down the staircase. I jump when Tyler appears around the corner, taking the stairs two at a time to reach me, with Winston following at his feet.

"You're still here," I squeak, trying to hide my wince from my scratchy throat.

"I'm here, sweetheart." Tyler lifts me in his arms and carries me down the steps like I'm light as a feather. He sets me down and helps me sit at the kitchen table. "I brought a few things for you earlier." He walks to the island and pulls out a mini pharmacy worth of medicine from a bag on the counter. "How are you feeling?"

"It's nice to feel clean, but I'm pretty exhausted." I rub my neck, every word I say feeling like sandpaper rubbing my throat raw. "Got anything for a wicked sore throat?"

Tyler pulls out a mini spray bottle. "Spray this into your mouth toward your throat. It tastes like honey."

I do as instructed, deciding it's best to trust the medical professional in the room. The relief I feel is instantaneous.

"Better?"

I nod. "Got any food in those bags?"

He pulls out a brown bag from the fridge. "I can reheat it in the oven." He reaches inside the bag and pulls out a sandwich.

Tears instantly pool in the corners of my eyes. "Is that—" I swallow down my thick emotion. "Is that a Hot Brown?"

"Sure is."

"Who told you?" My voice is barely a whisper, choked with emotion.

"You told me it's your comfort food whenever you're sick. That your mom always got you them growing up." He shrugs casually. "I figured you were too sick to get it yourself this time."

The memory hits me. I told him that on our *non*-date. The one Darla set us up on. "I can't believe you remember that."

"I remember a lot of things about you, Anderson."

I drop my gaze to hide my blush…and to avoid whatever hidden meaning is behind his words. I'm not ready to deal with whatever feelings he's having—or that I'm having—right now.

He clears his throat. "Do you think you can eat it? I picked up some chicken noodle soup if you want something more bland."

"The Hot Brown is perfect." No matter how sick I am, it's usually the only thing I can stomach.

I watch as he navigates my kitchen, opening a million drawers to find what he needs but not letting me get up to do anything.

The feeling is unfamiliar. But I think he's…taking care of me. No man has ever catered to my every need like this before.

I'm practically falling asleep at the table again when he sets the sandwich in front of me, along with a steaming mug that smells like minty tea. He returns upstairs to move the laundry while I eat half of my meal, starving since I've emptied my stomach in the last twelve hours. But I know not to overdo it and eat the whole thing. I sip the tea, and it tastes of peppermint and honey, warming me from the inside.

"You get enough?" Tyler reappears, perusing my plate.

"Yeah, I'll finish it later if my stomach does okay." Before I have the chance to put the leftovers in the fridge, he grabs my plate and does it for me. He walks back over as I'm yawning.

"That answers my next question." He smirks. "Come on. Let's get you in bed." Without asking permission, he slings my arm over his shoulder and pulls me into his side, taking most of my weight as he helps me up the stairs and back to my room. I raise an eyebrow, and his eyes twinkle with amusement. "Don't worry, I won't get in with you."

He somehow knows where my bedroom is, but I don't ask any questions since my energy is waning again. Tyler motions to my cozy chair that I sat in a lot when doing remote work. "Will you be okay there right now?" I nod, and he helps me settle into it, grabbing a fresh blanket and pillow from the top shelf of my closet and placing them on my lap. Winston curls up on the ground beside the chair, resting his head on his new stuffed duck toy. "Text me if you need anything."

"Okay," I murmur just before sleep overtakes me again.

Everything around me is fuzzy when I come to. I feel groggy, my eyes heavy with sleep. But I can tell I'm in bed with Winston lying dutifully beside me. I don't remember falling asleep here, but the sheets are silky and smell fresh.

The door to my room squeaks as it slowly opens, and I see Tyler peeking in. "Sorry, I didn't mean to wake you." He grimaces. "You doing okay?"

"My sheets are *so* soft." My voice is heavy in my groggy state.

"I'm glad you like them." My eyes are closed, but I can hear the smile in his words.

"You did this?" I burrow into them. "I love you."

"Ah, so you don't hate me?" His voice sounds teasing, but I detect a hint of vulnerability there.

"How can I hate you and all your rugged handsomeness?" I yawn, feeling like I'm going to be pulled back into a deep slumber soon. "If they put doctors with faces like yours on billboards, there would be a shortage of available appointments worldwide."

His laugh is beautiful, filling the whole room. "That's a high compliment. Especially coming from you." My bed jostles, but I'm too tired to open my eyes and see if it's him or Winston. "Does this mean you'll call me McSteamy now instead of Frankenstein or Doofenshmirtz?"

"You're not McSteamy." My brow furrows. That's the most ridiculous thing I've ever heard. I sigh, feeling my lips pull up into a content smile as I burrow under the clean sheets and snuggle Winston closer to me. "You're more of a McDreamy."

I stretch in bed, feeling more like myself after a few hours of rest. Aches and stomach pains aren't racking my body anymore. Instead, my stomach growls loudly like she's saying *how dare you deprive me of food.*

"Sounds like your appetite is back."

I gasp, jumping and opening my eyes to find Tyler beside me—err, underneath me. Pure mortification hits me when I realize what I did. I slept on Tyler *freaking* Reed's chest.

I'm unable to meet his gaze or even move. Maybe if I squeeze my eyes shut really hard and then open them again, he won't be there anymore. It's just a trick of my imagination.

"What are you doing?" Mirth fills his tone. I squeeze my eyes shut even harder. If there's ever a time for me to wake up with magical powers like Harry Potter, this is the moment.

I sigh when nothing happens, slowly opening my eyes to look at Tyler. In my bed. "What are *you* doing here?"

"In your bed?"

I pull the covers up, trying to hide my pajamas from sight. "Yes, and in my house."

"You let me in hours ago, and I remade your bed a while ago when the sheets were finished in the dryer. I carried you into your bed so you wouldn't hurt your neck sleeping in your chair." He rubs the back of his own neck, looking bashful. "When I checked on you later, you pulled me next to you, snuggled into me, and immediately fell asleep. I knew you needed your sleep, so I didn't move." Tyler leans over and pets Winston. "If it makes you feel any better, this guy eyed me the whole time. But I think we have an understanding now."

Winston licks his hand. The little traitor.

As I watch them interact, memories from the day flood my mind. No. For the love of biscuits. Please tell me I didn't call Tyler *McDreamy* and comment on his *rugged handsomeness*.

"You've been here all day?" My voice jumps an octave. I'm praying with everything in me that I'm wrong. That I just woke up from a crazy dream-turned-nightmare.

"My handsome self has been here since lunch." His lips tilt up at one corner into a cocky grin. "Though, I'm sure my appointments will be fully booked for the year if we use your billboard idea."

I press my lips together, wishing I could grab a paper towel and some cleaning spray and wipe away the humiliating memories on replay in my brain. "Can you please forget I said any of that?" I groan. "I'm sick and had no clue what I was saying. I didn't know you were actually here."

I lay my head back down before realizing that's a terrible idea because it means Tyler's chest is my pillow. I shoot out of bed like a Derby horse out of the gate…which is yet another terrible idea. It feels like the world is spinning around me. I grab my head and close my eyes, trying to stave off the dizziness. It would be *beyond* embarrassing to faint in front of Tyler.

Peeking an eye open, I watch Tyler get up from my bed and rush over to me. He takes hold of my forearms, steadying me. Once he seems certain I'm not going to keel over, a cocky grin pulls at his lips. "So you were *dreaming* I was here?"

"Stop putting words in my mouth." I suppress an eye roll.

"I will when you stop saying them."

I wish I could wipe the smug grin off his face.

Tyler lets go of his hold on me, takes a step back, and leans against the wall. I'm not sure if it's just because I'm still coming out of one of the worst stomach bugs I've ever had or not…but he has no business looking that good. Like an Adonis or a merman who lures you out to sea with his gorgeous looks.

I look around my room, trying to find a way to change the subject. I notice there isn't any more light streaming in through my window. "What time is it? Did I sleep the whole day?"

"You slept for a few hours. It's dinner time." He motions to the door. "Your friends are kind enough to be hosting Evie downstairs."

"Evie." My eyes go wide. "I'm sorry, I was so sick that I completely forgot to pick her up from school."

He shakes his head, smiling.

"What's funny about forgetting your niece?"

"You didn't forget her. Alyssa said the first thing you did was make sure that one of them could watch Evie. But even if you hadn't, your friends would've taken care of everything. People have your back, Kelsey." He puts a hand in his front pocket, making him look even more like a model. "You don't have to do everything on your own."

I bite my bottom lip, not wanting to read into the words he's saying. I *do* have to do everything on my own. That's the only way things will get done. No one else can achieve my dream for me.

My stomach growls again, louder than before, breaking the silence.

Tyler laughs. "Do you want the rest of your sandwich?"

I nod. "The soup too."

We walk to the kitchen, and Winston follows. He leaves my side the second he sees Evie with my besties, dropping his toy duck and trotting over to her with his tongue lolling. He gives her a big kiss on her cheek while she hugs his neck.

"No dogs at the table, Eves." Tyler shoots her a stern look.

"Sorry." She sits back up, keeping her eyes on the dog. "I'll give you the biggest hug ever when I'm done." He lays at her feet like he understood everything she said.

I glance at my friends sitting at the kitchen table with Evie, and find their eyes moving back and forth between Tyler and me like a ping-pong match.

I want to tell them there's nothing to see here. Just my friendly next-door enemy who isn't really my enemy anymore. Oh, and did I mention that I used him as my personal body pillow in my sick-induced slumber? Yeah...I think silence is the best option here.

I sit on a barstool at the island, not wanting to risk getting Evie or any of my friends sick, while Tyler reheats the leftovers. I devour the food.

He leans his elbows on the counter, smirking at me. "You know what animals are always hungry?"

I shake my head.

"Goats. They eat all day long. Sometimes they even eat things like paper or *clothing*." He presses his lips into a firm line like he's trying to hold it together. "You wouldn't happen to know anything about that, would you?"

My friends burst out laughing. Mallory wags her finger at him. "I'm starting to like you. You're savage, just like me."

"That's a high compliment coming from you, Your Savageness." He bows to Mal like she's royalty and not just a royal pain in my behind.

Evie giggles. "Do you think we'll see Snowball again? I can feed him some of the clothes I don't like anymore."

"I can honestly say I hope to *never* see Snowball again," I mutter.

Tyler snorts. "Now that you're feeling better, I should probably get Evie home so she can do her homework and get ready for bed. I also need to deep clean my fridge. There's this awful smell." He wrinkles his nose. "I already tried cleaning out the sink and trash can, but I can't figure out where it's coming from."

My stomach drops. I know exactly why his kitchen smells—the *Swamp Tush* candle I hid above his fridge with the lid off.

Evie hugs everyone goodbye, and I wave at her. Before Tyler can leave, I follow him toward the door.

"Thanks for taking care of me today," I say.

The smile he shoots my way looks genuine. "Anytime, Kelsey."

I rock on my feet. "Since you took care of me, it only seems fair that I save you the trouble of cleaning out your fridge." He stares at me expectantly. I take a deep breath and continue. "I might've done two pranks at the same time. The flamingo lawn ornaments and another one…"

"Please don't tell me there's a dead animal inside my house."

"No, nothing like that." I cross my arms. "It's a candle."

"A candle." He says the word slowly. "I don't know where you buy your candles from, but you should find a new candle shop."

I clear my throat, ignoring the way it still feels raw. "Well, you see, it's called *Swamp Tush*."

"*Swamp Tush*."

"Are you just going to keep repeating everything I say?"

"No, I'm just trying to understand." He crosses his arms, his eyes twinkling with amusement. "You hid a candle somewhere in my house that smells like literal butthole?"

"If I tell you where it is, can we call a truce on the prank war?" I shoot him my best pleading eyes, trying to look like Winston when he wants something.

"You mean the one you started and want to end on a win?"

"I only started it because I thought you were an evil jerk who thrived on waking me up before sunrise every morning and who hated dogs."

"So, you're saying the reason I had to change my phone number and need to air out my entire house is because I didn't wear headphones because I thought I soundproofed the room?"

I shift on my feet, wishing I was wearing my fuzzy slippers and not knowing what to say.

His lips tilt into a playful grin. "Relax, Anderson. I'm just messing with you." He shrugs into his coat. "I'll agree to your truce on one condition."

"Name it."

"Go on a date with me."

My eyes shoot up to his. I'm expecting to find the same playful expression there, but instead, he looks nervous and vulnerable. Like he just laid his heart on the line, and I have the power to crush it with one single word.

I hold up one hand. "Get pranked again." I hold up the other at the same height. "Go on a date with you."

I move my hands up and down like they're a scale and I'm weighing the pros and cons of each. Really, I'm trying to casually play off the whole thing while I'm freaking out inside at the fact that Tyler wants to take me on an *actual* date.

"I guess I can agree to your terms."

His face floods with relief. "Great." His smile is so bright it should be assigned wattage. "Once you feel better, we'll find a time that works."

"Sounds good," I manage to say, but the crack in my voice exposes me. I clear my scratchy throat and swallow carefully to collect myself. "Good night. And…thank you. For everything." *For taking care of me today.*

The tender way he's looking at me can melt me into a puddle if I'm not careful.

Tyler reaches out and gives my arm a squeeze. "Like I said, anytime. Sleep well." He leaves with Evie.

To hold up my other end of the bargain, I call after him, "By the way, you might want to look above your fridge."

Tyler looks back at me with a small smirk. "*Above* the fridge. Genius." With that, he shakes his head and continues his short walk home with Evie.

I shut the door and fall back against it, breathing heavily.

My talk with Darla might've convinced me not to fully close off my heart to love, but I'm still not sure it lasts. At least, I'm not sure there's a love out in the world that will last *for me*. And I don't want to risk hurting Tyler in the process of figuring out what I want for my future.

Although, I might already be in a position to hurt him. Tyler has been looking at me differently. I've tried to ignore it, but I can't anymore. Not with the gentle way he cared for me today, how he called me sweetheart, and brought me my favorite comfort food.

I sit on the ground. Winston bounds over, carrying the stuffed duck in his mouth. Tyler's even trying to get in the good graces of my dog. I groan.

I thought Tyler was trouble from the beginning, but—whether I like it or not—now I feel like I'm the one in trouble...of losing my heart.

# CHAPTER TWENTY-TWO

## TYLER

My phone buzzes in my pocket. Evie just finished eating the breakfast of champions—Lucky Charms—so it can't be much later than seven-thirty. It about killed me to give Evie something with basically no nutritional value, but the smile she's been wearing all morning is worth it.

I have no clue who could be calling so early on a Saturday morning, but I pull my phone out and see it's a local number. The thought crosses my mind that it could be an emergent patient, so I answer. "Hello?"

"Hi, is this Tyler?" The voice is feminine and sounds familiar, but I can't quite place who it is.

"Yes," I say warily, hoping it's not one of the overzealous women from Kelsey's newspaper ad that somehow got my new number. "May I ask who's calling?"

"This is your neighbor, Shayna."

I sigh in relief. "Is everything all right?" My mind jumps to the worst-case scenarios regarding Kelsey. She'd returned to work a few days after she recovered from the stomach bug, but I'm worried she caught something else or that she's hurt. I don't know why else her roommate would be calling me on a Saturday morning.

"I got your number out of Kels's phone because I think I heard her say once that you're into classic cars. Is that true?"

Random, but okay. "Yeah, my dad's a gearhead and taught me everything I know."

"I have no clue what any of that means, but Kelsey is putting on a classic car show for the residents at Sunrise Springs this morning. The man who was supposed to come in and talk about the cars came down with the flu. I know she'd never ask you herself, but is there any way you're free to come save the day for her?"

It would be a great precursor to our date tonight. Kelsey agreed to it when she was sick, and she hasn't backed out yet, so I'm taking that as a good sign. I smile. "As long as you don't mind watching an adorable five-year-old?"

"Deal. I love spending time with that cutie."

"Okay, what time does the car show start?"

"Uh, like thirty minutes."

I grimace, pushing up from the table and setting Evie's cereal bowl in the sink. "I'll drop Evie off in a few minutes."

"You're really helping Kelsey out. Thanks, Tyler."

I throw Evie over my shoulder, causing her to erupt in a fit of giggles. "What are you doing, Uncle Ty?"

"We're going to play a game. You get to pick out your own outfit, and we're going to see who can get dressed the fastest. Then you're going to hang out next door with Ms. Shayna."

Her eyes light up. "I'll get ready so fast." She runs into her room before I can respond, and I hear her chanting the words *girls' day* repeatedly.

I rush to my room, putting on a pair of jeans, a black long-sleeve tee, and a tan jacket. I'm pulling on a pair of socks when Evie bursts into my bedroom.

"I beat you!" She twirls. "I'm wearing all the colors of the rainbow. Do you like it?"

"Wow." I'm at a loss for words, taking in her pink sweater with green flowers on it, purple leggings, aqua-blue tutu, and orange socks. "What a *colorful* choice."

"Exactly." She smiles wide. "Now, can I see Ms. Shay?"

"Yes, once we get our shoes on."

With that statement, she sprints down the stairs. I follow after her, pulling on brown shoes while Evie slides on pink boots lined with fur. After dropping her off next door, I run through a local coffee shop's drive-through, grabbing a coffee for Kelsey the way she likes it—just a small dash of cream.

Once the coffee is secured, I drive to Sunrise Springs, arriving just on time. The parking lot is fuller than usual, but I immediately spot the six classic cars set up near the entrance to the building.

I park in the back of the lot and jog to the front where I find Kelsey pacing and biting her bottom lip.

She looks up from the ground when I stop in front of her. Her brows furrow, but a soft smile covers her lips, a welcome expression rather than the scowl I used to get from her. "What are you doing here?"

"I heard there's a nasty bug going around. Thought you might need some help with your event." I hand over the to-go cup. "I also thought you could use some coffee."

She takes a sip, closes her eyes, and hums. "This is perfect." Her eyes dart open. "Wait, how do you know how I take my coffee?"

I shrug, shoving my hands in my front pockets. "I just pay attention."

Kelsey blushes. "Thanks." Her mouth pulls to the side. "As for helping with the event…unless you know information about Chevys and Fords, then I'm not sure—"

"Oh, like the '63 Split Window?" I point behind her. "And that '72 Mustang over there? Yeah, I think I've got you covered."

She raises an eyebrow. "I know you told me your dad was a classic car fanatic, but I didn't realize you knew so much."

"Looks like we'll have lots to talk about tonight on our date." I shoot her what I hope is a flirty grin. She blushes, so I don't think I bungled it too badly. Her reaction fills me with confidence, making me stand taller. "For now, put me to work, boss."

"If you could just walk around the cars and answer the residents' questions, that would be amazing."

I nod and step aside as the residents slowly make their way from the building to the parking lot.

"Welcome to the first annual Sunrise Springs Classic Car Show," Kelsey greets them.

"Now, we're talkin'," Hank grumbles.

Kelsey smiles. "I had a hunch you'd like this event."

"Much better than the dancin' and flower classes."

I walk over to a lady standing near the Mustang.

"Didn't Mary Sue say she drove a pony like this one?" she asks.

I slide my hands into my pockets. "I'm sorry, but I don't know a Mary Sue, ma'am."

The woman harrumphs and walks away. I press my lips into a firm line. This is off to a great start.

I join a man at the next car in the lineup. "A '53 Five-Window Chevrolet?" He stares at it in awe. "I drove one on my pap's farm—little six-cylinder would pull harder than a fit-and-fiddle ox." He laughs before turning to me.

"I can't remember. Do those have a straight axle or leaf springs?"

"The one-tons had leaf springs in addition to the straight axle to handle the additional weight."

He clucks his tongue. "Man, what I wouldn't give to take one of these for a spin again."

"I'll have to check with Sunrise Springs and the car's owner, but I'll see if I can make it happen for you."

The man's mouth pulls up into a giant grin. "That's mighty nice of you."

I dip my chin in a nod and continue walking between all the cars.

A woman stops me with a hand on my arm. "Is this a Business Coupe?"

I sigh, grateful for a real question from one of the women. "Yes, it's a '46 Ford Business Coupe. Did you own one?"

"My daddy did. He was caught doing funny *business* in the backseat with his secretary in the office parking lot, if you know what I mean."

So much for a serious question. "I'm sorry to hear that."

"My mama wrung him out for everything he was worth, so it wasn't so bad."

I don't know what to say to that. Thankfully, one of the men approaches and runs his hand along the hood. "Do these things still run on leaded gasoline?"

I shake my head. "They don't sell leaded fuel for on-road vehicles anymore. Automobiles stopped being manufactured for leaded gas five decades ago."

"That long ago already?" The man rubs his mostly bald head. "Time flies, son. Don't let it pass you by."

I find Kelsey in the crowd and smile as I watch her interact with a few residents. Even from a glance, it's obvious they love her. Kelsey is the definition of a hard worker; she puts her all into everything she does, and it shows. Whether it's working here, with the dogs she walks, or with Evie, she's good at it all.

"Yoohoo, excuse me." A high-pitched feminine voice reaches my ears. I turn until I find a woman standing by a Triumph, gesturing me over.

"What's this called? A crumble seat?"

"No, a *rumble* seat. It's also sometimes called a dickey seat or mother-in-law seat."

She snickers. "Now, with a name like that, they're just begging for people to make jokes."

"I'd love to have my mother-in-law sit there during the middle of a downpour." Aunt D's laughter floats through the air. "Too bad she's long gone."

"Why are they called that?" Hank mutters.

I rub my hand along the rumble seat. "They got the term from horse-drawn carriages where servants or guards would typically occupy that seat. But once car ownership extended to more of the general population, they moved the extra seats to the car's interior for comfort."

"Huh." He grunts, his mouth pulling into a frown. "There's too much orange peel on this paint. Whoever did this paint job must've been blind as a bat."

I've been thinking the same thing, though I'd never say as much out loud. You can always trust the elderly and children to tell you how it really is.

The rest of the car show goes smoothly, except for the fact that I learned Aunt Darla had her first kiss in a Corvette that looked just like the one present today. I could've gone my whole life without knowing that information and been just fine. But it was nice to talk about the different engines with some of the residents.

I talk to the owner of the '53 Five-Window Chevrolet when he comes to take his car home. Once I've told him about the man who'd love to ride in one again, he immediately agrees to take him on a joy ride as long as Sunrise Springs okays it.

I search for Kelsey once all the residents are back inside and find her in the lobby. After she finishes talking with the man that I assume is her boss, she waves me over.

"You didn't have to stick around this long." She doesn't sound mad, exactly, just confused. Like the very thought of someone actually being there for her when she needs it most is a mind-boggling concept. "I feel bad that I've taken up a good chunk of your day when you could've been spending time with Evie."

"That's what happens when people care about you." I hesitantly step toward her like she's a stray dog that will bolt if I move too quickly.

Kelsey takes my hand in hers, intertwining our fingers. "I don't know what to say." She looks both ways down the hall. When she deems the coast is clear, she opens the door closest to us and yanks me into the room with her.

I stumble into the space, my breath stuck in my throat. Kelsey presses up against me as she flicks the light switch on, coating the tiny space in a warm glow.

"Why are we in a—" I look around us, laughing as I take in the shelves of cleaning supplies. Something stabs me in the back, and I wince. Thank you, Mr. Wooden Broomstick, for letting me know you're there. "Broom closet?"

"You told me if you kissed me, it would be because it's real." She tilts her head back. Her pupils are dilated, and her gaze is fixated on my lips. "Did you mean that?"

"You should know that I'm a gentleman. I don't typically kiss ladies in broom closets in independent and assisted living communities." I fist her olive-green sweater at her hips, pulling her flush against me. Kelsey gasps, and my lips twitch in a satisfied smile. "But I guess I can make an exception today."

I offer a beat of hesitation for her to push me away. Tell me this isn't what she wants.

She arches into my touch and whispers my name. "Tyler."

It's only two simple syllables, but I've never heard my name said that way—filled with want and need. Like she might explode if I don't kiss her right this minute. I want to hear her say my name that way over and over again, but for now, there's a much more pressing want coursing through my body. The sound of my name spoken softly from her lips is the green light I need.

My lips crash into hers. A soft moan escapes her, and I swallow it up with another kiss. Her lips are just as soft as I imagined and warm despite all the time we spent outside in the fall air.

While Kelsey isn't short by any means, she's tiny in comparison to me. If I'm going to kiss her like I want to—like I've been waiting weeks for—I need a better angle. I move my hands from her lower back down to her thighs, scooping her up.

Kelsey gasps, breathless. "What are you doing?"

I carry her a few feet back and set her on the countertop that I assume is some kind of cleaning cabinet. Right now, it's the perfect spot to thoroughly kiss the woman I haven't been able to stop thinking about. "Getting a better position so I can kiss you like you deserve."

Kelsey's cheeks flush strawberry pink, and I brush a soft kiss on each spot before covering her lips with mine again. Each press of my lips is desperate, wanting to explore every bit of her. Never wanting this moment to end.

She tastes as sweet as her maple latte, and I can't get enough of her. My hands explore her lower back while hers run along my arms and shoulders, up to my neck. This is the kind of feeling I've been chasing my whole life. We just click. There surely isn't a shortage of chemistry between us. And the way we move together, it just feels...right.

Our movements turn frenzied, like we're unsure if we'll get to experience this again beyond this moment, so we're enjoying it while it lasts. I kiss her until we're breathing as one, until I can't tell which breaths are mine or hers.

All the years of frustration and misunderstanding between us melt away in the roaring inferno our heated kiss nurtured to life—the sparks that had been patiently waiting all along ignited by the fuel of passion.

Whatever held us back or stood between us before is long forgotten amid our embrace.

I hope this isn't a fleeting moment. A one-time thing never to be repeated. Because I could spend a lifetime trying to find another woman who drives me so insane but also makes me laugh and *feel* more than I ever thought possible. As Evie would probably say, Kelsey is my unicorn.

When I finally pull back, I'm struck with the most beautiful thing I've ever seen. Kelsey is smiling up at me with her swollen, thoroughly kissed lips and her flushed cheeks, looking like I just told her she just won the lottery. Being this close to her, I notice the dusting of freckles on the bridge of her nose and cheekbones. I trace my fingers along them, hoping I'm given the chance to memorize them.

I want to know everything about her. The beautiful things, the hard things, and everything in between. I can only hope this moment didn't scare her away because I would like to repeat what just happened. Every day for the rest of my life, if I'm so lucky.

"That was…" She trails off.

"Yeah." I rub the back of my neck, one hand resting on her thigh.

We laugh as I lift her off the counter.

"How do you make that look so easy?"

"Lifting you?" I smirk, and she nods. "You're light as a feather."

"I'm really not."

"Then it must be all those early morning workouts of mine I know you're so fond of."

She shrugs. "I guess you can keep doing them as long as you use your headphones. You know, so you can lift me anytime you want."

"I'll carry you anywhere you want," I tease, pressing a kiss to her temple and pulling her into my chest. "You also just quoted one of my favorite movies."

Kelsey pulls back, looking unconvinced. "*Sweet Home Alabama* is one of your favorite movies?"

"I told you I was born and raised in Alabama, and now I have a beautiful woman quoting it to me. How could I not love it?" She smiles at the compliment, and I gesture to the door. "As much as I'd love to stay, I should probably get home to Evie. I have a hot date later to get ready for."

Kelsey shakes her head. "Right, of course." She moves past me, opens the door, and we nearly run right into my great-aunt.

Darla lets her hands fall to her sides dramatically like a toddler throwing a tantrum. "Why do I always get to the closet right after people finish necking? I always miss the show." She pouts.

I press my lips together, too embarrassed to say anything. And by the fact that my great-aunt just called it *necking*.

"Do people, um, *neck* often in this closet?" Kelsey's face is as red as a tomato, but I can't tell if it's from embarrassment or trying to hold back her laughter.

"Oh, yes. It's the hottest spot for couples in the building. The other one is the gazebo by the pond."

And now I'm thinking about how many people have touched the counter in that closet. I grimace, a shiver overtaking my body—and not the good kind.

What if Aunt D has taken her turn in there? Nope, not going there.

Laughter squeaks out of Kelsey's mouth. "Have you *visited the closet* with Ed yet?"

My head whips between her and my great-aunt. "Ed? Who's Ed?" They join together in uproarious laughter while I stand here trying not to gag at the thought of my aunt and whoever this Ed guy is doing what Kelsey and I just did in that closet.

Once they've calmed down, I ask, "Do I need to have a talk with this *Ed*?"

My new question sends them back into a howling fit of laughter. It's a wonder I even try. I hold up my hands, metaphorically waving a white flag. "You know what, forget I asked. I'm going home, but I'll pick you up at five?"

Kelsey looks at me with a heated gaze, like she's ready for round two tonight on our date. I know I sure am. "I'll be ready."

"You're going on another date?" Darla croaks, clutching Kelsey's arm. "Y'all have been holding out on me."

I skedaddle out of there before Darla ropes me into telling her all the details of the past week.

Besides, I have a date tonight, and I want to ensure everything is perfect.

# CHAPTER TWENTY-THREE

## TYLER

I'm nervous. Palms sweaty. Weak knees.

I shake my head. I need to get a grip before I'm singing about *Mom's spaghetti*. Maybe I listen to too much hip-hop music… But can you really listen to Eminem's "Lose Yourself" too many times? It's the perfect hype song in my workout playlist.

Okay, but in all honesty, I can't say I've ever felt this way before a first date. Though, I suppose it's a good sign because it shows how much I care. I want everything to go right with Kelsey.

I feel like I need to up my dating game, especially after our kiss earlier today. I'm not sure anything could beat that. Although, I'm hoping our next kiss will have a better location than a broom closet.

There's a knock on my door right on time. I open it, smiling at Kelsey's friend.

"Alyssa, thanks for agreeing to watch Evie tonight."

"Anything for Kelsey," she says, and I know she means it. Even though Kelsey may not have any family she's close with, anybody who sees the four girls next door together can see how fiercely they love and protect each other. Anyone would be so lucky to have friends like that.

Evie comes running down the stairs, and Alyssa squats to hug her. "Plus, I get to spend time with my best girl tonight. So it's a win-win. We're going to have a great time." Alyssa's eyes sparkle with mischief. "Maybe we can even take Winston on a walk since it's a little warmer tonight."

My niece bounces on the balls of her feet. "When are you leaving, Uncle Ty? No boys allowed, except Winston."

Looks like I've already got a little teenager on my hands, ready for her annoying uncle to leave her alone. But I'd take this excitement any day to distract her from missing her mom. I miss Tess more than I'd ever willingly admit.

"All right, I can tell when I'm no longer wanted. Have fun." I lean down, planting a kiss on the top of Evie's head. I wave goodbye to Alyssa before heading over to her house to pick up my date.

My hand trembles as I knock on Kelsey's front door.

I shake my head.

*Be cool, man.*

The door opens, and Kelsey steps outside with a soft smile, wearing a burgundy sweater that makes her eyes pop. She's wearing dark jeans instead of her usual leggings, but she still has her signature white tennis shoes on.

Kelsey's brown hair falls in loose curls past her shoulders, and the lipstick she's wearing matches her sweater perfectly. Although, I plan to mess it up later if tonight goes like I hope it will—with a repeat of earlier today. That was just a pre-date kiss, preparing us for the real thing.

"You look beautiful."

"Thanks." Her grin grows wider. "I guess you look Mc-Dreamy tonight."

I'm wearing the same outfit I was this morning—a black tee, jeans, and a tan jacket. I would usually dress a little nicer for a first date, but Kelsey sees me almost every day of the week in my scrubs, and I told her we needed to dress casually for what we're doing tonight. I at least styled my hair, though.

"Is McDreamy an adjective now?" I ask with a laugh.

"It's whatever I want it to be." She raises onto her tiptoes and presses a kiss on my cleanly shaven jaw. When she pulls back, she laughs and wipes her thumb along my jaw, probably wiping away her lipstick, although I wouldn't mind if she left it there, marking me as hers.

There's no way I'd contradict her tonight. Not when she looks like that.

"We should get going." I kiss her cheek and offer her my arm, leading her to my car.

"You're not going to challenge the fact that I'm using a nickname as an adjective?" When I shake my head, she leans her head back and laughs. "You've gone soft on me, Frankenstein."

"Maybe I'd do anything to see you smile." I open her car door, and she rests her forearms on it, peering up at me. Her lips tilt up at the corners.

"That's the right answer."

I close the door and walk to the driver's side. A dopey smile is plastered on my face as I sit beside her and turn the car on. I can't help it. It's just a byproduct of flirting with the girl I can't get enough of.

I pull out of my parking spot and start driving to our destination.

"Are you going to tell me where we're going?" she asks.

"Where's the fun in that?" I reach over and place my palm on her thigh, testing the waters for how the night may go. I know we kissed earlier, but that may not mean she's comfortable with physical touch tonight.

"You're lucky I like surprises."

She's definitely right about one thing: I'm the luckiest man in the world because Kelsey flips my hand over, wrapping her fingers between mine, and she doesn't pull away for the remainder of the drive into town.

When I park at the local dog shelter, Kelsey gasps. "What are we doing here?"

"I know how much you love dogs." I hop out of the car and jog around to her door, opening it before she can. The excited look in her eyes makes me feel like I just won the lottery. "So, I couldn't think of a better way to start our date than volunteering at the shelter."

"You thought right."

We head inside, and the volunteer coordinator leads us to the back. She talks through the volunteer form I filled out in advance and gives us leashes before taking us to the dogs.

Kelsey grabs my hand and squeezes tight. "They're so cute." It almost looks as if she might cry. I don't have anything against dogs, but I don't think they could ever bring me to tears. Okay, except for sad dog movies—I'm convinced you're not human if you don't cry during those.

The coordinator motions to the sign on the kennel in front of us. "We use a number system for our volunteers. Ones are the easier, more mild-tempered dogs, and fives are the harder ones to walk, usually reserved for the repeat volunteers. A five doesn't necessarily mean they're aggressive; it could just be because they're strong and pull hard on walks."

Once she's given us the tour of the rest of the facility, she asks, "Any questions?" Kelsey and I shake our heads. "Wonderful. Just make sure you note on the dog's chart once you've walked them and sign out at the front desk before you leave." She waves over her shoulder. "Yell for me if you need anything."

I leash up a level two dog that looks like a lab mix, but Kelsey walks up and down the aisles until she finds a level four dog who doesn't have many walks noted on his list.

She kneels on the ground and pets him. "You just want a walk like all the other dogs, huh? Isn't that right, Romeo?"

"With a name like that, he must be a little lover boy." I lean down and pet the boxer.

Kelsey leans down and pets his face. "He is the sweetest boy. Yes, he is." She has a real way with dogs because this "difficult" dog is like putty in her hands, wagging his tail and licking her hand.

We head outside and walk through the park area behind the shelter.

"Can I ask you a question?"

"Isn't that what you're supposed to do on dates?" She shoots me a wry smile.

"Hilarious." I clear my throat. "Why do you work so many jobs if dogs are what you're the most passionate about?"

"How do you know they're what I'm the most passionate about?"

"You're good at everything I've seen you do, but it's written all over your face."

She stops walking, looking out at the falling leaves around us. "If I tell you something, do you promise not to make fun of me?"

"I can make no such promises." I nudge her arm when her face falls. "I'm kidding. You can tell me anything."

"My dream is to open a dog rescue."

"Why would I make fun of you for having a dream?"

"You don't think it's a stupid childhood fantasy?" Kelsey looks up at me through her lashes, her vulnerable eyes searching mine.

"Stupid?" I scoff. "You want to help dogs in need. That's incredibly selfless." I intertwine my fingers with hers. "You're never too old to chase your dreams. In fact, I think it's one of the bravest things you can do. To never stop believing in your dreams, to never give up on them even when they may seem out of reach."

Kelsey swipes at her eyes, lifting her wrist with the leash. "You think I can do it?"

I shake my head. "I *know* you can." She smiles, and it's like a straight shot of serotonin to my heart. "Is that why you've worked yourself to the bone? You're saving money to open a dog rescue?"

"Yeah, and I'm close to having the funds I need now, thanks to this handsome, generous doctor who hired me to be his niece's nanny." Kelsey flips her hair over her shoulder.

"Is that so? He sounds like a swell guy."

"Swell?" She nudges my side with her elbow. "What is this, the 1800s?"

"Maybe I'm just trying to be a gentleman for you."

Kelsey steps closer, biting her bottom lip as she looks up at me. "What if I don't want you to be a gentleman right now?"

"I already told you I'd do anything to see you smile." I place my free hand on her waist and lean in close enough that I can feel her breath. "What would make you smile, sweetheart?"

She groans impatiently. "Kiss me, Tyler."

All my restraint goes out the window as she says my name again. I press my lips to hers.

Our movements are more soft and tender this time than the desperate kiss we shared this morning in the closet. My lips move slowly in time against hers as we explore each other.

My hand squeezes the dip of her waist. She runs her fingers through my hair. The gentle way her nails graze my scalp makes me moan.

I pepper featherlight kisses along her neck and jaw before she tugs my mouth back to hers for one more brief, yet longing-filled kiss.

Then Romeo seems to decide he's had enough of us ignoring him and whimpers loudly.

Kelsey pulls back, laughing. "At least that's a better interruption than Darla almost walking in on us."

She's got that right.

I rest my forehead on hers, not wanting to open my eyes. Not wanting this moment to end. It's obvious that she feels something more for me…but I'm not sure if she's anywhere close to where I am. Because I'm falling in love with the beautiful girl in front of me, and I don't know what I'd do if she didn't feel the same way.

It would feel like the worst tease in the world to have had a glimpse of what a relationship with her could be like—to have felt something so perfect with her—only to have it ripped from my grasp.

"I love it when you call me Tyler." I inhale the intoxicating lavender scent of her shampoo, barely able to hold myself back from pressing my lips to hers again.

Her eyes are hooded, making her look as love-drunk as I feel, as she peers up at me with a teasing grin. "Why?" She laughs. "It's just your name."

"I've always been Frankenstein or Doofenshmirtz or whatever other doctor name you can think of." I shrug.

"But I like how my name sounds coming from your mouth."

Kelsey blushes. "What else do you like about me?"

"Your eyes." I gaze into her beautiful hazel irises. "They're pools of warm honey and caramel that I'd be happy to be stuck in forever."

"I never took you for a romantic." Her eyes flutter shut, and her lips part as I graze her jaw with my thumb.

"You haven't seen anything yet, Anderson." Her stomach growls, breaking the moment. I smirk. "You hungry?"

She laughs. "Starving."

"Let's get you fed, then."

We finish walking the dogs around the park and drop them off in their kennels.

"I promise I'll be back to visit you soon." She places a kiss on Romeo's head. The dog looks absolutely smitten with her. I wouldn't be surprised if Winston had a brother soon.

We check out at the front desk, and I drive us about ten minutes down the road. I park in a city lot and open her car door again.

"Where are we eating?" she asks.

"I thought we could do an activity I knew you would love, and then I could take you to my favorite spot for dinner."

Kelsey lets me take her hand as I lead her down the block to a curbside food truck. I gesture to it with my free hand.

"A burger truck is your favorite dinner spot?" She raises an eyebrow. "You? The man who only eats healthy snacks? Mr. Gym Bro?"

"You won't be questioning it once you try it." I squeeze her hand. "Everyone deserves a cheat day. Especially for the best burger and fries in the city."

"I'll be the judge of that."

When we reach the front of the line, I look at her. "You okay if I order for us?"

She loops her arm through mine. "I trust you."

Those three little words may not seem like much to most people. But to me, they mean *everything* coming from her. I can't help but smile at her like a complete freaking idiot. The sun hits her face just right, making her look like a vision straight out of my dreams. How she went from being someone who annoyed me to no end to the girl I can't stop thinking about wasn't even gradual. It was hard and fast, and I wouldn't have it any other way.

"Sir, are you ready to order?" The cashier at the food truck speaks a little louder than normal, like he's already tried—and failed—to get my attention.

"Yeah, sorry." I don't even have to look at the menu. "We'll take two of the classic burger and fries baskets with extra house sauce on the side."

"Any drinks?"

"Water for me, and..." I turn to Kelsey.

"A Diet Coke, please."

The cashier rings up our total and gives me an order number after I pay. Kelsey and I grab our drinks, along with some extra napkins, and head to a picnic table nearby.

Once they call our number, I get up and grab the food.

"I hope you're ready for the best burger of your life." I set one of the containers in front of Kelsey.

"You're really hyping up this burger, so it better be good." She smirks.

I motion to her food. "Judge away."

Kelsey picks up her burger and takes a giant bite. She closes her eyes and moans.

I smile and take a bite of my own. "Good, right?"

"Good?" She scoffs. "This is amazing. The sauce is to die for." Kelsey pops a fry in her mouth. "Mmm, and the fries are fresh and perfectly salted. I can't believe I've been missing out all these years."

"I'm glad you approve." I dip a few fries in their house sauce—if I'm having a cheat day, I'm doing it right. "Tell me about your family."

"My family?"

I nod. "I know about your dreams now, but I'd like to learn about where you came from."

She sets down her burger and wipes her mouth with a napkin. "My family isn't like yours. I'm an only child, and my parents divorced when I was in third grade."

I take a sip of my water. "That sucks that you had to go through that at such a young age."

"It did."

"Was their divorce cordial?" I take another bite of my burger.

Kelsey blows out a breath. "Not at all. Their divorce proceedings dragged on for two years because they fought over every little thing. I'm sure their lawyers were thrilled once their divorce was finalized."

"Did they fight over custody of you?"

"Yeah, my mom won primary custody. But I think they only wanted custody of me so that the other person would have to pay them child support."

Although she's the one who knows her family dynamics best, I sincerely hope that's not true. I can't imagine a world where anyone wouldn't want Kelsey. "That's terrible."

She eats a few fries. "Yeah. My middle and high school years were spent going back and forth between their homes, with them both wanting information about the other parent. It was pretty exhausting. They bought me nice gifts, trying to outdo the other, too. My mom actually got me front-row seats to a Taylor Swift concert in sixth grade. That was where I met Shayna, Mallory, and Alyssa, so at least one good thing came out of their divorce."

"Again, that sucks, but I'm glad you got your best friends out of it." We both finish our burgers, and I dive back into the conversation. "You said you're an only child, but what about grandparents, aunts, uncles, or cousins? Did you have someone you could lean on throughout the divorce?"

She shakes her head. "My parents are both only children, too. And they waited a while to have me, so I lost all my grandparents by the time I was seven."

My heart breaks for her and everything she experienced at a young age, let alone any age. It had to be difficult to live through her parents' hostile divorce, but the fact that she did it alone—without any family to lean on—had to be the hardest part of all.

"What is your relationship with your parents like now?"

Her face falls. "It's been a few years since I talked to my father. I hear from my mother occasionally, but only when she needs someone to cry to about her latest boyfriend breaking her heart or when she needs money for rent."

I reach across the table, taking her hand and rubbing small circles on the back of it. "I hope you know that you deserve so much better than that. And while you may not have the best blood family, you *do* have family, Kelsey. Your friends would do anything for you."

She smiles softly. "I don't know what I'd do without them."

"Thanks for sharing with me. I know that can't be easy to talk about, but I like learning about you, Anderson."

Kelsey blushes and moves a rogue fry aimlessly around her takeout container. "Thanks for not telling me sorry, by the way."

"What?"

"You told me *that sucks* rather than that you were sorry for me, and I appreciate that."

"You're a capable woman who came through a tough situation. While I wish your past was easier, I know it only made you stronger on the other side."

She stares at me like I have four eyes. "Who even are you?"

"What do you mean?" I laugh.

Her eyes narrow playfully, but she also looks a little skeptical. "How do you know how to say the perfect thing?" She pulls her hand from mine and leans across the picnic table, grabbing my ear. "Are you being fed the perfect lines by one of my friends?"

"I'm not saying the perfect thing, just the truth."

She sits back and sips her Diet Coke. "I was wrong about you, McDreamy."

Hope rises in my chest. "As long as you're seeing the real me now, that's all that matters." I lean my elbows on the wooden table with a smile. "How about some rapid-fire questions?"

Her eyes glint playfully. "Try me."

"Favorite color?"

"Sage green," she answers immediately.

"Morning person or night owl?"

"I'm more of a mid-day kind of girl."

I'm not surprised by that at all. "Go-to karaoke song?"

"'…Baby One More Time' by Britney Spears."

I stop, my eyes wide. "Not a Taylor song?"

"If I'm singing it with my roomies, yes. They would be mad if I sang one without them."

"Fair enough. Beach vacation or mountain getaway?"

"Mountain getaway."

"Favorite ice cream topping?"

"Cheesecake bites."

"Sounds like we need to go on an ice cream date next," I say.

"In fall?"

"I didn't think you were the type of girl who would only eat ice cream at certain times of the year."

She smiles. "Correct, you passed the test. Next question."

"Biggest fear?"

"Losing the people I love."

I press my lips together, wanting to lighten the mood again. "Stay in or go out?"

"Go out."

That's not surprising since she's always on the move and working incredibly hard to achieve her dream.

Kelsey grabs my hand. "I want to know your answers."

"Blue. Morning person. 'Tearin' Up My Heart' by NSYNC. Mountain getaway. Peanut butter sauce. Bats. Go out."

"The morning person was obvious by your workout habits." She shoots me a teasing smile but then quirks an eyebrow. "But you're a big, strong man who's scared of bats? *That* I'm surprised by."

"I would save you from anything else—spiders, snakes, quicksand, a burning car. But bats…" I shudder. "Sorry, but you'd be on your own."

Kelsey leans her head back and laughs. It's the kind of sound I wouldn't mind hearing forever, especially if I'm the cause of it.

My gaze moves to the setting sun. "We should get home so I can get Evie to bed." I grab all of our trash and throw it out.

Walking back to the car, Kelsey leans her head against my arm, and it feels like the most natural thing in the world.

Though I don't know what the future holds for us, I hope this will become our new normal.

# CHAPTER TWENTY-FOUR

## KELSEY

AFTER PULLING ON A rainbow sweater, in honor of Evie's newest favorite color, I give Winston a kiss goodbye on the top of his head and make my way into the kitchen.

"It's time to go support our girl." I grab the floral arrangement from the kitchen table and smile at my three best friends. "Thanks for arranging this, Shay. It's beautiful."

"Only the best for Evie. Besides, every dancer deserves a bouquet after their recital." Shayna grabs her car keys from the hook. "Now, everyone get in Daisy Mae before we're late."

We pile into her lipstick-red SUV, lovingly named after one of Shayna's favorite Taylor Swift songs. She puts on her Taylor playlist but turns the volume down as Mallory and Alyssa turn to face me. Shayna eyes me in the rearview mirror.

I raise my eyebrows, looking between my friends. "What's going on?"

"This is our first night all together since your date last weekend. We want to hear your happies from the week," Alyssa says with a knowing smile.

"What, no crappies?"

"Oh, please." Mallory rolls her eyes. "You haven't been able to wipe the smile off your face all week."

"Was it the perfect date?" Shayna glances back at me once she pulls to a stop at a red light.

"I suppose it was." I've never thought about my perfect date. But if I were hooked up to a lie detector test and forced to answer what it was, I'd describe my date with Tyler in detail—volunteering at a dog shelter and spending the rest of the evening eating good food.

I tell my roommates all the details, smiling as I reflect on our day together.

"It's sweet how well he knows you." Shayna sighs. "I want to check out that burger truck. It sounds amazing."

I nod. "We should go for our next girls' night. I've been dreaming about it every day since."

"Have you been dreaming of his lips too?" Mallory puckers. I gently shove her arm.

"Wait, did he kiss you?" Alyssa doesn't look the slightest bit ashamed by her nosy question.

"Maybe." I dip my head, blushing as they hoot and holler.

"Was it everything you ever dreamed of?"

"Do his arms feel as muscular as they look?"

Alyssa and Shayna ask questions at the same time while Mallory sits silently beside me, her lips tilted up in a smirk.

"I'm not usually one to kiss and tell, but yes, it was very dreamy, and his whole body is as muscular as it looks." I fan my face. "He lifted me and put me on the counter."

Alyssa pauses the music. "On the counter? Where exactly did this kiss happen?"

"That was our first kiss. It was, uh, in the broom closet at Sunrise Springs."

"*First* kiss?" Shayna squeals. "As in, there's been more than one?"

"Did you just say it was in a *broom closet* at your job?" Alyssa turns around to face me.

"Yes to all of the above." I hold the back of my hands to my warm cheeks. "We might've kissed again behind the dog shelter and another time when he walked me to the door."

Alyssa claps. Shayna giggles in delight. Mallory nudges my elbow and asks, "Are y'all officially a thing?"

I'm shocked that she's the one to dig in with a question about my romantic life. Especially since she's sworn off romance since some guy—whom she makes us call the-man-who-must-not-be-named or hot cocoa man—took her on the best date of her life and then ghosted her.

Shayna parks in the packed lot of the school where the dance recital is taking place. The car is silent as my friends wait for my response.

"We haven't defined the relationship yet. It was only one date." I drop my voice to a whisper, saying words that both terrify and excite me all at once. "But I think I'd like for there to be more."

Alyssa and Shayna grab each other's hands, squealing happily for me.

Mallory's face remains completely serious as she says, "If he breaks your heart, I'll cut off his—" She cuts herself off with a shrug. "Well, you know."

We get out of the car, and Shayna grabs the bouquet from my hands. Next thing I know, I'm in the middle of a giant group hug.

"I love y'all for*evermore*."

"For*evermore*," they echo.

We pull back enough to cross our arms, making hand hearts with each other in a circle. These girls right here are my family, and I wouldn't have it any other way.

Once we're back inside, I glance around the space, trying to find Tyler. When I finally spot him, he's kneeling on the ground, hugging Evie in his manly arms.

"I'll be right back," I tell my friends. When I reach Tyler and Evie, she immediately jumps from his arms into mine, sniffling quietly. I shoot him a questioning look, but he goes wide-eyed and shrugs. Well, he's no help.

I crouch down to her level. "What's wrong?"

"I'm nervous that I'm going to mess up during my solo."

I run my hands up and down her arms. "Evie, you are so dedicated and talented. You've practiced every day for weeks; you know that dance inside and out. If you're on stage and you forget a step, that's okay because some of the best things in life aren't perfect."

She hiccups. "Like what?"

"Winston, for one." I blow out a dramatic breath. "He accidentally knocks things over with his wagging tail all the time because he's not perfect. But he's still the best, right?"

Evie nods her little head. "He's my bestest friend."

I smile. "And what about s'mores?"

"They're messy and get stuck all over my fingers." Evie purses her lips.

"But they still taste delicious, even though they're not perfect."

Evie looks thoughtful. "So, even if my dance isn't perfect, you think it will still be beautiful?"

"Exactly." I give her what I hope is a comforting and encouraging hug, trying to instill all the confidence I have in her.

My eyes find Tyler over the top of her head just as he's wiping away tears from his cheeks. Seeing the genuine emotion from him stirs up feelings in my heart that scare the daylights out of me, but I'm not sure I could stop them now if I tried. He smiles softly at me, and I return the gesture.

Releasing my hold on Evie, I nudge her arm. "But you know what?"

"What?"

"I know you're going to crush it." I reach my hand out in a fist, and she bumps it with hers, a small smile returning to her tear-streaked face.

A woman's voice comes over the speaker system. "We need all dancers backstage. I repeat, all dancers are needed backstage. Thank you."

I give her one last hug. "It's your time to shine, Evie girl."

All of my friends are suddenly around us, and Evie's grin widens. "You're all here!"

"You're family. Of course we're here." Shayna smiles.

Evie walks down the line, giving each of my besties a high-five.

"I saved us seats in the fourth row. I'll meet you there," Tyler says before taking her backstage.

My friends start heading into the auditorium. Shayna turns around when she realizes I'm not following them. "Are you coming?"

I shake my head. "I'll meet you in there."

"Have fun with your *boyfriend*." Shayna giggles.

"Yeah, she will." Alyssa wiggles her shoulders and hips.

"He's *not* my boyfriend. I just want to say hi."

"If by 'say hi' you mean suck face," Mallory deadpans.

"Y'all are the worst."

"You know you love us," Shayna calls back over her shoulder with a wink.

She's not wrong. They're my family—the girls who have stuck by my side through thick and thin, and I don't know what I'd do without them.

A few minutes later, I'm looking at the artwork in the lobby when arms snake around my waist, making me gasp. Not because I don't know who it is, but because Tyler's touch has a visceral effect on me every time.

He spins me around and presses a kiss to my lips. It's gentle but filled with so much feeling. When he pulls back, his eyes are a sea of emotion, tears pooled at the corners. He doesn't say anything, but he doesn't need to. With that tender kiss and the warm way he's gazing into my eyes, I can see how much he cherishes me.

Tyler shoots me an affectionate smile—one reserved for me—and leads me into the auditorium down to the row where Alyssa, Mallory, and Shayna are already seated. We scoot past them, and Tyler removes his jacket from the seats he was saving for us. I sit next to Shay, and Tyler takes the open seat beside me.

We shout our praise for Evie after she participates in her group ballet and hip-hop dances. When it comes time for her jazz solo, I move to the edge of my seat, wringing my hands together.

Shayna discreetly pulls out her phone to record it so Tyler can send it to his sister. I'm sure she's sad about missing this big moment.

The music starts, and Evie hits her opening steps like a seasoned pro. She moves effortlessly across the dance floor, executing all the moves to perfection, her personality written all across her face.

In the middle of her solo, Tyler reaches over and grabs my hand, squeezing it so tightly that I fear I might lose blood circulation. I think he might be even more nervous than Evie, but it shows how much he truly cares about her happiness. I guess that's what love does—it makes you *feel* so much more.

As we sit holding hands and watching his niece perform her solo, my heart feels close to overflowing. I've never experienced so many emotions at once before. I've been closed off for years to everyone but my besties, never allowing myself to get close enough to someone to risk getting in the way of pursuing my dreams—or getting hurt.

Evie finishes her dance with a slow curtsy. The whole auditorium is silent as the music fades. Once the crowd starts to applaud, our row erupts into cheers like we're her personal cheerleaders.

I glance over at Tyler, surprised to find tears streaming down his cheeks and a smile on his lips. Seeing how proud he is of his niece and how much he cares tugs at my heart.

He looks over at me and wipes his eyes, shooting me a goofy smile and squeezing my hand like he's thanking me for being there with him. He pulls me in for one quick, hard kiss that sends me into a daze.

With my heart pounding and mind reeling, I wonder if it's all worth it. If opening myself up to let someone in—if opening myself up to love someone and be loved in return—is worth the risk.

Right now, I'm feeling like it might be.

# CHAPTER TWENTY-FIVE
## KELSEY

"You were amazing, Evie," Shayna coos.

"The best dancer up there," Mallory agrees.

"And that solo…" Alyssa mimics her mind being blown. "Wow."

Evie beams under their praise before turning to me. I pull the bouquet out from behind my back.

"Are those for me?" When I nod, another smile blossoms on her face. "They're beautiful."

"Not as beautiful as your dancing tonight."

"Thanks, Ms. Kelsey." She hugs me, holding on tight while my friends head to Daisy Mae.

I squeeze her right back. "I'm always here for you, Evie girl."

She turns to Tyler. "You said something about ice cream?"

He laughs. "I should've known you'd never forget about sweets." Tyler's eyes find mine. "Do you want to join us?"

I consider abandoning my friends because ice cream coupled with a wonderful man and the cutest five-year-old is a tempting option. But I need to put our tradition first.

"It's girls' night." I gesture back to my roommates.

"I knew it was probably too much to hope for." He looks at the ground, shuffling his feet.

I shoot him a sympathetic smile. "I hope you two have the best time."

"Thanks." He nods his head toward my friends. "And tell them all thanks again for coming, please. It means a lot to Evie and me." Tyler kisses me on the cheek, and I wave goodbye before meeting my friends in the car.

"You had one job, Kels." Alyssa groans.

I stare at her. "Do you want to tell me what that job is?"

"You didn't kiss him goodbye." She pretends to faint. "Now we're going to have to watch a romcom at home to make up for my lack of romance."

"Does that mean you finally decided not to see Peter anymore?" I say, my voice filled with hope.

"Yeah. Surprise, surprise, he still doesn't want to get married." She runs her fingers through her blonde curls. "And don't think I didn't know it was you who messaged Austin to come over and cheer me up after."

I shrug, feigning nonchalance. "I have no clue what you mean."

"Mm-hmm." She shoots me a disbelieving look.

Shayna glances at me in the rearview mirror before turning onto the road. "But seriously, why didn't you kiss him goodbye?"

"I'm not going to kiss him in front of Evie when we haven't talked about what we are." Not to mention that I already kissed him twice inside...but my besties don't have to know *everything*.

She nods in understanding. "That makes sense."

I pull my phone out of my belt bag and gasp when I see the missed notification at the top.

"What is it?" Mallory asks, immediately sensing the change in my demeanor.

"I have a missed call from my mom."

The collective intake of breath in the car is audible. They all know how rare it is for her to call me.

"What does *she* want?" Mallory wrinkles her nose.

"I don't know. She didn't leave a voicemail."

"Maybe it was just a butt dial." Shayna sounds hesitant, though still the most optimistic of us.

"Yeah." My mind trails off, though I try to keep it from straying too deep into my childhood memories. If I let myself sit in those for too long, the sadness can feel overwhelming.

I'm quiet for the rest of the drive, only chiming in when necessary so my friends don't worry about me. But when Shayna parks in front of our house, my stomach drops. I can hardly believe my eyes. I close them shut before slowly blinking them open, feeling like they're playing a trick on me.

"Is that—" Alyssa gestures to our porch.

I nod, my mouth dry. "Yep, that's my mom."

"How does she even know where we live?" Mallory's tone is bitter. "She hasn't bothered to visit the past two years. So, why is she showing up now?"

"I'm about to go find out." I take a steadying breath and get out of the car, walking slowly to the porch.

My mother stands when she sees me, holding her arms out wide. "Sweetheart, it's so good to see you."

"What are you doing here, Mom?" I ask, keeping my distance.

"Now, where's the Southern hospitality I taught you?" She laughs. "Aren't you going to invite me in?"

I cross my arms, trying to hold myself together. "Are you going to tell me why you're at my house?"

"Can't a mother just want to see her only daughter's home?"

"At seven on a random Friday night without calling me first?"

"I did call. You didn't answer."

"I was at an event." I internally chide myself. I don't need to justify why I didn't answer her call. Thankfully, I'm given a moment to breathe when my friends exit the car and join us.

"Hi, Mrs. Anderson." Shayna's smile is bright, but I know her well enough to tell it's forced.

"Hello, girls. It's been a while." My mother runs a hand through her box-dyed hair. "And it's Ms. McGrath now." Apparently, she's reverted to using her maiden name since we last spoke.

"It sure has." Mallory glares at her.

My mother doesn't seem affected in the slightest, obviously lacking the wherewithal to know she isn't welcome. "Well, can I see your house?"

"I'll show you the living room." I step past my friends and unlock the door, ushering my mom in. All my friends follow with pitying glances that almost do me in. They move to the kitchen, where I'm sure they'll be eavesdropping while I show my mom the living room.

"Wow, this is nice." My mother looks around. "Very Victorian, and I like your decorating style."

"Alyssa's a pro at that." I pick at the threads on the knit blanket lying across the back of the couch. "Did you need something, Mom?"

She smooths her hands along her jacket. "I only need a place to stay for a little while. My boyfriend broke up with me, so I don't have anywhere to go."

I bite the inside of my lip. Of course, she isn't here to see me. It's just because she needs something now that she's spent all her divorce money and got broken up with for the umpteenth time.

"Do *you* have a boyfriend?"

I'm shocked she asked me a personal question, trying to pretend to be the kind of mother she never was.

"Kind of." I don't want to get into the complicated answer to that question with her.

"Do yourself a favor and end things now. All men leave, Kelsey. It's what they do. So, save yourself and get out before you end up heartbroken."

My stomach twists, and I'm hit with a wave of nausea. Her words stir up all the insecurities I've felt around dating my entire life. The insecurities I have when it comes to relationships because of her and my dad.

"So, where can I sleep?" she asks.

"We don't have a guest room."

"I'll sleep on the couch, then." She sits down. "Can you get me some water? I was waiting outside for an hour after my Uber dropped me off."

I walk to the kitchen without another word. I'm not at all surprised to find my friends standing there, obviously listening to our conversation.

Alyssa shoves a glass of water in my hand, barely half-full, and Mallory shoves a wad of cash into my other hand.

"What's this for?"

"Give it to your mom and tell her to get a hotel room for the night. After that, she's on her own," Mallory says with fierce determination. From the look in her eyes, I know she'd rather march right over to my mother and give her a piece of her mind. "She doesn't get to do this to you. She doesn't get to just walk in when it's convenient for her and drag you back down with her."

Shayna pats Mallory's back. "She's right. It's unfair to you."

I take a deep breath before walking back into the living room. I set the water on the coffee table in front of my mother and hand her the cash.

"I don't understand," she says, looking at me with a pinched expression.

"It's for you to get a hotel room. You can get a good night's sleep and then figure out what you're going to do next, but you can't stay here." My chest feels lighter saying the words I've wanted to for so long but have never been courageous enough to until now.

"Well, I guess I've just been a terrible mother to you, huh? Kicking your own mother out..." She huffs, standing without even taking a sip of the drink. "Don't come crying to me when your little boyfriend inevitably breaks your heart."

Without so much as a goodbye, she stalks out of the room.

When I hear the front door slam shut, I crumble onto the couch, feeling numb. My friends come rushing in. Alyssa holds my hand while Shayna runs her hands down my hair in calming strokes. Mallory sits at my feet, looking like she's holding back some strong words about my mother.

I let my guard fall, and tears stream down my face. Mallory grabs a tissue from the coffee table and hands it to me. I dab under my eyes.

"Do you want to talk about it?" Alyssa asks once the tears have slowed.

I shrug. "What is there to talk about? Y'all heard everything she said."

"But none of it is true." Shayna wipes a rogue tear from my cheek. "You're different from your mom, Kels. And Tyler is different than all the men she dates."

Alyssa nods. "He's an in-it-for-the-long-haul kind of guy."

"I know I'm not my mom, and thank goodness for that because I never want to be like her." I scoff. "But Tyler's not my boyfriend, and I don't need him."

"Kels." Alyssa squeezes my hand. "You've been the happiest version of yourself this week that I've ever seen."

Mallory sighs. "She's right. You've been humming and smiling constantly. It was honestly a little nauseating." Alyssa whacks her arm. "Ouch, what was that for?" Mallory rubs the red spot. "I was agreeing with you."

"Calling being happy *nauseating* isn't helping."

"I was saying seeing her *in love* is nauseating. Of course, I want her to be happy."

"In love?" I let out a hollow laugh. "I'm not in love."

"The way that you talk about him says otherwise." Shayna shoots me a sympathetic smile.

"Y'all know I've never planned on getting married." I swipe away the tears falling down my face. "I *can't* be in love. And obviously, with a family history like that"—I gesture to the front door—"I never should be. Love doesn't last."

"Love has lasted between us." Alyssa wraps her arm around my shoulder, pulling me against her.

"Fine. *Romantic* love doesn't last."

"Just because you haven't seen it doesn't mean it doesn't exist. I mean, think about my parents. They've been married for almost thirty years and still hold hands constantly."

"Exactly," Shayna says, then points at Tyler's house. "And just look at how Tyler has shown up for you. He took care of you when you got the stomach bug. He showed up to save the day at your job when the car expert backed out at the last minute. He took you on a date somewhere he knew would mean everything to you. Not to mention the way that man looks at you. The look in his eyes was not at all appropriate for a children's dance recital." She fans her face. "But seriously, I could keep going all night."

Alyssa squeezes my hand. "Don't you want someone who knows you down to your core—someone who sees you and takes care of you and helps you reach your dreams?"

I grind my teeth. "I can take care of myself."

"But would it be so bad to let someone else for a change?" Alyssa's voice is quiet, like she's scared to push me too far.

I can't be like my mom and let a man control my emotions. I can't let anything or anyone stop me from reaching my dreams. I shake my head. "I can't. Not right now."

And if I can't be around Tyler, that means I can't be around Evie either. As much as it would break my heart to upset her, I don't know what else to do. I can't do this. I can't risk everything for a man.

I look at Mallory, knowing she's the only one who could help me right now. "Can you watch Evie after school this week? Only until I find a new nanny for her."

Mallory nods. "Of course."

"Don't you think you're being a little rash?" Alyssa asks.

"Letting Tyler in and opening up to him was *rash*." I ball my hands into fists. "I should've known better than to think things could turn out differently. He'll walk away from me the minute I'm no longer convenient for him."

As much as my friends and Darla might argue that love can last, I don't think it ever will for me. I push up from the couch.

"Kels—" Shayna reaches out, trying to stop me.

I hold my hands up. "I need space and time to sort through my emotions." Before any of them can try to convince me otherwise, I head to my room.

Once I'm alone, I fall onto my bed. Winston jumps up, licking my face before setting his head on my stomach. I inhale a shuddering breath. "At least a dog's love is unconditional," I whisper, running my hand along his back. He's the only man I need.

As much as cutting Tyler out of my life might hurt now, I know it's for the best.

# CHAPTER TWENTY-SIX

## TYLER

"Eves. Kels. I'm home," I call out the moment I walk through the front door.

Evie runs out of the kitchen and hugs me. I crouch to return the embrace. Soft footsteps sound behind her. I look up, ready to pull Kelsey into my arms, but it isn't Kelsey standing in my kitchen…it's her roommate, Mallory.

My brows furrow. "Where's Kelsey?"

Mallory grimaces. "She's not here."

"What do you mean she's not here?" I pace across the living room. There's no way Kelsey would have one of her friends watch Evie in her place without letting me know first. "Is she sick again?"

She shakes her head.

I cross my arms, a smile pulling at my lips when I realize what's happening here. "Oh, I get it. She's trying to bring back our prank war."

Mallory reaches her hand out, stopping my pacing. "Maybe we should talk outside?" She tilts her head toward Evie, who is staring up at us curiously.

My stomach sinks, feeling like I swallowed a lead ton. "Sure." I open the front door for Mallory and follow her outside.

She pulls at the sleeves of her magenta cardigan, looking uncomfortable.

"You can tell me whatever it is. I can handle it."

Mallory sighs, looking at the ground. "Kelsey's not coming back."

"What do you mean?"

"Kelsey said she'd find you a new nanny. I can watch Evie in the meantime."

"Where is she?" I start moving next door, determined to see her and make sure she's okay.

"She doesn't want to see you, Tyler." Mallory's words stop me dead in my tracks.

"Why?" I can't wrap my mind around what's happening. Everything seemed like it was going perfectly the last time I saw her at Evie's dance recital. I haven't heard from her since then, but I assumed she had a busy weekend with her friends. I'm not going to be a controlling non-boyfriend and text her a million times until she responds.

"Did I do or say something?" I grab fistfuls of my hair, trying to get a grasp on what's happening. "I need to see her. I need to apologize for whatever I did to hurt her."

"You didn't do anything wrong."

I blow out a long breath. "I find that hard to believe if she won't see me."

"She just needs some space. I swear, you didn't do anything wrong." Mallory shifts on her feet. "Alyssa, Shayna, and I are rooting for you."

If her best friends are still cheering me on, maybe everything is okay. But then, why is Kelsey avoiding me?

She gestures next door. "I should get going."

Mallory starts to walk home, but I call out after her. "Will you please tell Kelsey that I want to talk? That I just want to understand what's going on so I can make things right?"

She nods. "I'll let her know."

When she's gone, I pull my phone out to send a message to Kelsey. A text feels too impersonal, but I'm not sure she'd answer a phone call. I open our text conversation and click the button to record a voice message.

"Hey, Kelsey." My voice sounds hoarse, threaded with heartache. "It's Tyler." I facepalm, biting back a groan at my idiocy. "You obviously already know that." Clearing my throat, I continue. "Anyway, I'm calling—er, well, voice messaging—to check in and make sure everything's okay. Mallory said you were going to find a new nanny, and I don't understand what went wrong. I would love a chance to talk things through with you, so please call me, or knock on my door, or send a carrier pigeon. Anything. Just please talk to me. I lo—"

I cut myself off. I can't tell her that I love her over a voice memo.

I can't lose her. Not now. Not after I've fallen for her. Despite my best efforts not to, I've been falling for Kelsey all along. For her spunk and ambition. For the ridiculous nicknames that she calls me. For the way she cares about everyone around her and would do anything for her friends. And it was hearing her encourage Evie at her dance recital that sent me over the edge. After that, my heart was hers. Simply, I've fallen for everything she is. I only hope I have the opportunity to tell her.

"I hope to talk to you soon." I press the stop button and hit send before I can second-guess myself. Even though I muddled my words, I want Kelsey to hear the emotion in my voice, to know that I care and want to work through whatever is pulling her away.

If she doesn't feel the same way, I'm not sure I'll ever get my heart back. Because I don't think there's another person in the world who can make me as happy—who can make me *feel* as much—as Kelsey Anderson.

The last two days have been the longest of my life. Kelsey didn't respond to any of my messages, so I resorted to knocking on her front door. Her roommates took turns answering it. No matter who answered, they turned me away, although their faces at least looked pained doing so. That, or they just pity me. I mean, Shayna gave me a dozen chocolate chip cookies when she turned me away. If that doesn't show how sorry they feel for me, I don't know what does.

It only has me even more confused as to why Kelsey is avoiding me, though. If I'd done something to hurt her, I don't think her friends would be looking at me like I'm a sad little puppy their parents won't let them bring inside. They'd be slamming the door in my face and calling me names that I couldn't repeat.

I take a deep breath, trying to shove my feelings down, before walking into Evie's room. "You ready for bed?" I ask with a forced smile.

She nods, already snuggled under the covers.

I tuck her in. "Now you're snug as a bug in a rug." Evie giggles, and I lean down to hug her. "Goodnight, Eves. Sleep tight."

Her face is crestfallen when I pull back.

"What's wrong?"

"Will Ms. Kelsey be back soon?" She rubs her eyes. "I miss her."

"I hope so, kiddo." I rub her back. "I miss her too."

I stay with Evie until her breathing slows. Once she's asleep, I head to the kitchen and treat myself to the last two cookies Shayna gave me. Sweets aren't usually part of my diet, but I've made an exception this week.

I stare at the crumbs on my plate, feeling like I've hit a wall. One that I can't break through on my own. I need female advice. There's no way I'm calling Aunt D or Nadine—they'd likely show up here in all-black outfits and insist we break into Kelsey's house. All the girls next door haven't told me what I can do to fix things, and I don't usually talk to my parents about women. That only leaves one option: Tess.

She'll never let me live this down, but she did say to call her if I needed help with a grand gesture. And I feel like a grand gesture is about the only thing that will help me get Kelsey's attention right now.

I pull out my phone and do the unimaginable. I call my sister for dating advice.

It rings twice before Tess's sleep-laden voice comes through the speaker. "Is Evie okay?"

I should've known that would be the first place my sister's mind went when getting a call from me at this hour. "Yeah, she's fine. Sorry."

"Then why in the world are you calling me at..." She pauses. "Two in the morning?"

I press my lips into a firm line. "Ah, I completely forgot about the time difference. Sorry, I'll let you get back to sleep."

Tess sighs. "You already woke me up, so you may as well tell me why you're calling, little bro."

"I need your help," I mumble.

"That's like music to my ears." She perks up. "Say it again."

"Oh, big sister. I need your assistance winning over my neighbor and telling her I love her. In a Taylor Swift way, or whatever it is you said before."

"I thought you'd never ask." I can hear the wicked grin in her voice.

Tess is never going to let me hear the end of this, but I'm desperate at this point. I'll do anything, even endure my sister saying she was right for the rest of eternity, if it means I might win Kelsey back.

———— ♡ ♡ ♡ ————

It's been pure torture waiting another day to put *Operation: You Belong With Me* into action. I still think the name is a bit much, but Tess insisted every grand gesture needs a name.

I already checked with Mallory that Kelsey would be home tonight. Now that Evie is in bed, it's finally time for this operation to begin.

With each step toward my workout room, I try to convince myself that Kelsey loves me, but I'll even settle for her just talking to me. I can't think of any other outcome than that.

My heart races when I step into my exercise room. I already did a practice test this morning to ensure that my soundproofing job worked *inside* the house. It works like a charm, so Evie won't wake up during this little operation. But Kelsey, on the other hand, is about to hear everything.

I unlock the window, slide it open, and make sure everything I need is within reach before I play "You Belong With Me (Taylor's Version)"—because Tess told me it's *crucial* to listen to her version—at full blast through my speaker system.

I hold up the giant poster board where I wrote *You ok?* exactly like Tess told me to. I guess this happens during the music video for this song. I'm just hoping it has the same effect on Kelsey today. That maybe she'll finally see that she belongs with me.

The chorus hits, and there's still been no sign of Kelsey. My heart sinks. This was a stupid idea. I don't know why I thought—

Kelsey's head pops out around her curtain. I can't read her expression from this far away, but she pauses. The seconds I wait to see how she responds feel like an eternity. My breath catches. My heart pounds. But I can finally breathe again when she slides her window open.

Her voice carries across the wind like a whisper. "What are you doing?"

I point to my sign in response.

She hesitates, but only for a second this time, before holding up a finger and disappearing from view. Thankfully, Tess gave me the idea to supply Mallory with a marker and some poster boards to put outside Kelsey's door. Now, all I can do is hope that she'll actually play along.

When she returns a minute later, I feel like a weight has been lifted off my chest. Instead of feeling like I'm giving an elephant a piggyback ride, hope blossoms inside once more.

Kelsey writes for a few seconds before holding up a sign that reads *Not really* in bubbly handwriting that doesn't match the tone of her message.

I hold up one of my premade signs that says *Sorry* followed by another one that could make or break how this night goes. *Meet me out front?*

She looks away for another minute before holding up a sign with only one word. One so simple that it doesn't mean much by itself. But to me, right now, it means everything.

My mouth tilts into my first genuine smile all week as I reread the sign—*Okay*.

I shut off the music, now that it's done its job, and rush outside, nearly falling down the stairs with the nervous energy coursing through my body.

Kelsey stands between our lawns with her arms crossed. I slow my pace, not wanting to scare her away.

Once I'm standing beside her, she tilts her head back, looking at the clear night sky above. "It's beautiful tonight, isn't it?"

I'm sure the stars look amazing tonight, but I only have eyes for her. "It really is."

She hangs her head, avoiding eye contact. I gently touch her chin, trying to get her to meet my face. She flinches, and I immediately drop my hand.

"What's wrong, Kelsey?" My voice breaks. "What happened?"

"I— It was my mom."

"Is she okay?"

"She's not hurt if that's what you mean." Kelsey inhales a deep breath. "She was here, waiting on my porch, when we returned from Evie's dance recital."

My stomach sinks. I wish I could've been there for her, holding her hand during whatever her mother did or said. "What did she want this time?"

"Her most recent boyfriend broke up with her. She ran out of the money she got from my dad in the divorce settlement a long time ago, so she showed up looking for a place to stay."

I reach into my back pocket, pulling out my wallet. "I can help put her up in a hotel or something."

She puts her hand on mine, stopping me. The feel of her soft skin on mine is like a jolt of electricity. My attraction for her pulses through me, but now isn't the time to act on that.

"I don't want you to use the money that you're saving to open the dog rescue." I look at her earnestly. "Please, let me help."

A single tear falls down her cheek. "My friends already gave her money for a room. I'm sure she's long gone now."

I put my wallet back in my pocket as her gaze finally meets my eyes. She looks as distant and heartbroken as I feel. "Why are you being nice to me? I've been avoiding you."

This is the answer I need. One that will help me know if I still have a shot with her. "Why have you been avoiding me?"

She flings her arms down, looking exhausted and exasperated all at once. "I can't be like my parents. They stayed together even after the love faded, and I was their casualty. I won't let that happen to me. I can take care of myself. I won't let anything or anyone stand in the way of my dreams."

"True love doesn't stand in the way of your dreams. It helps you reach them. It helps you surpass them."

"What does love have to do with it?"

I hold her face with both hands, needing her to see the sincerity in my eyes. Gently, I wipe away the rogue tear from her cheek. "I thought it was obvious?"

"What's obvious?" Kelsey's voice is breathless, her eyes trained on my lips.

"That I love you."

Kelsey's eyes dart to mine. "You...*what?*"

"I love you, Kelsey Anderson."

"You can't love me."

"Why not?" I whisper, running my hands through her hair.

"You might think you do now, but it won't last. It never does." She shakes her head, moving my hand with the motion.

"Just because your parents' relationship didn't last doesn't mean all love ends." I slide my hands down her arms and take her hands in mine. "Real love—unconditional love—is never-ending. It's accepting someone for who they are, down to their core. It doesn't have any strings attached." I squeeze her hand. "It's loving someone without expecting anything in return. *That's* how I love you. Beyond all reason. With every fiber of my being. If you can tell me you don't love me, that you don't want me, I'll leave you alone. It will be the worst pain I've ever gone through, but I'd step away because that's how much I love you."

I step closer to her. "But if there's the smallest shred in you that thinks you could return my feelings, then please believe. Believe that love is so much more than the cheap version you saw between your parents. Believe that my love for you isn't conditional and will fade away when life gets hard. Believe that I'm going to push you to achieve your greatest dreams and support you as you chase them. Believe that I love you and am never going to stop."

"But what about when life gets hard and you don't feel like this? When you don't love me anymore." Kelsey's head falls, more tears trickling down her cheeks.

I tilt her chin up, brushing a feather-light kiss to her forehead. "Love may start as a feeling. Something all-consuming and so happy you could never imagine feeling differently. But staying together is a choice, Kels. Feelings fade just like the sun disappears below the horizon every evening. But we must consciously *choose* to be together—to *love* each other—just as faithfully as the sun rises again each morning."

She wipes the tears from her eyes, and a small smile tugs at her lips. "You really are a romantic, aren't you?"

"Through and through." I kiss her temple.

"I love you, too," she says so whisper-soft, I'm not sure I heard correctly.

Pulling my head back, I search her eyes. "Did you just say that you love me?"

She nods. "I'm scared, Tyler."

"It wouldn't be called *falling* in love if it wasn't scary. It's a leap of faith." I wrap my arms around her waist. "But I'm always going to catch you. You don't have to *need* me, Kels. You just have to *choose* me." I pull her against me, our bodies pressed together, and rest my forehead against hers. "I can't promise that I'll never hurt you. That's part of being human; I'll never be perfect. But I can promise that I'll choose you every day. I'll apologize when I'm wrong. I'll support you and cherish you and love you like you deserve. You just have to let me."

Kelsey tilts her head back. When she looks into my eyes, gone is the distance and heartbreak. Instead, her beautiful hazel eyes reflect something I only hoped I'd see: trust. She wraps her arms around my neck and presses her lips to mine. It's different than any kiss we've shared because it's filled with a promise.

Of love.

Of hope.

Of a future.

*Together.*

I don't even realize I'm crying until Kelsey pulls back. She wipes the tears from my cheeks.

When we've both caught our breath, I ask, "What convinced you to talk to me?"

"Your persistence, for one thing." She laughs. "But how could I refuse when you went to the trouble of playing a Taylor song and holding up that sign just like the music video." She sighs. "That's every girl's dream."

"You can thank my brilliant sister for that idea." I smile.

"I love her already." She kisses my jaw, making me inhale sharply. "But not as much as I love you."

I'm about to show her just how much I love her, when my front door opens and little feet crunch on the grass.

"Ms. Kelsey, you're back!" Evie squeals, hugging both of our legs. "Please tell me you're never leaving again."

"I'm not, Evie girl." Kelsey looks right at me, her smile filled with the same joy and certainty I feel in my heart. "I'm home."

# EPILOGUE

## KELSEY

*One Year Later*

"It's time." Tyler hugs me from behind, pressing a kiss to my neck. I lean into his touch, savoring the peace that floods through me at his nearness.

It's hard to believe there was a time when I thought life would be better on my own, because now I can't imagine going a single day without Tyler Reed. My boyfriend. My encourager. My best friend. My future fiancé. That one's not really official yet, but I have a feeling it will be soon.

Life hasn't been all rainbows and sunshine over the last year, but I've come through all of life's trials stronger with him by my side. Tyler and my besties encouraged me to see a therapist to talk through my childhood, which has helped me let go of the past and fully lean into my relationship with him. He then met my parents and helped me set clear boundaries with them, holding my hand through the whole thing. I never would've made it through all the red tape to open my dog rescue without him, either.

But for each hard thing we've been through together, there have been a dozen happy moments—new core memories I hope I'll never forget. Like spending Christmas with

Tyler, Evie, Tess, and Darla. Winston and Romeo—who I convinced Tyler to adopt from the local animal shelter—worked together to steal the turkey from the table. The meat looked really dry, so maybe they were doing us a favor. But it started a new tradition of ordering pizza for dinner and eating it in front of the fireplace while watching Christmas movies.

"You've got this, sis." Tess runs over, pulling me into a bone-crushing hug. For someone as tiny as she is, Tess would be real competition for The Rock in an arm-wrestling contest.

She's been one of the highlights of this past year. Ever since she returned from her work trip to Africa, we've been inseparable. I introduced her to my besties, and she fit right into our group like a puzzle piece we didn't realize was missing. She also has helped me pull off some amazing pranks on Tyler, hence why we get along wonderfully.

"I know you'll be busy today, but I just wanted to say I love you and you're amazing." She squeezes my arms. "I'll see you Sunday for family dinner?"

I nod. "I'll see you then. Love you too." It's so nice to feel like I'm part of a family unit, something I never thought was possible.

Tess joins my friends, along with their significant others, Evie, Darla, Ed, and Nadine at the front of the crowd. They're my people—my family—and I wouldn't change it for the world.

Shayna, Alyssa, and Mallory are smiling from ear to ear as they raise their fancy to-go coffee in the air toward me. I don't even care that they won the stupid bet anymore because it led me to Tyler. However, I could've done without buying the fancy espresso machine…but at least I get barista-grade coffee for life.

"I'm so proud of you." Tyler kisses my cheek, making goosebumps erupt across my skin. "Your dreams are coming true."

"You're the person I want beside me when they do." I peer up at him through my tear-filled eyes. "I love you, McDreamy."

"I love you more, Anderson." He nudges me toward the front door, his teasing smile lighting up his whole face. "Now, give all these people what they're waiting for. Go cut your red ribbon, my little CEO."

I grab his hand, tugging him before he can walk away. "Stand with me?"

"Always."

Together, we move to stand in front of the small crowd.

"Speech!" Darla shouts.

"I don't have a speech planned, but I'll do my best." I laugh. "First, thank you all for coming to the Tails of Hope Dog Rescue grand opening. It means the world to me to have you all here. To have your support." I press a hand to my full heart. "I've dreamed of creating this organization my whole life, and it's truly an honor to share in its opening with all of you today."

I look back at the building, my dream come to life, and smile. "Every dog that will come through this organization, ready to be adopted by a loving family, will have a story—a background of abandonment, abuse, or neglect. But we get to offer them a better future. I can't wait for the photos of adopted dogs to cover the walls inside, sharing their stories for all to hear."

Taking in a shuddering breath, I continue. "Thank you for being part of that and for supporting me on this journey to find a loving home for every dog that comes through this organization. I couldn't do it without the love and encouragement of my *family*"—I look at all my loved ones in the front row—"and the support of this community." I motion to the building. "Without further ado, Tails of Hope Dog Rescue is now open."

Tyler hands me giant scissors, and I cut through the red ribbon. The crowd cheers as it falls to the ground.

He pulls me into a hug, and I inhale the smell of his deodorant and cologne. Being in his arms is my happy place, my safe haven. In his arms, I'm home.

My arms are still wrapped around Tyler's waist as the crowd moves inside to tour the facility, including the fifty dog suites and outdoor play area.

Darla waits until everyone else is inside before walking over to us. "Look at what you did here. It's beautiful, even though I still think you should've done a *duck* rescue."

We laugh together, and I shake my head at her antics, which, I've grown extremely accustomed to over the last year.

She wags her finger at us. "Now, when will you two give me some more great-great nieces or nephews to spoil?"

Tyler's hands squeeze my waist. "Aunt D, you need to let me propose first."

Darla taps her foot. "Well, what are you waiting for?" She waves her arm in a flourish. "Propose."

He leans in, pressing a kiss to my temple. "Soon." Although he's answering Darla, his words feel like a promise—an inevitable for the future we both want together.

With Tyler, the idea of settling down doesn't feel so scary anymore. I used to think that love didn't last, but he has shown me what love is every day. So, no. The idea of marriage no longer terrifies me. Instead, it makes me feel joyful and hopeful for what can be. And I can't wait to spend the rest of my life with the man who continually shows me that it's brave to open my heart—especially when I know he will never break it.

"You young people are always waiting for the *right moment*." Darla huffs, walking inside while shaking her head.

When we're alone, Tyler turns me around and lifts me up, kissing me in a soft, sweet way because he knows it won't be the last time. "You know, I've already given you my heart, so I may as well give you my last name." He presses his lips to the soft spot beneath my ear, making my back arch at his touch. "Kelsey Reed does have a nice ring to it."

I smile up at him, feeling more at peace than I have in my entire life. "I couldn't agree more."

———— ♡ ♡ ♡ ————

Read a bonus scene about Kelsey and Tyler three years in the future when you sign up for my emails at https://dl.bookfunnel.com/1oh6pxdnoh

Keep reading for a bonus epilogue!

# BONUS EPILOGUE
## MALLORY

*DECEMBER*

"Did we make a mistake letting Lyss and Shay pick the movie themselves?" I laugh, only half-kidding. "Knowing them, we're going to end up being forced to watch some sappy love story."

Kelsey bumps my hip with hers. "You're speaking to the girl who is sappy and in love now."

"Ugh, it makes me sick." I throw a popcorn kernel at her, shaking my head.

"Hey, if I can find love, you can too."

Tess gives me a fist bump of solidarity. "I feel you, girl."

"Thank you." I shoot a wide-eyed look at Kelsey. "At least someone still gets it."

"Just you wait. When y'all meet someone who can kiss as well as Tyler, you'll be changing your tune."

"Ew." Tess grimaces. "I thought we agreed to never talk about your physical relationship with my brother."

"Sorry, not sorry."

"Are y'all almost done?" Shayna asks. "There's a new romcom available to rent that I've heard great things about."

Tess and I groan. My besties are lucky I'd do anything for them, even watch fluffy romcoms.

"Be there in a sec," Kelsey calls back. She picks up the tray of drinks: four mugs of hot cocoa and one mug of peppermint tea for me because I refuse to drink hot cocoa ever since *the incident*.

I grab the giant bowl of popcorn and follow Kelsey and Tess into our living room. My gaze moves to the television, wondering what silly romcom they're forcing me to watch this time.

When I see the still picture of a man paused on the screen, my breath hitches. I lose my grip on the bowl. It clatters to the ground, spilling kernels all over our wood floor.

I haven't seen his face for three years, and seeing it now brings back all the stupid feelings I thought I'd gotten over a long time ago.

"What?" Alyssa moves toward me like she's going to protect me from an invisible force.

"It's him," I mutter, unable to look away from the screen.

"Who?"

"*Him*." I point to the television.

Alyssa rubs my back. "You're going to have to elaborate a little more than that, Mal."

"That's Griffin."

Shayna nods. "Oh, you're right. I thought he looked familiar. I think his name is Griffin Reynolds. Supposedly, he's the newest hot and upcoming movie star. Like the new Zac Efron or Glen Powell of our generation."

I shake my head. "No, I mean it's *him*. Griffin is he-who-must-not-be-named."

The room falls silent, all my roommates understanding my meaning.

"I'll find a different movie," Shayna mutters, exiting out of the picture of his face that sent shockwaves through my body.

"I can't believe *he's* hot cocoa man." Kelsey lets out a low whistle.

Tess looks around the room. "Okay, I'm going to need some context here. Who is hot cocoa man?"

I puff my cheeks up and blow out a long, slow breath. "That question has a long answer. And I'm going to need something a little stronger to drink than tea."

"Another time, then." She squeezes my arm, shooting me a sympathetic smile.

"But basically, just know that we hate him." Shayna huffs. You know it's bad when her sunny personality dissolves into storm clouds.

"Agreed," Alyssa and Kelsey echo.

Shayna clicks through the movies on the streaming platform. I grab a broom, and Tess helps me sweep up the popcorn.

"How about *Twisters*? Glen Powell is hot, but there's no romance."

I nod. "Sounds perfect."

I try to focus on the movie…to distract myself from the image of Griffin that's now seared into my brain. But my insides feel like the tornadoes on the screen, swirling around inside, wreaking havoc without a care for what's in their path.

My heart aches. I've always been one to put on a brave face, but it took me a *long* time to get over Griffin Reynolds.

Only now, seeing his annoyingly perfect smile, I'm not sure I'm over him after all.

———— ♡ ♡ ♡ ————

You won't want to miss Mallory's book, How He Got the Girl—a fake dating, celebrity romcom.

# ACKNOWLEDGEMENTS

ALL THE GLORY TO God! Thank you for putting a love of stories in my heart and for giving me the words to write this story.

I can't write a book without thanking my husband, Wade. I can never thank you enough for helping me live my dream. But you're my real dream. I love you forever.

Thank you to my real life besties for making it so easy to write this sweet female friend group. As Taylor would say, "I've had the time of my life with you." I love y'all!

This book wouldn't be what it is without my fabulous beta readers, Ashley, Kathryn, Meredith, and Steph. Y'all are the absolute best, and I never want to write a book without you! You gave me so much confidence in this book, and your suggestions were exactly what this story needed. Thank you so much for your time and feedback.

A big thank you to my critique partner, Annah. Your feedback on this book was invaluable, and your comments provided me with so much encouragement as I enter the world of romcoms. I'm forever thankful for you!

I still cannot stop looking at my gorgeous cover! Melody Jeffries, thank you for sharing your creativity with the world. It has been such a joy to work with you.

Thank you to my wonderful editor, Caitlin. Your encouragement and kindness means the world to me. I'm so thankful for your attention to detail. Thanks for helping make this story shine.

To my friend, Hailey Gardiner, who was taken from this world much too soon. Words can't express how much I've cherished your friendship the past few years. Your support meant the world to me throughout my author journey, but especially as I wrote my first romcom. I'm heartbroken you never got to read it, but your uplifting words will continue to push me forward for years to come. I'm so grateful I got to know you and be your friend.

To all my sweet readers, thank you for sticking with me (or joining me for the first time!) as I delve into the romcom space. You make every hour spent on writing so worth it. Thank you for reading my books and making my dream a reality!

Finally, thanks to Taylor Swift for writing songs worth writing love stories about.

# ABOUT THE AUTHOR

Amanda Schimmoeller is a closed-door romance author who writes sweet love stories for readers who love happily ever afters. Her books are filled with banter, heart, and characters you can't help but love.

She loves Dr. Pepper, salty snacks, and binge-worthy tv. You'll find her plotting her next great love story and living out her own fairytale in Tennessee with her husband and their dog.

Connect with Amanda at www.authoramandaschimmoeller.com

www.ingramcontent.com/pod-product-compliance
Lightning Source LLC
Chambersburg PA
CBHW050030120726
47903CB00006B/1978